One Last Deadly Play

A Novel By
FLO ANTHONY

T0204466

Wahida Clark Presents Publishing, LLC

60 Evergreen Place

Suite 904

East Orange, New Jersey 07018

973-678-9982

www.wclarkpublishing.com

ISBN 13-digit 978-1-936649-05-1

ISBN 10-digit 19366490550

eBook ISBN 9781936649198

Library of Congress Catalog Number

1.   Urban, Romance, Suspense, Gossip, Football, New York City, African-American, Street Lit – Fiction

Cover design and layout by Nuance Art, LLC

Book interior design by www.aCreativeNuance.com

Contributing Editors: Linda Wilson and R. Hamilton

Printed in United States

you...and my specials Jaizelle Dennis-Rome & Sandra Hall-Morris.... thanks for always having my back!

Many thanks to the wonderful people who went the extra mile to help me with my last novel.....Marva Allen, Hue Man Online, Vanesse Lloyd -Sgambati, Myron Mays Book Club, Toni Dozier, Cheryl Cisse, Falicia Fracassi of Fracassi Lashes, WDKX, Roz Nixon, Brown Girls Book Club, Basha Riddick, PBC Philly Book Club, Sisters Uptown Book Club, Sandra Trim-Dacosta, Langston Hughes Library, Frankie Darcell, Derrick Corbett, WDAS, Don Thomas, The New York Beacon, Kam Williams, Brian Niemietz,The New York Daily News, William Heller, Cindy Adams, The New York Post, The Philadelphia Sunday Sun, The Philadelphia Tribune, The Philadelphia Daily News, Phyllis Sims, Trudy Haynes, Will and Sheila Hart, Souleo, Arise TV, Pix 11, Audrey Adams, Tri-State Defender, General Motors, Westchester Alumni Chapter of Delta Sigma Theta, North New Jersey Alumni Chapter of Delta Sigma Theta, Brooklyn Alumni Chapter of Delta Sigma Theta, Mark Anthony Jenkins, New York Black Expo, Patrik Henry Bass, Essence Music Festival, Priscilla Burke, Black Caucus Foundation Weekend and Sandra Edwards.

To my cousins.... Claudette Anthony Bush, Josie Anthony, Reggie Anthony, Tawana Anthony, Karen Allen, Jamie Smith, Cheryl Williams, Sheila Johnson, Carolyn Downing, Margaret Jones and Conrad Tillard..... I love you......

To my God on Earth Claude Stanton.... Thank you for Unconditional Love......

Flo Anthony

ACKNOWLEDGMENTS

Giving thanks to God and my late parents Joe S. Anthony and Doris Johnson Anthony for giving me life.

Thank you Terrance Russ for introducing me to the most fabulous trio of women that I have met in a long time, Wahida Clark, Dr. Annie Hollingsworth and Nuance Clark.

Wahida, thank you for believing in me and through Clark Publishing Inc., once again allowing readers to enjoy the adventures of Valerie Rollins and Rome Nyland.

To my dear friends Jocelyn Allen, Khandi Alexander, Arcella, John Bernard, Ayanna Bynum, Shelley Brooks, T' Campbell, Suzette Charles, Janet Langhart Cohen, Paula Copper Cunningham, Bridget Davis,, Janis DaSilva, Angelo Ellerbee, Irene Gandy, Roger Goodell, Penn Allen-Griggs, Dawne Marie Grannum, Shannon Henderson, James Hester, Steven Hoffenbe LaToya Jackson, Karina Tartarski, Leon Isa Lee, Steven Marcano, Steven Manning, F Murray, Johnny Newman, Charles Oakl Renell Perry, Vivian Pickard, Georg Shafiroff, Helen Shelton, Micha Stewart, Trent Tucker, Rolonda Williams and Lu Willard....t' throughout life's journey.

As Khandi says: "We

To my line sisters Alpha Chapter, How Suzanne Randolp'

PART 1

CHAPTER ONE

Columbus

Columbus wished he had a clue to his true identity or where he really came from. The sole doctor on Crooked Island told Columbus that he suffered from something called "traumatic amnesia," a condition that must have occurred as a result of his near drowning. Some fishermen, who are part of the 350 residents on the island, pulled him out of the ocean half a decade ago. Since he had no recollection of ever even having a name, the guys decided to call him Columbus Isley after Christopher Columbus, who sailed down the side of the island in 1492.

Christopher Columbus called the island the Fragrant Isles. Legend said it was because of the refreshing scent of the cascarilla tree's bark, also called Eluethera bark. Thus, he had been named Columbus Isley, with his surname deriving from Isles. One of the fishermen who rescued Columbus said it was the last name of a famous singing group made up of brothers in the United States. Columbus couldn't remember having any brothers, but he did have a vague feeling that he had known a couple of men who looked like him.

As he'd done each and every morning at the crack of dawn for the last five years, Columbus Isley prepared breakfast for the guests at Morning Glory, a small lodge with only twelve rooms. He fingered the sparkling bottle-like emblem that hung from a thick gold chain around his neck after cracking the last egg. His friends had explained that it was a replica of a bat used to play an American game called baseball. The lodge provided only one television inside the bar, and it only got six local stations, so Columbus still had no idea what the game was. There was nothing even vaguely familiar about it to him.

Aside from the few tourists who actually traveled to the secret community located 583 miles off the Florida coast and the residents on the island, Columbus hadn't had much contact with the outside world. Only one telephone was in the lodge's office, and most residents depended on generators for electricity. There was no use of credit cards and only one bank. The mail boat came once a week, and only one flight arrived and departed twice weekly at Colonel Hill, a 4,000-foot airstrip on the southwest portion of the island.

Columbus, a black man with skin the color of honey and wild, curly, salt and pepper gray hair, piercing green eyes and the body of an African warrior, managed to catch the eye of a twenty-three-year-old white woman who originally came to Crooked Island accompanied by an addiction coach to overcome a problem with heroin. She also wanted to escape the fast-paced, drug-fueled modeling world in New York City and get her life and mental and physical well-being back.

Over the past couple of years, Ariel and Columbus had become very attached. One thing he remembered was how to make love to a woman, and how good his penis felt every time he entered her vagina. Just thinking about Ariel made Columbus's loins throb. He smiled. His lady was due back on Crooked Island on today's plane. Soon, they would be lying on a secluded beach, lost in a sea of lust.

His thoughts must have conjured her up. As Columbus got the coffee going, two milky-white arms wrapped around his waist. The beautiful woman's delicious smelling perfume engulfed him. He turned, pulled her to him, and then deeply kissed Ariel Pembrough, a bootylicious blonde with skin soft to the touch.

"You're back," Columbus said with a grin.

"Yes, I am," purred the supermodel, as her sky blue eyes glittered up at him. She stepped out of her yellow maxi sundress. She was panty-less.

Quickly locking the kitchen door, Columbus lifted her up on the counter and spread her legs. In the heat of passion he pulled his shorts down, then thrust his manhood into Ariel. These two lovers became one, losing themselves into each other.

"Well, that was a nice welcome," said Ariel as Columbus gently wiped her clean with a warm cloth as if she were a baby. She slipped her dress back on. Kissing her lightly on the lips, Columbus noticed the newspaper sticking out of her purse.

"What are you reading?"

"Oh, just an article about this wild murder case that's about to go on trial in Los Angeles today. It caught my attention because the guy in the photo looks like a lighter version of you. I thought he could be related to you or something. It says his name is Rolondo Jemison. It also involves the gossip columnist, Valerie Rollins. She's a friend of my mom's." Both names jarred something in his head. Columbus looked at the picture of the man. Sharp pains made him think his head was about to explode. A massive pounding in his chest quickly followed.

"Arrghhhh," he groaned as he collapsed on to the floor.

Chapter Two

Rolondo

Rolondo Jemison was on trial that Tuesday morning for multiple charges, which included impersonating his cousin, a missing baseball player named Royale Jones, felony drug possession, and kidnapping Wildin' Out, a prominent race horse that belonged to an African American jockey named Vance Dumas. Rolondo was also being tried for the murder of Vance's mother, Andrea Dumas.

Sometime during the trial, shortly after Judge Stanford Richardson asked the bailiff, "What is today's case?" a court officer pulled out a gun, shot another officer twice in the chest, and then tossed another gun to Rolondo.

"Thanks for nothing," Rolondo said, plowing two shots into his attorney's chest, killing her instantly as the bullets pierced her heart. Screams erupted as a mini exodus from the courtroom ensued. Armed with automatic rifles, two members of the jury stood and began wildly shooting anyone in sight.

Rome Nyland ducked for cover, then slowly stood and aimed at the court officer who had now become a perpetrator. He fired his gun. The NFL Hall of Famer turned private detective had been instrumental, along with his good friend Valerie Rollins, in aiding the Los Angeles Police Department with Rolondo Jemison's arrest. The bullet took the court officer down fast. At this stage of the melee, the only way to distinguish actual court employees from the perpetrators was that the good guys were either shielding people in the courtroom from bullets, or pushing them out the door as fast as they could. Rome ducked for cover again, then eased up, ready to fire.

Like a ghost, Rolondo had fled the courtroom. As his modus operandi usually indicated, Rolondo left havoc and bodies behind for others to clean up. With his exit, the bullets had ceased flying, and the LAPD's SWAT team stormed into the courtroom. Seeing they had matters under control, Rome dashed out of the door hoping to follow Rolondo's tracks.

Smooth as the cleverest of criminals, Rolondo Jemison had given the judge a hefty amount to solidify their arrangement. The Honorable Stanford Richardson, however, was one of the first people in the courtroom that Rolondo's boy capped. Inside the judge's chambers, Rolondo grabbed the duffle bag filled with cash from underneath the desk where the judge had stashed it. He then ran to the elevator that took him to the helipad on top of the courthouse.

As planned, Violet McClean aka Mrs. Vance Dumas waited for him with a makeup artist, Raven seated beside her. Although Raven worked at the MAC store in the Beverly Center, her boyfriend Roosevelt was a member of Rolondo's notorious gang, the Bugatti Blades. Raven had jumped at the chance to make a quick ten g's to transform Rolondo into a woman. Rolondo had been preparing for this day from the moment he was arrested. The dress bag Violet handed him held a mastectomy prosthetic bra that automatically gave him a 36 DD cup breasts. It also held a lace-front, black, long and curly wig that looked as if human hair naturally grew from his scalp. The gorgeous black St. John suit was designed to slay. Quickly, Rolondo changed clothes while on the rooftop. He had disguised himself as a woman many times for various schemes, so he strutted well in the four-inch Christian Louboutin heels that he slipped into. He sat on the opposite side of the makeup artist and told her, "Hurry the hell up!" The helicopter began its ascent into the blue sky.

Once the makeup artist worked her magic, Rolondo nonchalantly wrapped both of his hands around her neck and strangled every breath out of her body. Although Raven was tiny, she fought back fiercely, kicking Rolondo as well as attempting to remove his hands from her neck. Aside from him being too strong for her, Violet stepped in and held Raven's hands behind her back. The pilot never said a word. After all, he was a seasoned cop, who saw murders take place on a regular basis. Raven's still body lay at their feet, and Rolondo placed his two feet on her head for balance. He was ready to proceed with the mission at hand.

Within ten minutes, the helicopter started its descent onto the helipad on the grounds of the black dot.com billionaire, Victor Dumas's estate in the posh Bel Air community of LA. Victor Dumas was one of nine black billionaires in the world. At one time there had only been eight, but Michael Jordan reached billionaire status in 2014.

Violet's phone rang as soon as the helicopter touched down.

"Yes, Daddy. We're here," Violet said. "I'll put you on speaker."

"Hey, Sincere," said Janvieve.

"Hey, baby. That was some nice work you did back there. It's about time you stopped being a fuck-up. Now you and Violet get my grandchild, empty my brother's safe, and kill that bitch Valerie and anybody else who gets in the way.

"Violet, this is also your chance to redeem yourself from fucking up with Vance. I didn't plant you at Dumas Farms to watch you walk out on him." Thank God her father couldn't see her because Violet grimaced.

"I'm sorry, Daddy. I'm sick of that little prick Vance and his tiny dick, and I can't take that screaming brat. Do we really have to bring her with us?"

"Yes, you do. She is our billion dollar baby. Now get going, you two. And I'll see you tomorrow in Paris." The click on Sincere's phone ended anything else Violet or Rolondo might want to add.

Not even bothering to look back or down at the life he just ended, Janvieve Rochon emerged. Neither Caitlyn Jenner, Ayanna Bynum, nor Laverne Cox had anything on her. Rolondo's new personae, Janvieve Roshon, was now Violet's aunt. The two of them got out of the helicopter just as a member of Victor Dumas's security team approached them. When he saw Violet, he smiled.

"Oh, it's you, Mrs. Dumas. Is everything okay? Why did you arrive in an LAPD helicopter?" he asked. Before he could utter another word, Violet fired two bullets straight into his forehead. The guard's stiff body slammed hard onto the ground.

Undeterred by the murder, Violet and Janvieve entered the guest house, which was now Val's office. They found Amerani Logan, Valerie's assistant, there. She was busy packing up paperwork to take to her boss in New York, as well as emailing out MP3s of Val's radio show "Gossip On The Go With Valerie Ro" to the stations that carried it. Val would be taking the entire summer off from her show, but insisted she only email one week's worth of recordings.

"What's up, Violet? How are you?" Amerani asked with a happy expression but terror-filled eyes. She also forced a smile at Janvieve, whom she had a vague feeling she had seen somewhere before. As she extended her hand to the woman to introduce herself, she was so nervous she dropped the folder she had been preparing for Val. The contents flew over the entire desk.

Dammit! She must have seen Violet shoot that guard, Janvieve theorized. *Just our luck. Her acting skills are terrible! She's really trying to pretend she didn't see anything, but her eyes tell me everything. She gets an epic fail!*

"Nothing much," Violet answered politely. "I'm in town for the day and thought I would drop by to see my daughter and Val. Since Val is always working, I thought they'd be out here. Are they upstairs?" Amerani hesitated before answering.

"Well, Rome was afraid something might go down at the courthouse this morning, so he convinced Val to take the baby to New York to be with Victor and Vance. They took a red-eye flight last night. As usual, his inclination was on the money." Having no idea that he was standing right in front of her, Amerani continued, "Rolondo Jemison escaped from the courtroom a little while ago."

"Who is Rolondo Jemison?" asked Janvieve.

Playing along, Violet answered, "He's a career criminal who went on trial today for murdering Vance's mom, Andrea Dumas, kidnapping his racehorse, and I think drug trafficking was also one of the charges. I can't believe Rolondo was able to escape."

"Yes, it is unbelievable. I wanted to go to New York with them, but Val needed me to take care of some last minute things here, so she took Cantrese with her. Cantrese didn't even have time to pack a bag or call anyone. They left in a flash. Val even told her they'd buy her some clothes when they got to New York. I'm going to fly out tomorrow."

With a perturbed expression, Janvieve said, "I know you were probably thinking it was best to tell the truth, especially if you had any chance of getting out of here today with your life, but I've got some really bad news . . ."

Janvieve shook her head as she pulled out a pistol and pointed it at Amerani's head. "I'm sorry, honey. That is one trip you aren't going to make." She pulled the trigger. Amerani's limp body hit the floor.

Calmly, Janvieve told Violet, "Our plans have changed. We are headed to New York." His gaze shifted left, placing him in thinking mode. "Andrea once told me that Victor's safe is in his den. Let's at least clean it out. Sincere isn't going to like this."

"Yes, that's where it is. The safe is behind a portrait of Vance and Wildin' Out."

"Snap to it Violet. Let's go!" ordered Janvieve. "Money awaits. And so does death if the cops catch us."

Chapter Three

Violet

A s she had done her entire life, Violet followed
whatever instructions her cousin, whom she had
always called "Uncle" Rolondo but who was now
"Aunt Janvieve," gave her. Deep down in her heart she
knew that like her father's guidance, those instructions
weren't always the right thing to do, but it was almost as if
they had programmed her. This was the only way she knew
how to live.

"I love these black and white checks," Violet murmured
as she glanced at the interior of the little house filled with
MacKenzie-Childs home goods and furniture. "Looks like
Val is grooming Valencia to follow in her footsteps." She
remembered Val referring to the space as her 'bat cave.'
Valencia's yellow crib and matching rug had the courtly
checkered pattern on it in the corner next to a tiny table with
a tea party set and matching bib. For one slight second, there
was a tug at Violet's heart. Not looking back at her
daughter's belongings a second time, Violet led the way to
the inside of the huge mansion. Vance had given her the
combination to the safe shortly after they got married
because he also kept their important papers in it.

"You must really hate your husband and daughter a hell
of a lot, huh?" Janvieve asked. "You looked tortured."

Violet released a slight inaudible sigh.

"Daaamn! Vance must have really put you through hell. On second thought, your father's the one that put you in hell," Janvieve commented. "But it'll all be worth it in the end, you beautiful black China doll you. You'll see. So don't think for one moment that I can't tell you're torn up inside about everything that's happened."

"Did I ask you for a conversation, Uncle Rolondo? Oops, I mean, *Aunt* Janvieve."

"It doesn't matter whether you did or not. I'm offering, honey."

"Look, I grew up with Vance, and that little freak of a child did come out of my body. So sue me if I'm not completely heartless like you and Daddy."

"Honestly, I don't feel sorry for you one bit. You're coming out of this thing a billion dollars richer, so you will be all right. We all will be all right. Sometimes you have to do strange things for love, loyalty, and mountains of money."

Like marry your own cousin, Violet thought.

"Look at me, honey, I'm dressed as a woman!" Janvieve laughed.

Violet's face held a stone cold expression. As soon as she turned eighteen, following her father's instructions, she became Vance Dumas's secret lover. He was easy to seduce. That woman Vance married behind her back, Roshonda Rhodes, almost messed up her dad's plans. But Violet got pregnant following her father's orders once again. Vance and Roshonda became history. The only glitch in the whole set-up was that Violet hated their baby as soon as Valencia was born. Something in the back of her mind kept telling her that creating a child with her cousin made the kid a freak. She couldn't even look at her. She was sure a lightning bolt was going to strike her dead for participating in her father's incestuous deed.

"Here, take these!" Janvieve bumped Violet's arm. "Take a time-out from your reminiscing. Money first. Always!" After handing Violet a pair of white cloth gloves and putting on a pair herself, Janvieve quickly removed the portrait from the wall. Neither of them could believe what they found inside the safe. There were stacks and stacks of hundred dollar bills and at least fifty boxes of jewelry, all different sizes.

Violet's eyes sparkled with greed. *With this new found fortune, I can finally rid myself of my father's constant demands and Vance for good. I've gotta get away from here before I go crazy.* In one smooth move, she reached into the hidden pocket of her flowered Oscar de la Renta dress, pulled out the tiniest gun that anyone had ever seen, and shot Janvieve twice in the heart.

Eyes wide and filled with surprise, Janvieve's body slumped onto the couch next to the safe.

Violet ran into Vance's bedroom where she knew there still had to be some luggage, and grabbed a Louis Vuitton suitcase. Running back to the safe, she emptied all of the contents into it. *It's best to leave on my own now.* She remembered seeing a white convertible Jaguar F-type parked in front of Val's office upon her arrival. *So Amerani must be using the Jag now*, she thought. Still having the extra key on her key ring, she ran back outside and called for the rogue cop who had gladly accepted Rolondo's money to pilot the getaway helicopter.

"Officer, we need your help in here," Violet said, waving him over with a helpless expression.

The minute he started walking toward her, Violet fired two shots into his head, leaving him in a heap near the helicopter. From there, Violet McClean-Dumas casually strolled out the back door of her father-in-law's mansion, threw the suitcase filled with her new found fortune into the seat next to her, then drove off with possibly millions of dollars and jewelry. Still, she planned to kill Val and snatch her child. But for now those plans could wait. She would text her secret insider later and tell her she never made it to Los Angeles to visit Valencia. That way, only her father could connect her to what had transpired today. He would never rat her out, and there was no reason for him to know about all the goodies she had just found.

The world was now Violet's oyster!

Chapter Four

Valerie

Dead tired from all that rushing out of Los Angeles to possibly save her own life and others, Valerie Rollins, was just waking up. She glanced at the clock on the nightstand. It read two p.m. No matter what the circumstances were, she got up at the crack of dawn to do her radio show, "Gossip On The Go With Valerie Ro" every morning at four.

"I can't believe I slept until the afternoon," she said, taking a moment to look at her surroundings. *Okay. I'm in the Royal Suite on the twenty-second floor of the Ritz Carlton hotel on Central Park South in New York.* The bedroom was exquisite. Everything in the room including, the chairs, the tables, even the comforter was white.

A little before seven a.m., their flight had landed at JFK International Airport. A black Cadillac Escalade with security cars in front and back had whisked Val, Cantrese, a young lady she was grooming to work with her, the nanny Esperanza, Valencia (the baby girl of her soon-to-be stepson, Vance), to the hotel. Her fiancé Victor had been out in the Hamptons getting business together when they arrived. He should have been here by now.

The suite was uncannily quiet. *The baby, Esperanza, and Cantrese must all still be asleep too,* Valerie thought. Stretching her arms and legs, she turned on the television, and then headed into the bathroom. *I've got to get this day going.* She had given Cantrese money when they got to the hotel to run down Fifth Avenue and pick up some clothes once the stores opened.

Although the tension was high because of the impending threat, she still thought everyone could have a leisurely lunch here at the hotel together. They were safe here. She washed her face, and as she brushed her teeth, her thoughts were interrupted by Cantrese and Esperanza yelling and banging on her door.

"Come in. What's going on?" Val asked.

Cantrese was the first to answer.

"Turn to channel four. There's a special news bulletin. Rolondo Jemison escaped from the courtroom this morning. There was a bloodbath. They don't know where he is."

A look of terror spread over Val's face. She wanted to scream and cry, but she didn't want to frighten Cantrese or Esperanza. Val raced back into the bedroom and turned up the sound on the television. The reporter was actually interviewing Rome. That was weird. He hated doing interviews and normally left that up to her. But on Rome's orders she wasn't in Los Angeles. *When did this happen? And why hadn't Rome or Victor called me with this information?*

"Oh Lord, I never took my phone out of my purse when we got to the hotel this morning. Too tired." Val reached inside her Hermes Birkin purse. The phone was deader than a corpse. She plugged in the charger and put the phone on it immediately. Val listened carefully as Rome, wearing an Armani Collezioni suit with a black shirt and black tie, spoke to the reporter.

"I had a feeling that Rolondo would pull something like this. The prosecution's case against him was solid. He was getting ready to spend the rest of his life in jail and I knew that didn't sit well with him and he would do anything to be free," Rome said.

As usual, Rome looks good. In a previous life, he must have been the prototype for Will Smith's "Men in Black" movies because his entire wardrobe is black, Val thought.

"Mr. Nyland, is it true that you shot and killed at least one of his henchman today in the court room?" asked the reporter.

"Unfortunately it is. I have already turned my gun over to the LAPD, and after I check on my fiancée, I am headed straight to police headquarters. I felt it best to make sure no other innocent lives were lost today at the hands of Rolondo Jemison, so I did what I had to do."

"One more question, Mr. Nyland. Has anyone been able to locate former Major League Baseball Hall of Fame player, Royale Jones, whom Rolondo was impersonating?"

Rome shook his head.

"As far as I know, no one has found him as of yet. Mr. Jones is still missing. Excuse me, I have to take this call."

Since her phone was dead, Val picked up the phone in the room and dialed Rome's number. It went straight to voice mail. She hung up to dial Victor, but heard the front door to the suite open.

"Val, where are you?" Victor called out. Thank God, her man was finally here. She ran into the living room and gave him a tight hug.

"Honey, did you hear what happened in Los Angeles this morning with Rolondo?"

"Yes, sweetheart." He nodded sadly. "In spite of all that had transpired at the courthouse, just looking at you and hearing your voice brings a smile to my face. I love you so much, woman!" Although they had Esperanza and Cantrese as an audience, he kept hugging her. Then he kissed Valerie long and hard right in front of their staff just as his son Vance let himself into the suite.

Vance frowned, seeing their display of affection. "Oh, come on! That clown Rolondo is on the run, and all you two can do is make out?" Vance looked at his father and Val and shook his head. "We still don't know where Dad's brother Valerian is hiding out. I can't reach Violet. Our world is falling apart right in front of our faces. Are you both crazy?"

Val smiled as she looked at Victor and Vance. No father and son could be more opposite. Even dressed casually, Victor was always the epitome of elegance. Today, he wore head-to-toe Prada, a short sleeve cotton/silk multi-color shirt, beige slacks and Saffriano Logo drivers shoes. Vance, whose height was just slightly over five feet, looked like a mischievous little boy. He had on a white T-shirt, jean shorts, and bright red Giuseppe Zanotti sneakers.

As his phone rang, Victor told Vance, "No, we're not crazy. We're just madly in love and missing each other." He answered the call.

"Victor Dumas . . . Hey, Rome. I was just getting ready to call you to see what our next move is." As he listened, Victor's smile turned into a scowl. "Are you sure? I'll have the pilot get the plane ready to return to LA right away." He glanced at Valerie. "A serious crime scene! Oh God! Four bodies . . . Are you telling me I can't even come onto my own grounds?"

"Four bodies? What's going on, Dad?" Vance asked.

Victor held the phone a few inches from his face.

"Rome says we have to stay put in New York until the detectives say we can come home. Four people have been killed on our property."

Val's eyes narrowed. "What! Oh my God!" she said.

"He tried to reach you, but your phone went to voice mail." Victor put his mouth near the phone again. "Vance is here with us. I'll have him try to locate Violet. I think we're okay with security. I'll let Val know you will call her soon. Talk to you later, Rome." Victor motioned to everyone in the room to sit down.

"Darling, why didn't you let me speak to Rome, and why are you looking so frightened all of a sudden?" Val asked.

He put his arm around her and pulled her close as they sat down on the couch.

"As you've already heard, Rolondo broke out of jail this morning. There are a lot of dead people at the courthouse. Apparently, he used a police helicopter to escape. Rome just told me that our yard man showed up to the house a little while ago. There was a police helicopter on the grounds. Being just a yard man who works for a company, he had no numbers on any of us, so he called nine-one-one. When the police got there, they found several people dead. One of the officers on the scene is a friend of Rome's and was aware of his connection to us, so he called him. Rome is on his way there now.

"Val, thank God we got you and the baby out of there last night. That was a right-on call by Rome," Victor said.

Val grabbed the phone on the table.

"I need to check on Amerani. I'm praying she wasn't at work. Other than her and George, the house should be empty. I gave the rest of the staff the next couple of days off since none of us are there. Oh God, please let them be okay." Right away Val dialed Amerani's cell phone which went straight to voice mail. Then she dialed the landline in her office. It went to voice mail too. Dreadful tears flowed down her face. *It is after eleven a.m. in Los Angeles. There is no way that Amerani wouldn't have answered one of those phones.*

For probably the first time in her life, Val was speechless. She struggled to gather her thoughts. Rome had saved her life once again. There was no doubt in her mind that Rolondo had gone to the house to kill her and possibly Valencia. Most likely, when he discovered that she and the baby weren't home, he killed whoever else got in his way. She looked at everyone.

"First, we have to find out if Amerani and George are all right and who the other victims could be. Cantrese, keep trying to locate Amerani. Dial every number in the house, text her and send an email. When you're finished with that, I need to feed you guys. So go through the room service menu and order lunch. I have to get dressed. I will never forgive myself if something happened to my little Amerani."

This tragedy must have made its way into the second bedroom. The sound of the baby crying reminded them all that they were one and had to be strong for Valencia.

"I'll go see to her," Vance said quietly.

The last thing Valerie had imagined was for the summer she had always dreamed of in the Hamptons to start out with all of this murder and mayhem. But she was a resilient child of God and as usual, whenever she had to face adversity, she would make the best of it. She kissed Victor lightly on the lips, then headed into the bedroom. Knowing a warm bath would soothe her nerves, she turned on both spigots and steam rose up toward the ceiling within seconds. Quickly, she undressed and eased into the water, closing her eyes in prayer and finally crying aloud.

"Baby, it's going to be all right," Victor said as he entered the bedroom and locked the door. He'd heard Val sobbing and immediately went to comfort her. Kicking off his shoes, he removed his clothes and entered the bathroom. Victor lowered himself into the bathtub with Valerie. "Sweetheart, it really is going to be all right."

"No, it's not." Valerie wiped her tears away. "Why won't Rolondo and Valerian leave us alone? They're not going to stop until we're all dead or you give them all of your money. I know something happened to Amerani. She would have called me by now. She knows where we're staying, so even if my cell phone is dead, she would have called the hotel room."

Victor's sad, sympathetic gaze told her that she was right, but they had to stay strong. Hoping to ease her fear, stress, and grief, he kissed her on the shoulder once, then twice. Val closed her eyes as Victor kissed his way up and down the contours of her neck. An erotic sigh escaped her full lips. Victor touched one of her nipples as his mouth absorbed the other one. He wanted to show Valerie how much he loved and desired her and moved his tongue to her ear.

"Baby, we are still here on this earth, and we are together. Vance and Valencia are fine. We are fine. I'm praying for Amerani because that is all any of us can do. But as for Valerian and Rolondo, together we can beat them at anything they throw at us. We will win this war." He kissed Val deeply, then slowly moved on top of her. The Jacuzzi tub shot out relaxing warm water that soothed them both.

Their bodies moved in unison, giving each other all they had.

"You are so right," Val whispered, "nothing or no one can keep us down."

Just as they put all the horror of the morning behind them, a news bulletin from their house flashed across the television in the bathroom. The police were bringing a body out on a gurney. A tiny arm bearing the Cartier watch that Valerie had given Amerani for Christmas was sticking out. Val's worries had become a reality.

Val screamed, "Amerani is dead!"

Chapter Five

Janvieve

Janvieve awoke with a throbbing head. For a moment, she was disoriented. Looking around Victor's luxurious den, she realized where she was. *That stupid slut spawn of Sincere's actually shot me.* She slowly stood, removed her jacket, then the shell beneath it and felt the bulletproof vest she wore. After pulling the slug out of the vest, she felt her temple where the bullet had grazed her forehead and caused her to pass out. A small amount of blood was on her hand when she looked at it, but it had dried up, leaving just a slight scratch.

The first thing she had to do was to get out of here. She could hear people moving around the house. Years ago, Andrea had demonstrated to Rolondo that the bookcase in the den was actually the door to a safe room. Often, Rolondo was in the house with Andrea when that prick Victor was either in Kentucky or New York. As a result, Janvieve knew the keyboard access was right on the side and the code was Andrea's birthday, 9-18-60. She punched in the numbers. It was amazing how fast the bookcase slid open. Grabbing her purse, she dashed inside, then closed it fast.

Because of her loyalty to Sincere since they were kids, Janvieve hated Victor Dumas and all his brainiac wealth with a passion. *But shit, the sorry ass motherfucker sure does know how to live! This joint is mad stupid.* It wasn't a safe room. It was a safe paradise! She walked around the living room. Bright orange pillows adorned a beige sofa with a matching love seat. Two orange plush chairs were in front of what he knew was a bulletproof security window that no one on the outside could see. The high-round dining room table even had orange chairs around it. The television covered one entire wall. She clicked it, hoping to see what the newscasters had to say about Rolondo Jemison's escape. It was still early for the news, so she walked through the rest of the place. There were three bedrooms, which each had their own bathrooms and televisions. She recognized one of them as being a replica of a photo he'd seen of a room in the Taj Mahal in India.

Janvieve headed back into the living room. *Damn, I could use some blow right now.* She opened the fully stocked liquor cabinet and poured a glass of Chivas Regal scotch, swallowing it in one gulp, then poured another. "This liquor will have to do for now." She eased back on the couch and reached over to the panel of buttons on the wall. With a flick of a switch, a row of small paintings on the wall turned into monitors. *Hot damn! This system is tight!* She could see all over the house. She flicked a switch to the outside. The property was crawling with reporters, cops, and detectives. Janvieve spotted a familiar face amongst all the uniforms and plainclothes cops. She should have known Rome, who thought he was a real-life Shaft, would be hot on her trail.

"This bastard is like a damn roach that can't be stomped out. He has more lives than a frigging vampire! He just refuses to die." Janvieve simmered in her anger and slammed her right fist against the couch. At least three times Rolondo had tried to kill Rome. He would get him one day.

Janvieve watched as they loaded three body bags into Medical Examiner trucks and lifted one more into an ambulance. The only problem with this system was she couldn't hear what they were saying.

With hunger now nagging at her, Janvieve opened the refrigerator and wasn't surprised that the freezer was fully stocked with made-to-order frozen dinners. She found one with filet mignon, au gratin potatoes and string beans written on it. She unwrapped it, then popped it in the microwave oven that was built into the wall. For now, she would have a delicious dinner, get drunk and chill out here for the night.

She decided not to call Sincere or Violet. Maybe it was best that they think Rolondo was dead for the time being. Janvieve was sick of those two anyway. All Sincere ever did was call him stupid. But, Rolondo was far from being stupid. He knew the real bulk of Royale's fortune had never been touched. Some of it was stashed away in banks in Florida and New York. But a few million dollars was locked away in a vault under the Holy Temple of Mary Magdalene Church in Sag Harbor, which was out in the Hamptons in New York. Janvieve had even learned from a preservationist who expressed interest in the property that the Underground Railroad's last stop had been under that church for slaves who traveled up from Virginia and the Carolinas. There was a room concealed beneath a still-extant trap door under the main sanctuary.

Rolondo and Royale used to spend summers in Sag Harbor with their cousin Claude when they were young. The three of them were the same age. Rolondo and Royale were the sons of identical twin sisters who had married identical twin brothers. Claude's mom, Victoria, was their mothers' older sister, and his dad was their fathers' older brother. The three of them looked like triplets although Rolondo's complexion was a little lighter than his two cousins. He also used the last name Jemison instead of Jones because of all the trouble with the law. The fewer people tracking him down from the sordid past he had lived, the better it was for him.

Sincere was also their cousin. His mom Valerie was their mothers' middle sister. Janvieve laughed.

"I guess since Sincere and Victor are half-brothers, that means Victor is Royale, Claude, and my half-cousin." *That's a funny thought. It's also crazy that the name Valerie is so intertwined in Victor's life. His mother's name had been Valerie, his father's mistress's name was Valerie, and now he is engaged to that celebrity snitch-bitch, Valerie.*

Tomorrow, Janvieve would figure a way to slip out of this joint and go get what was rightfully hers. Not trusting the pilot, she had carried the Marc Jacobs handbag off the helicopter that Violet had given her. The purse had new identification cards and a passport for Janvieve Rochon in it, as well as a burner cell phone. Before leaving the helicopter, Janvieve had stuffed as much of the judge's payoff money as she could into it and more into her panties, shoes, and stockings. Thinking she was slicker than grease, Miss Violet had been too dumb to look inside the purse. Janvieve kicked off her shoes, pulled off her skirt, undies and stockings. Bills tumbled out. It also felt good to let her dick swing freely. She wished she had a woman to stick her dick in. She had been in jail for almost two years. There had to be a maid around here whose pussy she could tear into after all the heat left and before she got out of here. She organized the money. As soon as she snuck out of here, she would buy some clothes and a plane ticket to New York. She would catch up with Violet and put her to sleep soon. It was time to get this party started!

Janvieve took another gulp of scotch as she watched Rome and two detectives enter the den. This safe room had been built early in Victor and Andrea's marriage, so she was hoping that Rome didn't know it existed.

"Rome Nyland definitely has to die sooner than later," Janvieve whispered. "His fucking around with my life has to stop! In the meantime, I have one last deadly play to render before leaving Los Angeles."

Chapter Six

Turquoise

Turquoise had been purposely avoiding Rome's calls since this morning when she heard on the news that the man she thought was Royale Jones had shot his way out of a courtroom. She didn't want to hear Rome's little innuendoes about her and Royale/Rolondo, or whatever his name really was.

Nut brown, boasting an hourglass figure with a derriere that rivaled both Serena Williams and Nicki Minaj's, and her hair cascading around her face in twists, Turquoise Hobson was stunning. Dressed to the nines in an Anthony Vaccarello black and silver studded dress and leather ankle boots with metal detail by Hedi Slimane for Saint Laurent, Turquoise sat at the bar at Craig's restaurant on Melrose Avenue in West Hollywood waiting for a new client, Samantha Stephenson. She had met the young woman earlier in the day at an Open House she'd hosted. Turquoise owned her own real estate firm, and the home she was selling was located in Calabasas.

Samantha's husband had recently been traded to the Los Angeles Dodgers from the New York Mets. She happened to be driving past the house after visiting another player's wife in the area, saw Turquoise's sign outside and decided to stop in and take a look. She and her husband were staying in a hotel. Therefore, she wanted to find something fast. Turquoise jumped on the opportunity, offering her services to be their exclusive realtor. They made an appointment to meet at her office the next day. Then Samantha mentioned that she was meeting a few other players' wives that night at Craig's and suggested Turquoise join them for dinner. Turquoise accepted the invitation without hesitation. All she could think of was how professional baseball players' wives could turn into clients, and more clients meant more money.

In actuality, Turquoise had been wanting to check out Craig's for some time. It was owned by Craig Susser, who had worked at Dan Tana's restaurant for years. The place was on fire. All of the A-list celebrities like Paula Patton, Chrissy Teigen, Kim Kardashian, and Dwayne Wade and Gabrielle Union dined here. Maybe she would get lucky and run into one of them this evening. Turquoise spotted her client Samantha.

The two women exchanged greetings and were just being seated in a private VIP Room. They were the only diners in there.

"They seat all of the baseball players and their spouses back here," Samantha explained with a smile.

"Lovely. This is how I love to roll," Turquoise replied as she glanced around. A waiter came over and asked if they would care for a drink.

"I want to try something different," said Turquoise. "What do you suggest?"

"Our house specialty is the skinny margarita. It's made with George Clooney, Randy Gerber, and Mike Meldman's ever-popular tequila and combines Casamigos Blanco, fresh lime juice, agave nectar, and pomegranate juice. I guarantee you that it is delicious!"

Samantha giggled. She looked like a young Louise Vyent, who was one of the most sought after black models in the nineties. Her black curls bloomed around her face like flowers.

"Well, I don't know who those other two guys are, but anything that George Clooney owns is more than good enough for me," Turquoise agreed.

"The Gerber guy is married to the model Cindy Crawford. Two skinny margaritas for us!"

"Okay. I'll get the drinks and give you two beautiful ladies time to look over the menu."

Turquoise smiled at Samantha. She was a lovely young woman.

"Are your other friends on the way?"

"No, they all had to cancel. You know how busy people get. So tell me about yourself, Turquoise. It's obvious you have a hot man with all that ice you're wearing. Girl, I need sunglasses just to sit next to your hands. That rock on your left hand must be at least ten carats, and that canary diamond heart on your right hand is simply stunning!"

Although she was disappointed that she wasn't having dinner with more potential clients, Turquoise politely answered.

"I'm engaged to Rome Nyland. You may have heard of him. He used to play in the NFL. Now he's in business for himself. He's a pretty generous guy."

"Oh wow! Of course I've heard of him. I saw him on television this morning. I guess he was in the courtroom when that guy Rolondo something or other broke out of jail. Generous is an understatement. Isn't that heart ring from Tiffany's? I was at the flagship store on Fifth Avenue in New York with my husband not too long ago and looked at one just like it. Girl, I love me some blue boxes from Tiffany."

"I'll be glad when the drinks arrive."

Turquoise didn't want to talk about the heart ring. She didn't even know why she continued to wear the bauble. Well, actually she did. It was just too gorgeous for her not to sport it every day. She had told Rome she had inherited the ring from her Aunt Winifred who had passed away when he asked where she got it. She thanked her lucky stars when their drinks arrived before she had to comment on it.

Setting the drinks down in front of them, the waiter asked, "Have you two ladies had a chance to look at the menu yet?"

"No we haven't," Turquoise told him, "but I've been reading so much about the honey truffle fried chicken that I'll have that and the chopped salad with no cheese to start.

"That sounds like a plan to me. I'll have exactly what you're having. I love me any kind of fried chicken."

"Thank you, ladies."

Turquoise took a sip of her drink.

"Oooh, this is good."

Watching Samantha lift her glass to her lips to take a sip of her margarita, Turquoise noticed she wasn't wearing a wedding ring. Instead, there was a pave diamond ring encrusted with a Wildcat head on her finger. She also had on a matching necklace. That was odd. Royale had played baseball for the Los Angeles Wildcats.

"You mentioned this afternoon that your husband played for the Dodgers. Isn't that Los Angeles Wildcat jewelry that you have on?"

"You must have misheard me. I told you he played for the Wildcats." Samantha moved in very close to Turquoise and stuck a gun into her side. "Don't you dare scream or make even the smallest sound. Listen, you are going to get up and walk out of here with me very fast. We are going to take a little ride. And don't even think about calling your wannabe cop fiancé. I took your phone out of your purse the moment we sat down. Oh. One more thing. Rolondo would like his ring back. Raise up slowly. I'll lead you out. One false move and you are one dead, trifling gold digger."

Turquoise had never had a gun pulled on her before. She totally froze and did what Samantha asked. As Turquoise stood, Samantha snatched the heart ring from Tiffany's off her finger. Then she grabbed her engagement ring off her left hand.

"I want this one too."

With a magician's sleight of hand, Samantha also snatched Turquoise's five-carat diamond heart necklace that she had received as a birthday gift from Rome. Then she quickly whisked her out of the restaurant and pushed her into the seat of a bright red Bugatti.

Samantha drove to her apartment building, which wasn't that far from the restaurant where two men were waiting in a burgundy Lincoln Navigator. Samantha told Turquoise, "If you want to stay alive, just do what you're told."

"Why are you doing this? Who are you?" Turquoise reluctantly got in the truck with the men.

Samantha spat in her face, then whispered, "We are the Bugatti Blades. We know who we are. But you forgot who you were. See you in purgatory, bitch!"

The Navigator sped off erratically.

Wearing both of Turquoise's rings, Samantha waved to a young kid as if nothing had just transpired as he approached her.

"Hi, Miss Samantha."

Reaching into her Michael Kors purse and pulling out money, Samantha smiled at him.

"Hey, baby. You are just the young man I want to see. I have to go to New York City for a few days. Here is fifty dollars. Look out for my car."

"You got it. No problem, Miss Samantha."

She kissed him on the cheek, then scurried inside to get packed for her trip. Her job was done here.

Chapter Seven

Rome

Earlier that evening . . .

Pick up, Turquoise!" Rome said as if the words would reach her telepathically. Her cell rang.

"Hey, baby," she purred. "I just noticed that you've been blowing up my phone. What's wrong?"

"Thank God I finally got you. I've been trying to reach you all day."

"I was way down by Palm Springs showing a house, and there was no reception out in the desert. I already heard about Rolondo breaking out of jail. Are you all right, sweetie?"

"I'm fine, baby. It's a good thing I got Val out of here last night though. All clues point to Rolondo possibly hightailing it to Victor's house first. Several people were killed, but as usual the SOB got away."

"Rome, I swear it seems as if Val is all you ever think about most times."

"Turquoise, did you hear what I just said? Val could have been hurt and you too. So, I'm concerned about your well-being rather than who I think about most. People were killed. Did any of that register?"

"Yes, baby. It did. And that's terrible!"

"Yeah, it is. Look, I'm afraid Rolondo might come after you."

"I wasn't anything to Rolondo other than his real estate agent. He doesn't want anything from me."

"Babe, why don't you cancel all of your appointments for the next few days and fly with me to New York? I would feel much better if you and Val were in the same place. I'll come and get you now and help you pack. We'll check into the Four Seasons in Beverly Hills for the night and take the first flight out in the morning. How about it?"

"Rome, I have too much on my plate for that. I just can't stop everything I'm doing and go to New York just because that lowlife's on the run. Look, I have to go. I'm at Craig's right now. I'll call you as soon as we finish dinner. Maybe we can have a nightcap later."

"But, baby . . ."

The phone went dead in Rome's ear as he sat inside his Cadillac SRX. "What was that all about?" he asked himself. Regardless of what she said, he was still worried about her. She mentioned she was at Craig's. He knew it was on Melrose. He would swing past there and at least follow her back to her place just to be sure Rolondo wasn't staking her out. His phone rang. It was Val.

"Hey, I was just getting ready to call you."

"Hey. A lot of my media friends have been calling me now that word is out about the home invasion. They're telling me that three people are dead. I saw the watch I gave

Amerani on the wrist of someone being carried out of there. Who are the deceased?"

"A woman who had no identification on her was found strangled in the helicopter. There was a full case of make-up and wigs in the seat near her. So my assumption is that she was a makeup artist, and Rolondo may be moving around in drag. The police pilot is also dead. It serves him right for being a dirty cop. Unfortunately, your security guy George was also killed. The police are notifying his family now."

"Oh my God! Poor George. Victor and I will call his people to take care of any arrangements and compensate them, but no amount of money can replace a life. I feel so terrible. All he was doing was his job. He shouldn't be dead. Please tell me about Amerani. Was that her?"

"I'm sorry, Val. Amerani had already arrived at the house before the perpetrators got there. She was shot twice in the head. She's still alive, but in a coma. The doctors told me that her prognosis doesn't look good. The paramedics took her to UCLA Medical Center. However, I told the police not to tell the media she's alive, and you can tell Victor, but do it privately. Don't let anyone else hear you, not even Vance. If she makes it, she will be able to identify her shooter, so I don't want Rolondo or anyone else who might have done this to try to finish the job."

"I understand. I am so relieved that she's alive. Rome, she was one of the kids from a shelter that I mentored. She doesn't really have anybody. Hire private nurses to sit with her around the clock and get security to the hospital. Put her under the assumed name of Margaret Scholz. Text me all of the hospital's information. I want the city's best neurologists in on this."

"I got you. What are you going to do about the media?"

"Well, since we are already having a press conference on Thursday to announce the polo team, we might as well wait until then to address what happened today, and by then we should know more. We have tomorrow to pull it all together. I guess we're here now for the time being. Can you get here for the press conference?"

"Yeah, I am out here in the streets now trying to see if Rolondo's cronies will tell me anything. I'm going to run up on this rapper, Cayenne, who's down with the Bugatti Blades. For the right amount of money, he'll dime out his own mother. Maybe he can give me a few clues. I'll be in New York some time tomorrow night. Book me a room."

"You got it. I'll put some feelers out and see what I can find out also. See you tomorrow. And Rome, please try not to get killed tonight. We need you."

"Yo, baby girl. I am the grim reaper, so he can't get me. Later." Rome decided to check up on Turquoise at Craig's before he went to look for the rapper.

Upon arriving and showing the maître d' Turquoise's picture, he learned the maître d' was looking for her also. She and another woman had skipped out after they had a couple of drinks and ordered dinner. Rome gave the guy two one-hundred dollar bills, then hightailed it out of the place.

This was crazy. There was no reason for Turquoise to walk out on a bill. She had his black American Express card, and she was making good money. *Who was this new client she was meeting anyway?* He dialed her cell. No answer. Instead of calling her office, he decided to drive on over to North Canon Drive in Beverly Hills. It didn't take him long to get there. He didn't have a good feeling once he arrived.

On the ground floor, it was pitch black. He tried the door. It was obvious she wasn't there. He tried calling her cell again. Still no answer.

Rome got back in the car and headed toward Turquoise's townhouse in Ladera Heights. He had a key, so when he arrived he let himself in.

"Baby. Turquoise, are you here?" He searched every room and thought of every place she could possibly go and came up with nothing. Defeated by his findings, he sat down and punched up his friend James Pace, a lieutenant in the Los Angeles Police Department.

Pace picked up on the first ring.

"How's it going, man?"

"Not good. My fiancée Turquoise is missing. I think it could have something to do with Jemison's escape."

James sighed.

"Man, I never wanted to be the one to have to tell you this, but that girl Turquoise Hobson has been playing you this whole time. She went to see Rolondo once after he was arrested. He paid off one of the correctional officers. We could never be sure who it was, but everyone knows he let the two of them get it on in a private interviewing room. The guys here are pretty sure their little session was videotaped."

"Wait a minute, Pace. What the hell are you saying?"

"No one has seen it, Rome, but Rolondo sure bragged about it. He made countless collect calls to her office number, but after that escapade, she never accepted his calls. All he talked about to other inmates was getting even with you and her."

Rome couldn't believe what he was hearing. He balled his hand into a fist and banged on the truck's Dashboard.

"James, we have been boys since college. How could you have kept this from me?"

"You know that's police business. I couldn't say anything to you. Listen, I tried to give you hints. For some reason you never caught on. When is the last time you spoke to her?"

"A few hours ago, but I went past the restaurant where she told me she was eating. There was no reservation in her name, so I showed the maître d' her picture. He told me she'd left without paying the check. She's not answering her cell, and she's not at her office. I'm at her house, and she's not here either. My gut says Rolondo got to her."

"Or the slut is somewhere with her legs wide open for another guy," James murmured.

"James, what the hell did you just say about my girl?"

"Look, man. I'm sorry about all of this. We have to give this until the morning. If she doesn't show up by then, we'll get right on it. I'm sorry, Rome. Sit tight."

"Yeah, man. If there is a sex tape with my woman and Rolondo out there, I need to get my hands on it. I'm disappointed in how you did me, man. I don't care about police business. We've been boys too long for you to withhold information from me like that. This is my life and future with this woman we're talking about. Later!" Rome had no intention of "sitting tight." He had to round up a couple of Rolondo's little gang minions and get ahead of this chaos and fast.

He refused to dwell on what James had just told him about Turquoise and Rolondo. In the back of his mind he had always known something was going on with the two of them. Val had begged him not to get engaged to Turquoise. First, Davida, his son's mother cheated on him, and now Turquoise, only the second woman he had ever loved, had done the same thing. Being a nice guy was now a thing of the past. He was going to be like every other player out there. His new motto was "the more notches on his jock strap, the merrier his life would be."

Chapter Eight

Columbus

"Is he alive?" Ariel screamed as the nurse placed smelling salts under Columbus' nose.

Columbus coughed.

"Yeah, man. He alive. He coming to now," Nurse Louisa answered.

After Columbus collapsed that morning, Ariel had gotten two guys who also worked at the bed and breakfast to carry him to the only clinic in Colonel Hill on Crooked Island. There was no hospital or doctor there, and Louisa was the only nurse. She gave Columbus a small sip of water. He coughed again and opened his eyes.

"Columbus! Baby, you're alive. I was so scared I was going to lose you," said Ariel.

He looked Ariel directly in her eyes.

"My name is not Columbus. My name is Royale."

Is his amnesia really over? Ariel wondered what that would mean for their relationship. "Are you sure that Royale is your name, like the man who is missing in the newspaper article?"

He nodded, then spoke to the nurse.

"Can I go back to my room at the lodge now? I just need to rest. I'll be okay."

Louisa could not believe the handsome stranger suddenly remembered his name. He hadn't had an inkling

45

of who he was for five years up until today. How did this happen?

"Of course you can. Do you feel any pain?"

Columbus shook his head. The fewer words he spoke and the less the people here knew about him for now, the better off he would be in the long run. He jumped up, grabbed Ariel's hand tightly, then pulled her out of the clinic.

"Baby, slow down. What's your rush?" Ariel said, nearly running to keep pace with him.

"My rush is I have to get back to my life right away."

"But, Columbus. Your bosses are going to need you back at work."

"I told you my name is Royale. I am finished with that job. I need to get to Miami tonight."

"Miami? Why there?"

"I don't want anyone to hear what I have to tell you. Let's go sit on the beach. We can speak privately there."

"Okay."

As Columbus and Ariel approached the white sandy beach, for the first time in five years, tranquil feelings rather than anxiety engulfed him. The water's many shades of clear blue helped create a serene effect. Columbus spotted two empty chairs. The couple sat in them watching the flamingos frolic in the water. He finally spoke.

"Ariel, that newspaper article you showed me this morning jolted me back to life. The man in the picture that looks like me is my cousin Rolondo. I remember now that the two of us were on my yacht which was docked on Fisher Island in Miami. I caught him looking for a very important document that has information on it pertaining to a safe that I have hidden in Sag Harbor. We had a huge disagreement over the contents in the safe. He wanted them bad enough to see me dead."

Ariel gasped.

"Wow! Your own cousin? That's lowdown."

Columbus nodded in agreement.

"I used to be a professional baseball player. When I was playing I made big money, and I bought some very valuable things that are in that safe. Those long dollars stopped coming in after I retired. I wanted to stay papered up, so I got caught up in getting fast money with those three goons who have been hustlers since we were kids, but all the contents of that safe belong to me and me only."

"Three goons and all hustlers. I've run into quite a few of those," Ariel commented.

Columbus understood her comment because of her previous addiction.

"I remember Rolondo slugging me and knocking me down. Then my head hit the edge of the boat. After that, I heard a large explosion. I saw Rolondo run off the boat. The next recollection I had about anything that transpired that night or before it in my life, until you showed me that newspaper article this morning, was the guys pulling me and that small rubber dinghy out of the water five years ago.

Up until today, my life started at that moment. I need to get off this God-forsaken island tonight."

"I'm so glad that you know who you are, baby, but how are you going to get out of here tonight? You don't have any identification, plus, the plane back to Miami that I flew in on has already left by now."

Columbus picked up the medallion that had hung around his neck all of these years. The piece of jewelry was humongous. It was five-inches long and four-inches wide. He now remembered that it was fifty carats of diamonds. Slowly, he unscrewed the base of the bat and put his two fingers inside of it. First, he pulled out a wad of bills held together with a rubber band. Behind that came a card folded in half. Finally, he pulled out a key.

"It's all still here. I always kept at least $10,000 on me and my passport. The key is to my safe deposit box in Miami. It has more money in it. My cousins never knew about the bank where I keep the box. I can give one of the fishermen here a thousand dollars right now, and they will take us to Miami. I can clear customs with this card. I'll ask Trevor. He'll do it. Let's go." There was also a map folded up inside with the numbers 3-4-61 written on it, which was the birthdate of the only woman other than his mother that Columbus had ever loved.

Not uttering a word, Ariel got up from the chair and followed Columbus. She didn't know if he was telling the truth about who he was, or if he was just delusional. She had always thought that medallion around his neck was costume jewelry. Who knew all that stuff was inside of it? She kept coming back to Crooked Island to see him because he was the most handsome man she had ever laid eyes on, and the sex was the best she had ever had. Well, even if he didn't have more money stashed away in some safe deposit box, ten grand could buy her quite a few new outfits and some shoes in Miami. Plus, if he really was this Royale character, there might possibly be a whole lot more than just ten grand in her future. Last, she was not as sober as she let him or her damn man think. His little stash could buy her a lot of fun. Her thoughts were interrupted by Columbus's next question.

"Ariel, before I passed out you mentioned that your mom knows Valerie Rollins, the gossip columnist. Does she know where I can find her?"

"I'm sure she does. That article says that Val was very instrumental in the arrest of your cousin Rolondo. She thought he was really Royale Jones, which I guess is you."

"That's impossible. If anyone knew Rolondo wasn't me, it was Val."

"How do you know that?"

"Years ago, Valerie Rollins was in love with me."

"Wait. I'm confused. I thought you just indicated that you don't know where she is. How was she in love with you?"

Columbus sighed. His entire past was beginning to replay in front of him like an old television movie that no one really wanted to watch again.

"Let me rephrase that. We were once in love with each other. I went to college at the University of Michigan in Ann Arbor, which is Valerie's hometown. She was home working while on summer break from Howard University where she went to school. We met and started hanging out. One thing led to another, and we fell hard for each other. Although I was only twenty, I had never met a woman like her, and at the time I didn't think I would again."

"And just why is that? What made her so special?" Ariel asked, more out of jealousy than curiosity.

"She was as funny as a comedian, had a heart of gold, really smart, loved everyone she came across, and to top all of that off, she was fine!" Columbus grinned slightly.

Clearly you were crazy about her. It's all in your eyes, Ariel thought. *Maybe you still are . . .*

He continued. "That summer she even competed in the Miss Black Michigan pageant. I couldn't wait to wake up every morning just to see Valerie. When she got back to Howard in the fall, she discovered she was pregnant with my child. I wanted her to have an abortion. I was on the verge of a huge baseball career."

"Don't tell me. She wanted to keep it," Ariel commented.

"Right. She did. I drove to Washington, DC in the middle of one week to convince her not to have the baby, but then I decided to ask her to marry me. Before I could propose, we had a huge fight at her dormitory. She fell backward down some stairs trying to run from me."

"That's awful!"

"The long and short of it is she lost the baby in the fall. I went back to Ann Arbor. Val never came home from Washington, DC for the summer again. I graduated and went on to play baseball for the Los Angeles Wildcats. We never spoke again. But more than thirty years have gone by since then, and neither of us ever got married. She must still love me."

"That's being presumptuous."

"Maybe. Every time I used to see her doing a report on TV, I wanted to try to get her number. But I never had the nerve to try to reach her, and it wouldn't have been real hard for me to do that because I heard she was like a sister to my boy Darryl Strawberry. I'm sure he would have given me her number. I actually called the *New York Post* where she worked a couple of times, but hung up as soon as I heard her voice. I've done some pretty rotten things in my life."

"As we all have," Ariel said with a light shrug, remembering the licks she pulled off just to get her fix. But she had, had enough of his reminiscing about Valerie Rollins.

"Maybe that's why God cast me away here for five years. It may be thirty years later, but I know that there is no way Valerie Rollins thought that Rolondo was me!"

"You sound as if you still are in love with her. She's engaged to the billionaire Victor Dumas now."

Thankfully he didn't have to respond to what Ariel had just said because Trevor was walking toward them.

"Look, there's Trevor. Let's see if he can get me out of here tonight. Yo, Trevor."

"Hey man. I was just coming to check on you. Is everything okay?" Trevor asked.

"It's better than okay. I know who I am."

"That's great, Columbus! I mean uhhh . . ."

"Columbus is fine, Trevor. Listen, I found a few dollars. How much will it cost to take Ariel and me to Miami tonight on your boat?"

"How much you got?"

"One thousand US dollars." At the mention of that much money Trevor's eyes shone with greed, greedier than a person ending a fast.

"I can do better than getting you the boat, man. A small private plane just dropped off a couple of guests. Give me the money and let me see if the pilot can take you back to Miami with him tonight. How soon can you be ready to leave?"

"I'm ready now, brother. There's nothing here I want to take with me. I don't even need to say good-bye to anyone. Ariel, go get your things. I'll wait here for you."

Trevor returned to the beach an hour later and waved to Columbus and Ariel to join him.

As they walked toward Trevor, Columbus whispered to Ariel, "For now, and even when we get to Miami, keep calling me Columbus. I have to find out what my cousins are up to before I let them know I'm back. If Rolondo was masquerading as me, he must think I died in that explosion. I don't want him to find out I'm still among the living until I'm ready for him to know. I wonder if Valerie is in cahoots with him and how she met the so-called great Victor Dumas."

"Do you know Victor?" Ariel asked.

"I've never met him, but yeah, I know about the lucky ass, rich geek. I grew up with his wife, Andrea. My cousin Sincere is Victor's half-brother. He doesn't deserve to have all that money he's got. Some of it should be Sincere's."

Within minutes, Trevor had whisked them away to an airstrip. Once there, they approached the door of a small plane. The pilot shook Columbus's hand as he and Ariel boarded the tiny twin engine plane.

"Welcome aboard."

Columbus scooted into one of the small seats. Just like time had stood still, no matter how little this plane was, he was once again flying private. He thought, *The real Royale Jones is coming for all of you motherfuckers. I am going to take back all that belongs to me, including my woman Val.*

Victor Dumas, you better watch out!

Chapter Nine

Valerie

D ear God our Heavenly Father, please deliver quick justice to the evil, greedy, and wicked men who are endangering our lives. But also, please bring some peace and healing into the lives of my loved ones. I need them to be safe, Father. Please send a breakthrough our way. Thank you, Father. Amen."

Looking out of the suite's window at the busy New Yorkers walking up and down Central Park South, Valerie reflected on all that had transpired over the last twenty-four hours. Rolondo was on the run, Amerani was in a coma, and Turquoise was missing.

"What are you thinking about sitting here all alone, baby?"

Val looked up. She had been so lost in her own thoughts that she hadn't heard Victor come in. She smiled as he kissed her. She released the anxious breath she held and spoke her truth.

"That this trip happened so quickly. Here it is just the third week of June. We planned to fly into New York for Thursday's press conference to announce the Dumas Diamonds Polo team, but now some crazy fool is on the loose wanting to do harm to us, and all of our plans are ruined."

"Sweetheart, that's not true. We're going to do as we planned. Believe me. It'll all be over. It's just a matter of time." Victor kissed her lightly on the forehead.

"What about heading back to Los Angeles to finish packing for the summer?" Valerie and Victor had been preparing to head to the Hamptons from July First until Labor Day. "I was so excited about having our own place there. And I couldn't wait for the season to begin. But now we're holed up waiting for . . . a deranged lunatic to be captured."

"You worry too much. We can only do what we can do. Right now we aren't allowed back on the property anyway."

"That's true, sweetie. I'm going to calm down. Besides, I just prayed. I do need to chill out." She took a deep breath. "So how were your meetings?"

"Great. Vance's polo crew is on point. The new game from Dumas Electronics will be out in October, in time for the New York Toy Show and the holidays. The farm house will be ready for the guys to move into by Friday. The staff is moving in tonight to start accepting deliveries by tomorrow. Our house isn't as ready as I would like it to be, but it's livable."

"That's a positive."

"If Rome says it's okay, we can go ahead and move in over the weekend."

"I'm sure it's beautiful. Listen, I spoke to Rome a little while ago. He needs to speak with you. The safe in the den was emptied out. He said you need to have someone call your insurance company. How much money was in that safe?"

"About $20,000. I had just emptied it out to give Vance enough cash to use for essentials for the polo team." Victor and Vance made the decision to further integrate the game of Polo by forming a Polo Team comprised of all Black players to compete at the Bridgehampton Polo Grounds over the summer. The city of Philadelphia, Pennsylvania, had actually produced the first African American Polo Team. Philly's Work to Ride Polo Team first made history in 1994 when it became the only African American team in the country.

"Oh no, babe!"

"There's more bad news. The jewelry in there was worth five million dollars though. It all belonged to my mom and Andrea. I was saving it for the baby, or if Vance has any more daughters."

"That's what I told Rome. It's all listed with the insurance company, right?"

Victor nodded yes.

"Okay, when Rome gets here in the morning we'll get the list out to all of the pawn shops in Los Angeles. It will be okay, honey."

Victor chuckled.

"You sound like me now."

"I do, don't I? Are you hungry?" Val asked. "I sure wish we could go out to eat. I need some air."

Taking Val's hand in his, Victor responded, "Yes, I am hungry, and we can at least go downstairs to eat. My security went over details with the hotel security, and we can at least move around the hotel. Put your shoes on. Let's go."

"You don't have to say another word, handsome man. Auden Bistro and Bar it is." Val slipped on her Gianvito Rossi lace pumps that matched her animal print gold dress from Ashley Stewart, and then she raced out the door with Victor to the elevator. They ran smack dab into Vance and Roshonda. Vance spoke first.

"Dad. Val . . . I thought you had to stay in the suite."

"No," Victor told him. "It's pretty safe for us to move around now, as long as there is security in the hallway up on the floor that we are staying on. My guys are spread all over the hotel. Along with the hotel's security looking out for us, we are good to go." He turned his attention toward the woman accompanying Vance. "And how are you, Roshonda?"

"I'm fine, Victor. Hello, Valerie. I'm sorry about running into you two like this. Vance and I didn't plan for you to find out about us like this."

Valerie laughed.

"I told Victor a month ago that you guys were back together. One of my spies ran into you at L'avenue restaurant in Paris having dinner. Hey, you all are adults. Does Violet know that you're back together?"

Vance smirked.

"I don't think so, but I plan to tell her tomorrow. Dad, I don't want to hear it. Violet signed a pre-nup, and she left Valencia and me. That is called abandonment. It's not like I threw her out." The elevator arrived and all four of them got on.

Val knew the only thing in Vance's life that Victor had ever disapproved of was Roshonda. She had been one of Victor's deceased wife, Andrea's lovers. As far as Victor was concerned, the girl would always be nothing but a high-priced call girl. Suddenly, the air turned very frosty between Victor and Vance.

"We are going downstairs to eat. Care to join us?" Val asked, breaking the ice.

"Fine," said Vance, as the elevator doors opened. "Nino and one of Roshonda's friends are meeting us in the restaurant. We can all eat together. There's Talfor now."

Although Val had told Victor that Vance and his first wife Roshonda could possibly be back together, she knew from his expression that seeing their reunion live and in person was giving him a headache.

"She may be one of the most beautiful women walking the face of this earth, but when it comes to my son, I don't trust the girl!" Victor muttered.

"Victor!" Val stated with a narrowed right brow. She then whispered in his ear, "Well, since they're back together, you can at least stop paying her to stay away from him. That certainly was a waste of money."

Roshonda followed Val's lead as Vance and Victor lagged behind them.

"I can clearly tell Victor's not happy with me," she complained in a lowered tone to Valerie. "What do you think I should do?"

As they entered the restaurant, Valerie's phone buzzed. *Saved by the buzz*, she thought.

"Go ahead and be seated, Roshonda. This is a very important text." As Valerie read through her text messages, she gasped. "Oh no! I have to call Rome right away."

A short moment later, Victor and Vance arrived at the dinner table at the same time as Nino Lopez. Dubbed the black Nacho Figueras because he had the same chiseled looks and swagger of the Argentinian polo player who also modeled, Nino was African American and Puerto Rican, best known as "Blacktina." Prior to graduating from Stanford University, he had played on the school's polo team. Like Vance, Nino wore a black polo shirt embroidered with Dumas Diamonds Club in red. Nino shook both Vance and Victor's hands and gave them each a bear hug.

"Vance, Mr. Dumas, I am sorry I couldn't be here earlier for the meeting. My flight was delayed," Nino said.

"Call me Victor. No problem. Please sit. Let me introduce you to the ladies."

"There is no need for an introduction. A gentleman is always familiar with such beautiful women. Ms. Rollins, Mrs. Dumas, and Ms. Redd, photographs and television do not do the three of you justice. Your beauty in person is indescribable."

Blushing, Val told him, "I see my description of you as the 'Chocolate Casanova' is right on target."

"I love it every time I hear you say that name on the radio or put it in print." He turned toward Talfor. "Talfor, it is an honor for you to be my dinner companion this evening. I lusted after your *Sports Illustrated* swimsuit issue cover." She smiled, but Val could tell Talfor was not interested in him. She probably thought of Nino as a horse-riding fool. Her critical eyes said a lot more than her smile. He probably didn't even have six figures to his name and couldn't even buy her a Chanel bag, let alone an Hermes Birkin. Valerie knew a woman like Talfor would set her sights on a man like hers, Victor Dumas, because he was more of Talfor's mark. Valerie took in the beautiful woman's extremely low-cut strapless dress that left little to the imagination. Her breasts practically popped out as she leaned into Victor.

"Victor, I am so excited to finally meet you in person. When Roshonda told me that she and Vance were divorcing, I said to myself, 'What a shame that I never got to meet his handsome daddy.' And look, now they're back together, and I am having dinner with a powerful man like you. Who would have thought that would ever happen?"

Diverting his eyes from her breasts that Talfor had stuck right in them, Victor put his arm around Val and said, "Have you met my fiancée Valerie?" He turned to Val and gave her a long kiss on the lips. Vance shook his head.

Val extended her hand to Talfor, who nonchalantly shook it.

"We actually have met before, Talfor. I was on the set in Paris when you and Michael Jackson filmed that video back in the nineties. Remember Michael took all of us out for dinner at Regine's afterwards?"

"Yes, I vaguely remember seeing you there."

"By the way, Talfor, I'm also good friends with your ex-whatever he was to you—Rodrigo's wife, Countess Tatiana. Dumas Electronics developed a high-tech security system for their houses throughout the world, as well as specialized computers that can't be hacked into after her old ones were totally compromised."

"Oh, that's really great," Talfor said, nodding while putting on an unenthused grin.

Vance couldn't take the tension at the table any longer. He jumped up to go to the men's room, knocking the candle over. Valerie picked up her glass of water and threw the water on it, narrowly missing Talfor.

"Thank God I didn't get you!"

As Vance scurried away, the waiter arrived with several bottles of Cristal, chardonnay, merlot, more water and pitchers of orange and cranberry juice.

"Mr. Dumas took the liberty of ordering this ahead of time. Would anyone like a mixed drink?"

Everyone at the table shook their heads no. The private server for the evening started pouring the drinks.

"I'll give you all moment to look over the menu, and I'll be right back to take your orders."

As the group sat there perusing the menu, neither they nor the security who sat at the surrounding tables noticed a distinguished looking guy and a lovely young lady take a seat at the adjoining bar. They sat away from Victor and Val's table, but close enough to overhear what was being said.

Vance rejoined the table.

"So, Nino. Special polo shirts, pants, and riding boots were delivered to each of you guys' rooms for you all to wear to the press conference on Thursday, just in case any alterations are needed. You have your own security guard and a valet just until we move out to the farm on Friday. We'll start working out with the horses on Saturday."

"That sounds perfect, man. Thanks for everything. These polo shirts are dope. I couldn't believe there were twelve of them hanging in the closet of the hotel room."

"We owe that and the outfits for the press conference to Val. She has become the Dumas Family Fashion Director."

"That's right," Val told them. "I want the Dumas Diamonds Club to shine!"

"Are you all ready to order? Can we start with you?"

One by one, they all gave the waiter their orders. "Does anyone want anything to start with?"

"No thanks," Victor told him. "You can pour us another round of drinks. So Roshonda, does anything other than Vance bring you to New York? Are you taping your reality show here?"

"No, I'm off until August, so I decided to spend the summer here with Vance. I've never been to the Hamptons before. It definitely sounds like a place where I need to be."

"And just where do you plan to stay? Vance is staying on the horse farm with his team."

Roshonda looked at Valerie, hoping to get some help shutting Victor and his non-stop questions up, but Val never went against Victor. She kept sipping her wine with no intentions of getting into this conversation. Vance came to his first wife's rescue.

"Actually, Dad, I'm in the process of renting Roshonda a house out there for the summer. She's coming out with us on Friday. I have a realtor that will take her around starting Saturday."

"Oh really?" Before Victor had a chance to react fully, Valerie did the only thing she knew would work to calm Victor down. She made sure the tablecloth and napkin covered her hand, which was on his thigh, and she slowly caressed his penis with gentle but firm strokes.

The food had also arrived. Food and sex were always a sensual mind-blowing combination. Hopefully Victor would take his mind off how much he hated Roshonda. Val removed her hand, then whispered in his ear, "Be good. There's more to come later." And in a regular voice she told everyone else at the table, "Just bow your heads and silently thank God for this food we are about to receive and that we are all here together safe and sound. Have a great dinner, everyone."

Val's little under-the-table seduction scene with Victor hadn't gotten past the eyes of the man watching them from the bar. As everyone at the table said "Amen," he told his companion, "They won't be safe and sound for too much longer."

Chapter Ten

Violet

After ditching the Jaguar on a side street in downtown Los Angeles, Violet had hopped on a bus to Las Vegas. The petite, curly, red-haired China doll clutched her suitcase on her lap tightly. Violet wasn't comfortable putting it under her seat or in the overhead bin. She still hadn't had a chance to count her new found fortune. She laughed to herself, knowing she had gotten greedy just like her dad Sincere.

From the second she went to live with her father Sincere in Schaumburg, Illinois, he formulated a well thought-out plot for Violet to infiltrate his brother's property, Dumas Farms in Kentucky. He worked it out with Andrea Dumas, who was married to Victor and also the mother of their son, Vance. Andrea, however, still considered herself as Sincere's woman. On the street she was previously known as Sincere's "bottom bitch." Andrea really had the wool pulled over Victor's head.

As soon as Violet turned fifteen, Andrea introduced her to Victor as an old friend's daughter and got her a job on the farm as a stable worker. Violet explained to Victor that she was an emancipated minor and produced the paperwork to prove it. He didn't have a clue that she was his niece and his son's cousin. Back then, Victor didn't even know her father existed. Since Violet was just a teenager, Victor also enrolled her in school and let her stay in the main house, instead of the farm workers' houses. She became a new member of the family. How quickly Violet had now been overtaken with greed like Rolondo, and even Andrea, God rest her soul.

Early on, Violet recognized that Andrea often abandoned Victor and Vance like stray animals, preferring to fly off to Paris to shop or party with Sincere in Las Vegas and Los Angeles. Violet, however, didn't need any money now. Her father-in-law was worth $4.7 billion, which her husband Vance was the sole heir to. Vance Dumas was worth a couple of hundred million dollars of his own money, and her daughter Valencia had a $500 million dollar trust fund. This crazy shit she was doing to help her father get his hands on Victor's billions was crazy and it had to stop!

As the bus pulled into Las Vegas, her phone rang again. It was Cantrese for the umpteenth time. Violet had actually recommended her for a job with her father-in-law, then begged Victor and Valerie to hire her before she walked out on Vance, so she would have a spy in the house. They both grew fond of Cantrese Gambrel, and she had quickly become sort of an assistant/maid to Val. Violet waited until she was safely within Las Vegas City limits before answering her phone, in case they might be tracking her whereabouts. She pressed the "accept" button.

"What's up, girl?"

"What do you mean what's up? Do you know what happened at the Dumas mansion today? People are dead. What did you do, Violet?" Cantrese asked.

"I didn't do anything. I never made it to LA. I decided to stay in Las Vegas instead. Drake is performing at Caesar's tonight. He invited me to the show." Previously, Violet informed Cantrese that she would be making a surprise visit today to see the baby and would compensate her with $1,000 to turn off the security system. Violet didn't want any recording of what was going to go down at the time. Nor did she want Cantrese to place her suspicions on her at this moment.

Cantrese let out a long sigh of relief. She indeed had informed Violet that everyone would be home that day, and her father-in-law and Vance were in New York, getting their team of all black polo players together to compete in the Veuve Cliquot Polo Classic.

"Word? Well, it's good you didn't go there. If you had, you might not be alive to talk about it now."

"Why? What happened?"

"Rolondo Jemison broke out of jail. It looks like he headed straight to Victor's. Now, some girl who Val thinks is a makeup artist named Raven Lawson is dead. Our security guard George is dead, the cop who flew the helicopter that was found on the grounds is dead, and poor Amerani is dead."

Violet wondered if she had heard Cantrese correctly. She hadn't mentioned Rolondo or a second woman.

"That's terrible! Did they find Rolondo there too?"

"No, it's as if he disappeared into thin air. Those four were the only bodies that the police and Rome found at the house. Why haven't you answered your phone all day? Vance has been calling you. Until the police or Rome and Val can get a grip on where Rolondo went, or where Victor's brother Valerian is, Rome wants everyone in New York here at the hotel with security together."

Violet had seen all the missed calls from Cantrese, Valerie, her husband, and father all day. She had been avoiding all four of them. *That fucking Rolondo must have been wearing a bulletproof vest when I shot him. Damn . . . damn . . . damn . . .* She knew he was fast on her trail.

"Don't tell any of them that you spoke with me. Okay? I'll call Vance in a little bit. Keep your mouth shut, and there will be another grand in it for you and just maybe, a new Chanel bag to put your latest payment in. I'll send the money by Western Union tomorrow. I'll text you the MTCN number." Violet knew Cantrese was grinning into the phone.

"I gotcha. I love the way you do business, girl. Later."

Violet headed off the bus, then hailed a cab and told the driver, "Take me to Caesar's Palace, please." She planned to check into the hotel and finally count her money. After that she would deal with Rolondo's whereabouts, as well as calling Vance and Sincere. If her father got on her nerves too badly, she would give his whereabouts up to Rome. Or better yet, she would just kill him! The thought had occurred to her many times in the past. She was sick of him running her life. Most likely, her dad and Rolondo would look for her at the farm in Kentucky, so it was safer for her to hide out here for a few days until she could get a grip on things.

In the meantime, Viva Las Vegas!

Chapter Eleven

Janvieve

It had been a long day hiding out right here in the safe room of Victor's house. Biding her time before leaving had proved advantageous for Janvieve. First, she had discovered $10,000 hidden in the back of one the closets in the master bedroom. She quickly added that to the stash in her briefcase. Most important, she had found a map of the house and safe room in the desk drawer. It showed that the window in here was fake. When removed, it opened into a tunnel that would take her right outside of the gates and onto the street. Janvieve was just waiting for it to get dark so the guards at the gate wouldn't see her as she made her escape. She knew that Victor's house was in walking distance to the Beverly Hills Hotel. If she could just get there without being seen, she could check in there, and then head to New York in the morning.

On the five o'clock news, she had learned that Victor and Valerie planned to hold a press conference on Thursday at the Ritz Carlton Hotel. She also saw the breaking story about Rolondo's escape from the courthouse and the murders that took place on Victor's property.

Maybe Janvieve would sneak in the press conference and stay in the back. Perhaps Rolondo and Violet hadn't been able to get their hands on that baby yet, but she intended to make sure their original plans came to fruition. Janvieve looked through the small overnight bag that Violet had also given her.

"Hmmm . . . I guess since she thought I was dead there was no need to take it with her." The bag contained toiletries, a pair of flat shoes, makeup and a change of lingerie and clothes. *Not bad! These items will at least get me to New York tomorrow. After that, I'll shop for a proper wardrobe befitting of a socialite such as myself.*

She glanced at the monitor that showed the front of the house. She couldn't believe her own eyes. There wasn't a security guard or a police car in sight. Janvieve was definitely a woman who knew when to seize the moment. This was her chance to blow this joint and head to freedom.

Without hesitation, Janvieve put on the flats, grabbed her purse, the duffle bag and the briefcase filled with money and pushed the window open. Then she rushed into the tunnel. It was only a few short yards before she saw a ladder leading up to a trap door. Strapping all three of her belongings to her body, she hustled up the ladder, then slowly lifted the trap door and looked out. The street sign said she was on Stratford Lane, which fortunately looked pretty secluded. She climbed out and ran as fast as she could, not stopping until she got to the next street. Thank God Rolondo did all that working out in prison.

Janvieve could hear the sound of traffic coming from the other side of the hedges across the street. She dashed over and looked through them. She was on Sunset Boulevard and saw the Beverly Hills Hotel looming up in front of her. It would be easy for her to get a room there for tonight. Although a few people had started coming back, there was still an unofficial boycott going on against the hotel ever since its owner, the Sultan of Brunei, implemented the anti-gay Sharia law in his country. As soon as Janvieve booked a room, she would also have the concierge book her a flight to New York tomorrow, then try to track down Violet's whereabouts. Getting rid of that Judas-like heifer was going to be fun.

Just as Janvieve crossed the street on Sunset to make her way up the hotel's driveway, a black SRX aggressively honked the horn. She jumped out of the way of the car. She hadn't realized she was crossing the street on the green light. The driver slowed up and rolled down the window.

"You need to be more careful, miss. I could have hit you. Are you all right?" Shockingly, Janvieve realized she was looking straight into Rome Nyland's face.

Lowering her head quickly, she mumbled, "I'm fine," then dashed up the driveway. Janvieve couldn't believe that Rome hadn't recognized her, and she had come so close to being caught.

Chapter Twelve

Rome

As Rome drove down Sunset Boulevard, defeated and alone, he let his mind get the best of him. Nevertheless, a figure growing larger in front of his windshield suddenly registered in his head. He slammed on the brakes. The woman moved out of his path in perfect time. He asked if the woman was all right, then advised her to be careful. *Why does that woman look familiar?* Rome thought. But after the day that he'd had, the last thing on his mind was another slick sister. He had a lot of ground to still cover before this day ended. He put the car in drive and merged into traffic.

Although Rome was pissed for looking like a jilted, played-for-a-fool idiot to Pace, he kept heading to South Central to look for his confidential informant (CI). It was now around seven o'clock. Rolondo's escape this morning seemed like years ago. He suddenly realized that he hadn't taken the time to eat all day.

His informant, Cayenne hung out at a laundromat that doubled as his recording studio over on Crenshaw. He would scoop the boy up, then head out to North Hollywood and take him to eat at Sweetie Pie's on Lankersheim Boulevard. Taking Cayenne over there would mean they could talk privately while chowing down on the restaurant's smoked half chicken, mac-n-cheese, and fried corn on the cob that he had been reading about. Then they'd wash it all down with some sweet tea. He hadn't even had a glass of water today. Comfort food sounded real good about right now.

As Rome pulled in front of Cayenne's spot, "Agent 99 calling," popped up on his dashboard. That was his nickname for Valerie.

"Hey, I was just getting ready to grab some food and then call you. I can't find Turquoise anywhere. You are not going to believe what James Pace just told me."

"Turquoise is the reason I am calling you. I already know that she's missing. One of my friends saw you at Craig's and overheard you asking about Turquoise. Rome, my news isn't good. He says he saw a woman who fits Turquoise's description getting into a red Bugatti. He couldn't see who was driving. You and I both know that could have been one of the Bugatti Blades' cars or even Rolondo's. It's hard to believe that creep would still be in Los Angeles with so much heat on him, but he is pretty bold. Do you think she left the restaurant with him?"

At this point Rome didn't know what to think about his fiancée's actions.

"Val, James told me that Turquoise went to see Rolondo while he was in jail, and he bragged to inmates that they made a sex tape."

"I didn't think you would ever have to worry about anyone ever seeing the tape."

"Say what?"

"No one was supposed to ever see the tape."

"Val, what are you talking about? Are you telling me that you knew about this?"

"Yes, a source told me a while back that Rolondo's crew somehow had the tape and wanted a million dollars not to put it on the internet. I'm sorry, Rome. I bought it to protect you and to keep Turquoise in line. I confronted her about it. She begged me not to tell you and swore that she would never communicate with Rolondo again."

"What is wrong with everybody? Why do you and James feel I need protecting? I am a grown ass man. Who the hell else knows about this tape and that Turquoise was sleeping around on me?"

"Only Victor, but he's never seen the tape. I had to tell him because that's where I got the money to buy it."

"Where is the tape now?"

"That's a problem. It was at the house in Victor's safe."

Rome couldn't believe how this day just kept getting worse.

"Well, Miss Thinks-She's-Debra-Do-Right, as I told you, the safe was empty, but I think I did see some videotapes on the floor. However, I couldn't care less about that tape now or who sees it. Whatever happened to Turquoise, I don't ever want to see her again. I'll have James put an All-Points Bulletin out on a red Bugatti. After that, she's on her own. I'm going to eat, check out Cayenne, and then I'm out of Los Angeles. I'm spending the rest of the summer in the Hamptons with you. And Missy, we're not finished discussing your little tape caper."

"Rome, don't hang up. I have one more thing to tell you."

"What now? Is Turquoise a madam who owns a strip joint or something?"

"Well, at least you still have a sense of humor. No she is not. This information isn't about her. I think I know who the dead woman in the helicopter was. My sources say she could be a makeup artist whose name is Raven Lawson. Her boyfriend is an actor that hangs out with the Bugatti Blades. No one has seen her since she left for work this morning. She told a friend who works at MAC in the Beverly Center that she was going to get paid ten grand for a job she had today."

"I'll text that info to Pace and get him right on it. Thanks. Nice going."

"Okay, Rome. I'm sorry about all of this."

"So am I. I'll see you tomorrow."

"Will do. Bye, Rome."

Rome shot the text about the dead girl's possible identity to Pace, then opened a hidden compartment underneath his seat in the car. He pulled out a stash of hundreds, then counted out ten thousand dollars before heading to Cayenne's laundromat.

Two years ago, Victor had made Rome his director of security due to the fact they worked so well together when he hired him to look for his wife. Val had actually been the one who received the tip that Andrea had been killed in Las Vegas. She had accompanied Rome there. That's where she and Victor had met and fell in love. Now Victor paid Rome a salary of $2 million a year plus another $500,000 for expenses. Rome never knew when or how much cash he ever needed to spread around, so he had a safe built into his car. He was still in shock over what he had learned about Turquoise. Had he ever really known his fiancée? He prayed she was still alive, but at this moment his feelings for her had ceased to exist. Right now he was more interested in finding Rolondo.

Cayenne was standing in front of the laundromat talking to some guys as Rome pulled up and motioned the young man to come over. A stocky guy with long dreadlocks, Cayenne always dressed in a suit. His theory was that it made him look and feel like a true businessman, and if you looked the part, you commanded more respect among your peers. He looked at Rome suspiciously as he approached the Cadillac SRX.

"Yo, bro, you cool and all, but you can't keep rolling up on me like this. I don't want my boys to think I'm a snitch." Rome handed him the wad of cash. "Well, I guess a brother could answer a few questions, but not here."

"Get in. I'll treat you to dinner."

Cayenne yelled at his crew, "Yo, I'm going to take care of some business with my man here. He's financing my pee-wee football team. I'll catch up with you all later at the spot."

As Cayenne got in the car, Rome asked him, "Pee Wee football team? If you really need money for that purpose I will give it to you. Just get me the particulars on it, and I'll cut you a check."

"Cool."

The guys rolled up to Sweetie Pie's around thirty minutes later, parked the truck, then stepped up to the window where they put in their order. It was one of those beautiful Cali summer evenings, so they chose a table outside. Rome spotted one of Val's best friends, George Pryce sitting at a nearby table. George was a veteran publicist who had once represented Death Row Records back in Suge Knight's heyday. He was also the former publisher of the first magazine for black men, *MBM*. Rome recognized the guy with him as his client, Roy Albert Andrade, the author of a book titled, *Virula*. Val had the ad for the book on her website. He waved at them as he and Cayenne sat down. When the waitress brought their food over to their table, Rome dug into the smoked chicken and baked beans right away. Cayenne opted for the turkey leg, and side splitter, which consisted of four side dishes.

"So," asked Cayenne in between bites of turkey, "what's this all about, Rome?"

"You may look stupid, but you aren't. Don't play with me. Who broke Rolondo out of the courthouse, and where is he?"

"Giving out that kind of info can get me murked. I need a lot more than ten grand."

"You know that's not a problem."

"Okay, some cat named Claude arranged the escape. I don't know where Rolondo is now, but Sincere is also looking for him. Word is, your peep— Vance's ex-wife— is also involved. Sincere is also looking for her fine ass."

"Roshonda?"

"I don't know what her name is. All I know is both she and Rolondo are missing in action."

As far as Rome knew, Claude/Sincere/Valerian were all one and the same person, so that didn't make sense. Plus, Roshonda had seemed so repulsed by Rolondo when they knew him as Royale. But she had been pretty angry when Vance left her to marry Violet. Hooking up with Rolondo could be her revenge against him.

"Where does this Claude live?"

"He used to be in Las Vegas, but now I hear he rests in New York, but not in the city, somewhere called the Hamptons."

"How about Sincere? Where is he these days?"

"As far as I know he's out of the country."

"You're playing me for stupid again, Cayenne. You know that Claude is just another alias that Sincere goes by."

"All right. You keep thinking that, man, and I'll keep thinking that you really are stupid. I don't know where you got that wild idea, but Claude and Sincere are definitely not the same cat. In fact, they're cousins. Personally, I think Rolondo is probably headed wherever Claude is. I hear there's a lot of bread involved, a whole lot, even bricks of gold and silver."

Rome listened, taking in everything that Cayenne was telling him. The waitress's voice broke into his thoughts.

"You gentlemen want anything to drink?"

"I'll have a sweet tea," answered Rome.

"Let me get some lemonade," Cayenne requested.

"Cayenne, do you know anyone who drives a red Bugatti?"

"Yeah, one of Claude and Rolondo's women. I don't know her name, a bad sister, looks like a supermodel. She's got the last Bugatti out there. After Claude murked that billionaire woman, Andrea, the crew's Bugatti connection dried up."

Rome corrected Cayenne.

"Don't you mean when *Rolondo* killed Andrea?"

"No, I meant what I said. All evidence pointed to Rolondo killing Andrea, but the real murderer was Claude. The man is more invisible than Casper the Friendly Ghost. That's why he broke Rolondo out this morning. It was a code of ethics type situation."

"Code of ethics, huh? Hmm . . ."

Rome couldn't believe how much information he and Val had missed on this case. This wasn't like either of them. But he knew the reason they were no longer on point. They had both been distracted, him with Turquoise and Val with Victor and all of her new found wealth. Victor gave Valerie money and jewels more than regular dudes sent flowers to their women. It didn't surprise him that Victor had paid for that sex tape. The man would do anything to please Val. But he was now realizing that he and Val had become so wrapped up in their long awaited individual love lives, that they had lost all sense of concentration on work. As a result, Rolondo had killed more victims and was on the lam. He would speak to Val about all of this when he got to New York the next day. They had to get back on track in order to stop Rolondo, Valerian, and now this Claude character, who they both had thought was Valerian.

"One last thing, do you know where I can find Rolondo's woman who drives the Bugatti?"

"I hope you got a huge stash of paper somewhere because this is going to cost you big time." Cayenne eyed Rome with a serious gaze that Rome returned. "Yeah, okay . . . So, one of my shorties stay in the same complex. I saw her and Rolondo coming out of the building a couple of times before he got locked up. It's called the Palazzo East Apartments on West Third over in the Fairfax District, right by the Grove. Just look for the Bugatti. She normally parks it out in front."

"Okay, sit tight. Order some dessert. I'm just going to run out to the car. I'll be right back." Rome didn't want Cayenne to see where he kept PCFS, which was short for Petty Cash For Snitches. Val had given the money he used for informants that nickname. He ducked in the car and pulled out five grand, then went back to the table.

Handing Cayenne the cash under the table and dropping a fifty dollar bill on top of it for the waiter, Rome told him, "Enjoy your dessert. I'm sure you can get back to your spot okay. I have to bounce. I'll be in touch about the check for your football team. Thanks." Rome stood up to leave.

"It's always a pleasure doing business with you, man." No sooner had those words left Cayenne's mouth, than two of Rolondo's henchmen approached. One of them opened his jacket revealing a gun.

"Step off, man. You ain't the only one packing heat," Cayenne said, placing a hand near his waist as he rose from his seat.

"He's right," said Rome. "Is there a problem?" He too made a slight show of his weapon.

The guys looked back and forth between Rome and Cayenne, then turned and calmly walked out of the crowded restaurant.

Cayenne sat back down to enjoy his dessert. Because of the impending threat, Rome thought it wise to drive Cayenne back where he picked him up, except he parked one block away. They shook hands, then parted ways.

In one last ditch effort to find Turquoise and Rolondo before leaving for New York, Rome decided to check out this apartment building and see if he could spot the Bugatti, then possibly talk to this chick who might know something.

After that, he was heading back home to pack for New York. It was time to get the hell out of Los Angeles!

It didn't take him long to get over to West Third Street near The Grove. The Palazzo East apartment complex he was looking for was huge. Looking up at it, Rome remembered that a murder/suicide took place here a while back. An unknown rapper who was a good friend of boxing champion Floyd Mayweather Junior, shot and killed his beautiful wife, a dancer on the VH1 drama series "Hit The Floor," then he turned the gun on himself. Two young talented lives were just wasted! That had been a really sad story.

Cayenne was right on the money. It wasn't long before Rome spotted the red Bugatti. He didn't have a warrant or anything to search it, so he decided to write down the license plate, text it to Pace, then walk around and see if he could find someone who knew the owner. He parked his car, got out, and walked up to the car. As he punched the numbers on the license plate into his phone, Rome felt a small metal object in his waist. He turned his body with a swift body kick, and "bam!" The perpetrator was on the ground.

"Don't hurt me, mister!" squeaked a small voice.

Rome stared down into the face of a kid who could only be around eleven or twelve years old. He snatched the little sucker up, successfully removing and closing the knife he clutched in his fist, then put it into his own pocket.

"Who are you, kid? Moves like that against the wrong person will only get you killed, not make you a killer."

The kid squirmed as Rome held a firm grip on him.

"Miss Samantha paid me to watch her car while she's out of town. Who are you?"

"Never mind who I am. How much did this Miss Samantha pay you?"

"Fifty dollars."

Rome dug the last cash he had in his pocket out.

"Here's $200. Now, what is your name, and where did Miss Samantha go?"

"Not that it's any of your business, but my name is Antonio Wright. She went to New York. Why you trying to steal her car?"

"I'm not trying to steal it. I'm just looking for your friend."

"Are you a cop?"

"No, I'm not a cop. I'm looking for a friend of mine that Miss Samantha knows. Her name is Turquoise." Rome took out his phone, then showed Antonio a picture of Turquoise.

"I know who you're talking about. I saw her earlier tonight, but she left in a burgundy Navigator with two guys. She didn't go to New York with Miss Samantha."

"Are you sure?"

"Yeah, I'm sure. Because after they left, Miss Samantha came back out with her suitcase, gave me the money, then left in a cab."

"What are you doing out here anyway, kid? Do you live around here?"

"No. I make more money here running errands for the people in this building than my friends do carrying bags at the mall. I need extra cash for school and to help my mom."

"Well, be careful. You have a number? Maybe I can use you to do some work for me."

"Sure. It's 323-555-1789."

"Okay. I'll be in touch. One more thing before I leave. Did Miss Samantha say when she was coming back from New York?"

"No, she didn't. Hey, Mister, can I have my knife back?"

"Not in this lifetime, Antonio." Laughing, Rome got back in the truck and drove off. He would text this new info to Pace, and then get on a flight first thing in the morning. It looked like the friendly skies to New York also led to Rolondo, the mysterious Claude, and now this woman Samantha!

The Big Apple had better get ready for Rome Nyland!

Chapter Thirteen

Violet

After the taxi pulled in front of the world renowned Caesars Palace Las Vegas, Violet walked into the lobby, and she could feel the electricity. This joint was jumping! Lining the walls were posters of Jerry Seinfeld, Celine Dion, Elton John, Mariah Carey and Rod Stewart, who were all performing concerts here. Before she could get to the desk, one of the hotel's hosts approached Violet.

"Good evening, Mrs. Dumas? How are you? Let me take your bag." Violet held on to the treasure-filled suitcase tightly.

"No thank you. It's not heavy."

"Are you going to be staying with us? If so, do you want your usual Penthouse suite? There is one available. Will your husband be joining you?"

"Yes, I am checking in for a few days and would love the usual suite. No, unfortunately, my husband isn't coming. He's in New York with our daughter. I can just go to the desk and check in."

"Nonsense, Mrs. Dumas. We can take care of all that for you. Just let me get you an escort upstairs." He motioned to a bell man. "Take Mrs. Dumas up to penthouse one and see that she gets settled. I will just charge everything to the Dumas' account and send someone up with your keys. Your husband and late mother-in-law, may she rest in peace, have always been two of our most generous and special guests. Just leave everything to me."

Violet followed the bellman onto the private elevator. She was tired. She needed a hot bath, a meal, and sleep. Tomorrow morning, she would deal with all of these challenges.

As she walked through the door of the palatial suite, her cell rang. Vance again. Handing the bellman a twenty as he closed the door behind him, she reluctantly answered it.

"What do you want, Vance?"

"Hello to you, too. Where are you?"

"In Las Vegas for a Drake concert, even though my whereabouts are none of your business."

"I couldn't care less where you are, Violet. I don't know if you are aware of it, but Rolondo Jemison broke out of jail this morning. It looks like he went straight to Dad and Val's house, where your baby Valencia also just happens to reside. You do remember her, don't you?" Violet played dumb.

"Is Valencia okay?"

"Not that I believe you give a damn about our daughter, but yes, she's fine. Rome thought it was best for her and Val to be out of LA during Rolondo's trial. That was a good call on his part. He thinks you would be safer here too. I can send the plane for you. Maybe you might reconsider and play polo with us this summer."

Like Vance, Violet was small in stature. Horseback riding must have run in their blood. She learned very fast, soon becoming the protégé of Vance, who was the most famous African American jockey in the world. The last thing Violet wanted to do was be stuck in New York with them.

"You don't need me. I heard you got that Falaki chick from Kenya to play on your little polo team."

"Yes, Falaki is playing, but we can also use you. You were the best player on our team in Kentucky."

A little over a year ago, Violet was an accomplished jockey and had won the Cash Call Futurity Race with her horse, Tres Jolie.

"And as I said, Rome wants you here. It would also be nice for you to see the baby. She gets bigger every day. You don't even know what she looks like now."

"Thanks to your darling soon-to-be stepmother, Miss Holier-than-Thou Valerie, I do know what Valencia looks like. She texts me photos of her every damn day. You guys are stupid, spending all that money for clothes from Gucci and Burberry on a baby!"

"Val buys her all of those clothes. She's my daughter. She can dress her in Chanel. It's fine with me. Are you coming to New York or not?"

"No, I'm not coming to New York. I'm thinking about moving here to Vegas."

"Fine, but the way you spend my money flying all over the place and shopping, you need to stop complaining about how Val dresses your daughter."

"Good-bye, Vance." Once their call ended, Violet exclaimed, "Ugh! Yuck!"

There was a knock on the door. Violet figured it must be the valet with the keys. She opened the door. Instead of the valet, a woman she hadn't laid eyes on or heard from since she was a little girl stood in the door way. With a huge smile spread across her face, the woman greeted Violet.

"Hello, daughter. May I come in?" Betty Lum asked.

Too stunned to answer, Violet opened the door. As her mother walked in, she looked her up and down. Betty Lum looked like an older, yet shorter version of Kimora Lee. The years had been good to Betty. She was tiny in stature like Violet and beautiful. Her jet-black hair still hung to her waist just as Violet remembered. She was dressed impeccably in a Jacquared dress by Louis Vuitton and crystal-embellished sandals by Stuart Weitzman. She carried a signature Louis Vuitton purse. Betty walked over to the bar.

"Do you mind if I fix myself a drink?"

Still too stunned to talk, Violet nodded yes. Her mom poured a glass of Hennessy straight, gulped it down.

"Where's Rolondo?" Betty asked.

"I don't know where Rolondo is," Violet replied.

"Look, Violet. Your father sent me here. I can't believe you don't know that he has a GPS tracking device on your phone, and therefore, monitors your every move. Now, Sincere wanted to kill you for not following his instructions, but I convinced him not to kill his only child. I am going to ask you one more time. Where is Rolondo?"

"I don't know. He turned on me. He pulled a gun on me, and I ran out of Victor's house as fast as I could, then jumped into my Jag and drove off." Before Violet could bat an eyelash, Betty slapped her.

"Liar! I gave birth to you. Don't you think I know when you're lying? That Dumas money that you aren't sharing with your father or me has made you go soft!" Betty looked down and saw the duffle bag, grabbed it, unzipped it and shook all of its contents onto the floor. Stacks after stacks of one-hundred dollar bills and dozens of jewelry boxes in multiple sizes fell out of it.

"I suppose Santa Claus just dropped all of this down the chimney for you. Better yet, it looks like you had a field day at the Dumas mansion. Don't just stand there. Child, you had better answer me. Didn't you just hear me say that your father wants you dead?" Betty put her hands on both of Violet's shoulders and shook her. Tears trickled down Violet's face.

"When did you and my father hook back up?"

"There is no time for tears now. You silly goose, your father and I never broke up. I have always lived in Chicago in his house. Now, you need to come clean and fast. For the last time, where is Rolondo?"

"I don't know where he is. I thought I killed him, but the cops didn't find his body, so I guess he got away. Please tell Dad I'm sorry. When I opened that safe and saw all of that money, I just wanted out of this life. Please don't let him kill me."

"Baby, you were born into this life. Your only way out of it is when you die. But you don't need this money that is on the floor." Betty released the grip she had on Violet's shoulders. "You are the wife of Vance Dumas. Have you lost your mind? Now, if you don't want to leave this earth right here and now, call your husband and tell him to send one of those Dumas jets to pick up you and your mother and take us to New York."

"But—"

"Let him know that we'll be ready to leave here first thing in the morning. Don't look at me as if I am talking to you in a foreign language. I am coming with you to make sure this job gets done this time." Betty walked around, assessing the posh suite. "It's about time I met my grandbaby and son-in-law."

She doesn't want to meet Valencia any more than I enjoy seeing her, Violet thought. *It's all about money. Money . . .*

Betty folded her arms and paced in front of Violet. "I met the great Victor years ago. I am also sure that the famous Ms. Valerie Rollins and I are going to become great friends, and then, as soon as we kidnap that baby and take all of

Victor's money, you are going to kill them all. I've been out to the Hamptons before with your father and Andrea. It's time I experienced it again. Call him. I brought you into this world, so I can damn well take you out of it."

The bellman finally knocked on the door. Violet let him in. He was accompanied by a waiter from room service.

"May we come in?"

Violet nodded yes.

"Management took the liberty of sending you a complimentary bottle of Cristal, chocolates, and strawberries, Mrs. Dumas. Where would you like everything?"

Betty took the liberty of answering for Violet.

"Over by the bar. Please open the champagne and pour me a glass." They had yet to pick up the spilled bag off the floor, so Betty grabbed a stack of hundreds, pulled two bills off of it, then handed one to each of them. She put the rest of the stack in her purse.

Astounded by all the money lying in the middle of the floor, the bellman simply stepped over it, pretending that it wasn't even there as he made his way to the bar.

"That will be all."

"Thank you very much, ma'am."

All of this was too much for Violet to comprehend. She had never even been sure that her mother was still alive. Sincere had never discussed her. And here she was in the flesh, standing right before her, giving her orders and taking money that didn't belong to her. She watched as her mother counted the cash.

"There is only a little more than $20,000 here. You pulled that stupid backstabbing stunt on your father for this little bit of chump change?"

Violet didn't answer her. She had been under the assumption that Victor kept millions of dollars in his safe. Once again, Vance was a liar.

Betty then looked through a few of the jewelry boxes. She placed one huge diamond cocktail ring on her finger.

"Sincere gave Andrea this ring. I was so jealous. The man never gave me anything but grief. This jewelry is all old. Call Vance immediately before I kill you myself for these stupid mistakes right now. This money and jewelry now all belong to me."

Violet picked up her cell phone and dialed her husband.

"What now, Violet?" he asked.

"I changed my mind. I want to come to New York in the morning? Can you send the plane for me?"

"What changed your mind?"

"I was looking at Val's texts and figured I should see the baby. Book me my own suite though. My mother is also coming."

"Your mother? Since when did you get a mother?"

"I've always had a mother, and she's here in Las Vegas with me now. She wants to meet her granddaughter."

This information didn't sit well with Vance. Whoever this woman was, she had to be cleared by Rome's security staff before she would be able to come near his daughter.

"What's her name?"

"Betty Lum. What's with all these questions? Are you sending the plane or not?"

"Yes, I'll send the plane tonight. I'll have a car pick you and your long lost mother up at eleven in the morning. Caesar's security called Dad's office, so I know you are there."

Violet sighed. GPS tracking on her phone, snitching hotel security fake cops . . . this all had to end.

"Good for you. See you tomorrow."

Betty handed Violet her purse.

"Why are you giving me my purse?"

"We are going downstairs to the Forum Shops. You are going to dust off your Dumas credit card and buy your mother a new wardrobe for New York. As you can see, I don't have any luggage with me. When I'm finished, you can buy me dinner at the Palm. Chop-chop! Let's go."

Not knowing what else to do to end this new madness, Violet reluctantly followed Betty out of the door.

Chapter Fourteen

Columbus

Walking through Miami International Airport, Columbus was having a hard time grasping the fact that he had lost five years of his life and money. As he and Ariel passed a Thomas Pink, a store that carried mainly men's clothing, he glanced down at his shirt, shorts, and sandals. He looked like the beach bum he had become over the past half decade. He needed to change into something decent right away.

"Let's duck in here, baby. I need to at least get a shirt and a pair of slacks to change into. I'll do some heavy shopping after we hit my safe deposit box tomorrow."

Ariel was still slightly in disbelief of Columbus' story, but she followed him in the store anyway. At least he had nine thousand dollars. That would do for now.

A salesman cautiously approached them. He stopped short and turned his nose up at the sight of Columbus. Judging by his unkempt appearance and shabby old clothes and sandals, the salesman was positive that Columbus had no money to spend in the store.

"May I help you with something?"

"Yes, thanks, man. I need to get a couple of shirts and maybe some khaki slacks. I think I wear a seventeen neck and need the pants to be thirty-four/thirty-four. Let me get that shirt hanging there in blue and one in white. And two pairs of the pants hanging there in my size will do. I want to wear one set out."

"And how will you be paying for these items?"

Columbus unscrewed his medallion. When he pulled the wad of hundreds out, the salesman changed his entire attitude. A broad smile suddenly materialized on his face.

"We have quite a few items on sale, sir. Perhaps you would like me to show you something else."

"So now it's sir, is it? When I walked in here, you looked at me like you were smelling shit. Didn't your mother ever teach you not to judge a book by its cover? No, I don't want shit else from you or your stank-ass attitude. Just ring me up and show me where the dressing room is so that I can change my clothes."

As the now embarrassed salesman took his money, Columbus glanced down at the man's feet. He was wearing a pair of black Nike sneakers that looked like they might fit him.

"On second thought there may be one more thing that you can sell me. What size shoe do you wear?"

"Eleven."

"That's my exact size. Here's another $200. Sell me the sneakers that you're wearing. I'm sure you keep an extra pair of shoes here at your job that you can change into."

"Yes, I do. The shoes are yours. Let me get you rung up and show you the dressing room."

Leaving the store with Columbus dressed in his new clothes and sneakers, Ariel was in awe. Wearing this type of attire, Columbus looked even more handsome. He had never acted like he did just now in the guest house on Crooked Island. He was always very humble and soft spoken. They reached the airport's exit and stepped out into the Miami night.

"Hail us a cab, baby. Tell them to take us to the Delano on Collins Avenue, South Beach."

"Isn't that real expensive?" She didn't want him to blow his entire fortune tonight, at least not before she had a chance to get her paws on some of it.

"I remember it being very reasonable. We'll be okay there for at least a couple of days."

"Whatever you say." Following her man's instructions, Ariel extended her arm and yelled, "Taxi!"

A cab came to a screeching halt in front of them. Columbus held the door for Ariel as she climbed in. He motioned to the cab driver to put her overnight bag in the trunk, then got in next to her.

"The Delano on South Beach on Sixteenth and Collins Avenue," Ariel told the driver.

Columbus rolled down the window. This wasn't the night for air conditioning. He needed to breathe Miami's air. The cab drove steadfastly toward the beach. Columbus didn't want to let Ariel know just how nervous he really was. He had no idea what was waiting for him back here in the United States. When he and Rolondo had the fight on the boat that day, there was about $20 million hidden away in Sag Harbor. There should also be at least $100,000 in his safe deposit box back at the Sun Trust on Washington Avenue. He would be there in the morning when they opened. He looked at Ariel. Sitting next to him in this cab, she didn't seem as glamorous as she did back on Crooked Island. He wondered if she was really who she claimed to be, and if he could trust her. Tomorrow he would get a laptop and a cell phone and rejoin the living. As soon as he was able to get online, he would see if he could discover who Miss Ariel Pembrough really was.

The taxi pulled in front of the Delano. This upscale art deco hotel with a sleek Philippe Starck design sits along the ocean in South Beach, with its trendy dining and nightlife. Everything in the entire hotel was white on white. Columbus paid the driver and exited the car after Ariel.

"Listen, I know I told you to keep calling me Columbus, but my passport card is in my real name, Royale Jones, so I have to check in with it here. Okay?"

"Gotcha. Lead the way."

Ironically, even though Royale's hair was now a mass of salt and pepper colored curls, as opposed to the Caesar cut that he used to sport, the hotel's desk clerk recognized him right away.

"Mr. Jones, it's been years. We've missed you here at the Delano. I saw on the news the other day that the authorities in California thought you were still missing. I'm glad to see that you're okay. Will you be checking in?"

Oh boy. He was going to have to ask this clerk to keep his identity on the down low. Royale struggled to remember the man's name before realizing he was wearing a name tag.

"Hello, Greg. I've been out of the country. I want to check in, but we don't have a reservation. Do you have any rooms available for two or three nights?"

"You are one of our best customers. Of course we have something available for you. Let me see what I can find." Greg punched a few keys on the computer. "You're in luck. Your regular poolside duplex bungalow is available for $2,269 per night. To welcome you back, I can give you a discount rate of $1,500 a night. Do you want me to put it on your account with us?"

"Is it still active? I haven't used it in five years."

"That wouldn't make a difference if your bill was paid. He hit the computer again. "Yes, it's still in effect. You have a zero balance. I just need to update your information. Is your address still the same?"

Columbus hesitated. He had just sold his house here in Miami when he had the fight on the boat with Rolondo. He had actually been living on the boat at the Marina.

"Can I give you that information in the morning? I'll also have a new phone number then."

"That won't be a problem, Mr. Jones. Here are the keys. The bellman here will escort you to your bungalow."

"Thanks, Greg. One more thing . . ."

"Yes?"

"Please don't let too many people know that I'm here. I would really appreciate it. I want to stay a little quiet for a while."

"No problem, Mr. Jones."

"Columbus—I mean Royale, don't you think this is too much for you? We can get a regular room. I don't mind." Ariel was still in shock that Columbus had just spent $1,500 on a hotel room. Back on Crooked Island, he slept on a cot in a room behind the inn's kitchen.

"No, this is fine. I always stayed in this suite when I needed to get away from everything to clear my head. Isn't this how you supermodels normally roll?"

Ariel simply smiled.

When the bellman opened the door to the bungalow for them, her mouth opened wide. She had never seen such splendor. There was a white on white living room with a beautiful couch and a fully stocked wet bar. A spiral staircase led to a master bedroom upstairs.

"This is beautiful. You must have had some kind of life before you wound up on Crooked Island."

"If you only knew. I'm starving. Let's go to the restaurant. Do you want to change your clothes first? That dress looks a little worn for the fancy dining room here." Ariel didn't have anything but shorts and a few tank tops in her bag, other than the sundress she was still wearing from this morning when she had arrived on Crooked Island.

"You never complained about my clothes on Crooked Island. My clothes were good enough for you there. No, I don't want to change my dress. I'm fine. Let's go eat."

Columbus eyed her attire in a severely critical manner.

"I mean . . . unless you want to purchase a few dresses for me tomorrow. I just didn't think I'd need anything extravagant on the island . . . and . . ." She shrugged.

She's rambling, nervous, even scared, Columbus thought. *What is she hiding?*

As Columbus and Ariel entered Delano's Italian restaurant, LeBron James and his wife Savannah were on their way out. Royale lowered his eyes to the ground. It had been years since he played professional baseball, but no matter how much time passed, or what the difference in their ages were, athletes usually recognized each other. He wanted as few people as possible to recognize him or know where he was. They followed the hostess to a table outside by the pool where they were quickly seated. She told them she would send the waiter right over.

"Did you see LeBron James and his wife Savannah?" Ariel asked.

"How could I not see them? They walked right past us. This hotel has always been a melting pot filled with celebrities. I used to even see Beyoncé and Jay Z here quite often. But before my accident I heard they started staying at the Setai whenever they come to Miami."

"Good evening. Can I get you some drinks?" the waiter asked as he approached them.

"Neither of us drink alcohol. I'll take a cranberry mixed with orange juice."

"Actually, I would like a glass of merlot."

Royale looked at Ariel suspiciously.

"Won't that mess with your sobriety?"

"No, it will be fine just this one time. We've had quite a shocking day."

"One merlot and a cranberry mixed with orange juice coming up."

Royale didn't like the fact that Ariel had ordered something alcoholic. He remembered the horrible state she was in when the addiction coach first brought her to Crooked Island.

"What's up with you drinking? I was there when you went through all of those tremors. I helped your coach clean up your vomit."

"I never had a problem with drinking. I had a problem with drugs. I repeat, we have had quite a shocking day. First I thought you were dying. Then I find out you're some rich and famous athlete who has thousands of dollars hanging around his neck all these years. I'm surprised that you don't need something to take the edge off."

"I have never needed anything to take the edge off. My cousins and I have been around the drug business since we were teenagers. The first rule of dealing is that you never

ever sample the product. But . . . you are right though. It has been a tough day, so I will see how you handle the wine."

The waiter arrived with their drinks.

"I'll give you two a minute to study the menu," he said with a slight nod.

"Actually," Royale told him, "I'm ready to order now. I'll have the meatballs to start, then the truffle tagliatelle and the tomahawk ribeye bisteca. How about you, Ariel?"

Practically downing the entire glass of wine in one gulp, she told the waiter, "I'll have the petite filet mignon and another glass of merlot." Before Columbus could utter another word about her drinking, Ariel quickly asked him, "Why don't you want anyone to know you're alive?"

"I need to locate my three cousins first, then sneak up on them before I come forward. All of them have money and possessions that belong to me. The first place I am going to head is to Sag Harbor. I need to empty out my safe. It's in a church I bought for my cousin Claude to pastor. He should be able to lead me to Sincere and Rolondo. Then, I am going to kill Rolondo."

"You don't mean that literally, do you?" Ariel's eyes widened.

Columbus did not answer her. A flash of Victor Dumas on the television in the adjoining bar suddenly got his attention.

"I'll be right back." When he reached the bar, he asked the bartender to turn up the sound. Victor was talking to a reporter with Valerie standing next to him holding his hand.

She had put on weight over the years but hadn't aged a bit. She was still beautiful.

"I have issued a five million dollar reward for anyone who can give the authorities in Los Angeles any information on the whereabouts of Rolondo Jemison, or my brother, Valerian Davidson. Mr. Jemison is a dangerous fugitive, who is wanted for multiple murders. I feel that my brother may have information that could lead us to him."

"Mr. Dumas, after the tragedies that happened today at your house in Los Angeles, as well as these men being at large, are you and your son still going ahead with your plans to enter the Bridgehampton Polo Tournament?"

"While this has been a horrific day which resulted in great losses of loved ones for many people, including my family, we are forging ahead with the Dumas Diamonds Polo Club. My fiancée has purchased an apartment building right here in New York City that will serve as a home and educational facility that will aid in stopping gang and gun violence throughout the city for the many young people who have become influenced by groups like the Bugatti Blades."

"Valerie, can you tell us about this project? It sounds wonderful."

"Not now. We are having a press conference right here at the Boat House in Central Park on Thursday at noon. Please feel free to come. I'll tell you all you need to know then. Now, if you will excuse us. As you know, it's been a long, long day for Victor and me. It's time for me to get this man to bed. Thank you."

"Thank you, Victor and Valerie. This has been Sarah Jeffries reporting live from The Ritz Carlton Hotel in New York City for ABC News."

Val kissed Victor lightly on the lips for the cameras as well as to infuriate Talfor, who was watching them closely. She was not a jealous woman, but she had to let the girl know Victor was way off limits where she was concerned. She waved at her as she and Victor, flanked by more security than the secret service, headed to the elevator bank.

Columbus had noticed Talfor Redd standing in the background and didn't miss Val looking at her right after she kissed Victor. He and Talfor had a fling back in the day. She had a penchant for nose candy and ménage à trois back then. Perhaps she could be helpful to him in bringing down Victor. It wouldn't be difficult for him to reel her back in. She would screw him or anybody else for a Chanel bag and some cocaine.

Well, now he knew where to find Val and Victor. He would also attend this press conference on Thursday at the Boat House in the Big Apple. After that huge reward Victor just offered, shadowing the two of them could lead him to Rolondo and Sincere. He wondered when Victor had discovered that Sincere was his brother. A lot had happened in five years. There was a lot of catching up to be done. He had to get a phone and a laptop the minute he left the bank to see what was going on in the world.

Columbus arrived back at the table just as the servers were bringing out their food.

"Ariel, as soon as I go to my bank in the morning, we'll go over to the Bal Harbour Mall and do some shopping. We're heading to New York tomorrow night. I'll get the concierge to book us on a flight and get me a reservation at the Ritz Carlton. I would stay with you, but I have a lot of business to get done."

Ariel thanked her lucky stars he didn't want to stay with her. She lived in a one-room studio apartment on the fourth floor of a walk-up on Manhattan's upper West Side. The totally false personae she had created just for Columbus would be blown right away if he saw the way she lived.

"I understand, baby. We can get together at night when you finish your business."

"It's settled then. Big Apple, here we come. Bon appétit!" Columbus said with an inviting grin.

The waiter returned with another glass of merlot. And as much as Ariel tried not to gulp it down too fast, she emptied the glass in mere seconds.

Although Columbus didn't look up from his plate, he still caught how fast her wine glass returned to the table empty. *Ariel Pembrough, I'll definitely be checking you out the moment I get my hands on a computer.*

Chapter Fifteen

♥

Rome

On Wednesday morning an exhausted and extremely frustrated Rome sat in first class trying to piece together Turquoise's disappearance. Victor had wanted to send his jet for him, but Rome felt safer taking such a long flight with people around him. He had calmed down a little over the way Turquoise had betrayed him with Rolondo, whom they had all thought was Royale. Well, not all of them. Val had said over and over she remembered Royale being a bit heavier and darker. She had even joked that perhaps he had gotten his skin bleached and gone on a diet. The funny thing about her statement was that she never mentioned where she met Royale in the first place. He had always assumed that she must have seen him play baseball.

As soon as he allowed his mind to rest, the state of his busted relationship came back to him. But so did his disturbing conversation with Pace about Rolondo and Turquoise's sex tape. His gut stirred. He had wasted almost two years of being with Turquoise. Without realizing it, a tear trickled down his cheek. He no longer wanted to marry her, but a part of him still loved her, and he certainly didn't want her to be dead.

"Are you all right, sir?" Rome looked up at the woman who was sitting across from him. She seemed very familiar.

"Amethyst? Amethyst Printup." He quickly wiped the tear away. *Shit, I hope she didn't see that.*

"Rome Nyland?" She looked closer at him. "My God. How long has it been? I didn't realize who you were." They couldn't stand up to hug each other because the plane was taxiing down the runway to take off, so Rome reached across the aisle and squeezed her hand.

Rome and Amythest had both been Olympic hopefuls in 1980. Amethyst was a figure skater and Rome was on the relay team. They had both trained at the sports facility at UCLA. However, neither of them ever made it to the Olympics that year. Amythest broke her ankle during the trials. Rome made the team but was a victim of politics. In 1980, the United States led a boycott of the Summer Olympic Games in Moscow to protest the late 1979 Soviet invasion of Afghanistan. In total, sixty-five nations refused to participate in the games, whereas eighty countries sent athletes to compete.

Rome laughed. "I had a rough night. I guess I'm looking old and tired this morning. My own son probably wouldn't even recognize me."

"Naw, you don't look rough. You are still one of the most handsome men in the world. I heard that you had a son with that girl Davida, who was a cheerleader when we were in college. Are you two married now?"

"No, we never got married. We still hung around each other for a long time after we graduated. My son is eighteen. He goes to Morehouse. Davida always told me she had no interest in becoming any man's wife. Then out of thin air she married some doctor around three years ago. I was pretty hurt but life goes on." He thought it was best not to mention Turquoise. "How about you? Are you married?"

"Sadly, I'm a widow. Colon cancer took my husband away six years ago. We didn't have any children. I still miss him very much."

"I'm sorry. Do you still live in Los Angeles?"

"No, I live in New York. I was out here for my cousin's wedding. It was on Sunday. I stayed an extra few days."

The flight attendant handed each of them drinks they had previously ordered as well as menus.

"I teach ice skating."

"Really? Well, no big shocker there though."

"No, I guess not."

"You were always a great figure skater."

"Thanks."

"So if you don't mind me asking, where are you staying now?"

"I own a brownstone up in Harlem and built a tiny rink behind it."

"Very fitting."

"I'm also a nurse at a private practice. I actually met my husband at Sylvia's Restaurant in Harlem after he was diagnosed. He was telling the bartender about his diagnosis. I was sitting next to him and offered a few medical suggestions. We ended up eating together that night and every night afterwards for the next two years until he went on to heaven. I didn't have a long time with him, but it was a beautiful one."

Rome didn't know what to say. Her life was sadder than his. He looked at her and smiled. She should be about the same age as he was, fifty-four. Amethyst was still gorgeous.

In the past he had never fallen for those light bright types. He liked his women dark brown like his mom had been. Val always said that Davida and Turquoise looked like twins. The way those two had put him through the ringer, maybe it was time to switch up his taste in women. Perhaps heading to New York would lead him to the light at the end of the tunnel, or at least a little walk on the dark side with sex in the friendly skies. He needed some sort of distraction to take his focus off Turquoise's betrayal. Plus, he couldn't stop trying to figure out how the woman Samantha was connected to Rolondo, and if she had turned Turquoise over to the bastard. Yes, five hours traveling cross country with a beauty like Amethyst was just what he needed right now. It was as if fate had intervened.

"Let's ask the flight attendant for some champagne and toast to our surprise reunion!" Rome attempted to lighten the mood.

Amethyst was down for that. She'd had a crush on Rome Nyland the entire four years they were at UCLA. He never had eyes for anyone but that Davida though. This might be her lucky day.

"Cool. Bring on the bubbly!"

Hell . . . maybe they could even join the mile high club before landing. If only Rome could stop the never-ending torturous thoughts of Turquoise's betrayal and her strange disappearance. He asked the flight attendant for a bottle of their best champagne and wondered, *Where the hell is she?*

Chapter Sixteen

Valerie

All Valerie had been doing since she got up this morning was trying to locate Turquoise. It was as if the woman had vanished into thin air. She was currently finishing up a call with Turquoise's assistant, who seemed so spooked by her boss's sudden disappearance, that Valerie was sure she was going to have a nervous breakdown at any moment.

"Okay, Sylvia. The computer tech guy will be there soon to pick up Turquoise's laptop as well as your main computer to take it to the police station. We've already got a trace on her phone. Is the security guy there yet that Rome sent over last night?"

"Yes. There are actually two guys here with me."

"That's good. Now just conduct business as you normally would. If any one that calls or comes by there today looks or acts the least bit suspicious, you dial 911 right away. You hear me?"

"Yes."

"And by all means if your boss contacts you or shows up, call me right away. Rome's plane will be landing here at three, but he's in contact with me by email from the plane. Okay?"

"Yes, Val."

"Don't worry. We will find her, and don't you worry about getting paid on Friday if Turquoise doesn't surface. Whatever your weekly salary is, we have it covered."

"Thank you so much. Bye, Valerie."

"Bye, sweetheart." Val rubbed her forehead. Just for one day, she wished she and Victor could live a normal life. From the moment they met in Las Vegas when she had discovered that his estranged wife, Andrea, had been killed, their life together had been packed with nothing but murder, mayhem, and malicious people. She loved this luxurious life that Victor was providing for her, but life sure had been a lot calmer when she was struggling.

They had been trying to get married for over a year, but one thing or another came up that prevented them from planning a ceremony. First it was Violet giving birth to the baby, then Violet leaving Vance, and Val having to take care of Valencia. Now, Rolondo was running around loose, people were dead at their house, and Amerani was in a coma, not to mention Victor's safe being emptied. To top everything off, Victor had told her before he left for his Manhattan office this morning that Violet's mother, who used to be in cahoots with Andrea and Valerian was also on her way here. At this point they all needed divine help.

"Jesus Lord, please help us, dear Father."

"Did I hear you call my name?" Victor, wearing a sexy smile on his face, walked into the third bedroom of the hotel suite that Val had converted into an office.

"No, you are my god on earth, but I was talking to the main one upstairs."

He stooped down to kiss her.

"How's it going so far today? Any progress on locating Turquoise?"

"No, all we know is she was last seen getting into a burgundy Navigator. LAPD has an All-Points Bulletin out on that make of truck. They will stop everyone they see driving one.

"Charmion called me. She booked a two-bedroom suite for Violet and her mom up the street at Trump International Hotel. Their flight gets in about the same time as Rome's. He emailed me that Vance, you, and I, along with him, would go over to the Trump International with extra security to speak to Violet and her mom at five."

"Okay."

"We need a break from everything that's going on. Once we get the lowdown on those two, I want to have a nice family dinner at Ricardo's Steakhouse in East Harlem tonight." Until Valerie moved to Los Angeles a few years ago to take a regular job on a daytime chat show, she had lived up the block from Ricardo's. It had been her main hangout. Although the show was canceled after its first season, she opted to stay in LA because the rent on her two-bedroom house in Hollywood was actually cheaper than her walk-up apartment in East Harlem.

Two years ago, when her soror, Dedra, committed suicide in Val's home, she moved in with Victor. At first it was supposed to be a temporary arrangement until her house was repaired. But cupid's arrow hit Val and Victor hard. The two became inseparable, and she had been living with him ever since.

"I still don't know if I think it is wise for all of us to go roaming around New York City without knowing where Rolondo may be lurking," Victor interjected.

"With Rome with us, we will be safe to eat somewhere other than this hotel. I will invite Violet and this Betty chick, but I don't want any trouble between Violet and Roshonda. So I'm hoping Violet won't want to come with us."

"Me and you both, baby." Victor set a box from Piaget on Val's desk. "I thought this might take a little bit of the damper off you from yesterday. Plus I thought you needed something new and sparkly to wear to tomorrow's press conference."

Though she responded to the present with, "Honey, I told you to stop giving me gifts," Val secretly loved her fiancé's generosity. She opened the box. A gorgeous gold cuff by Isola Della Giudecca, Venice, encrusted with a huge starburst of rubies and white, pink, and yellow diamonds was inside. She immediately put it on her wrist. It was gorgeous. "I love it! Thank you, baby."

Victor locked the bedroom door and unbuttoned his shirt.

"Why don't you show me just how much you love it? I wouldn't mind a little afternoon delight." Val lifted her maxi-dress over her head, snatched off her bra and panties, then undid the zipper on Victor's pants.

"Neither would I, baby." Just as the two soul mates fell back in the bed, Val's phone buzzed. Reluctantly, she looked at her text message:

Thought I had lead on the burgundy Navigator, but when I followed one on Crenshaw, a woman and child got out. No Turquoise or two dudes. Sorry.

Val was sorry, too. She kept the information near the forefront of her mind. But right now it was time for some good, stress-relieving lovemaking. She kissed Victor gently, then deeply as they lost their individual selves, merging into a sensual almost musical bond of one rhythm. As the two fell into a calming sleep, one final thought picked at Val's brain. *Where had Turquoise disappeared to?* She would definitely have to get back to looking for her.

PART 2

Chapter Seventeen

Yohance

The Three Points Sports Bar on Dean Martin Drive on Sin City's West Side hadn't seen any real action in almost the two years since Andrea Dumas' body had been found inside. However, the club's managers' still kept it cleaned, well-stocked, and the Los Angeles Wildcats memorabilia that decorated the walls looking shiny and new. The woman locked in the bedroom in the back was coming to.

"Help me," she moaned. "Where am I?"

"Don't worry about where you are, bitch. I got you."

"I need to use the bathroom." She tried to sit up, but realized she was chained to the bed, so she fell back on it. That's when she realized she was naked. She tried to cover herself with the sheet on the bed. Why was she so woozy? Had she been drugged?

"It's too late for all that covering up, baby. You don't have a damn thing to hide from me. I have seen everything that you got and more. We had so much sex last night that I know where every pimple is inside and outside of your booty." Yohance sneered at her.

"I'll take you to the bathroom. But first, let me give you this little shot of feel-good. I feel like partying some more.

You know, you are one fine specimen of a woman." Before the woman could protest, the man shot her up with heroin. He pulled her up.

She struggled to stand because her legs felt like rubber. Who was this man, and what was he giving her?

"Hell, let me just carry you into the bathroom." The man, who was actually only nineteen, picked her up and carried her into the bathroom. He sat her on the toilet, then ran a bathtub full of water. He placed her in the tub.

"Here's a wash rag and some soap. You should be able to wash yourself. Don't get any idea about going through that window. It's locked, and you are butt ass naked. And I will shoot you without even thinking about it. I'll be back soon with something for you to eat. Enjoy your high!" He slammed the bathroom door behind him and locked it.

She tried to focus. She remembered going to dinner at Craig's with the new client. Beyond that, the rest of the previous night was a total blur. Who had brought her here and why? Why did they keep shooting her up with some drug to keep her so out of it? And why had that kid taken her clothes and shoes? She had to gather her wits together and find a way to escape so that she could contact her fiancé. She had to get out of this awful place! Tears flowed down her face. Had Rolondo told that girl and these guys to do this to her? If so, where was he?

"Dear God, please just get me out of here." She fell back into a nod in the tub.

Up at the front of the Three Points, four members of the Bugatti Blades, Shemar Woods, Reggie Rodriguez, Bruce Abroms and Maximillian Moore were playing an intense game of poker. Yohance Allen, who had been keeping guard over the woman who was being held captive, got a beer from behind the bar, then observed their game.

"How's your patient liking her medicine, man?" Reggie asked.

"I put her in the bathtub so she can clean herself up. I think it's going to take one more day to really get her hooked. As soon as we get her where we want her to be, Pastor Claude wants to turn her out right away."

Bruce gave Yohance a surprised look.

"That fast? He gonna put her on the ho' stroll here? That woman must have done something real bad to him."

"No, not to Pastor Claude. She was one of Rolondo's women. Pastor Claude says she did him real dirty, and turning a stuck-up slut like her into a drug-addicted street ho' was much better revenge than killing her. By the way, Max, you, and I are driving her to New York City. She's joining his stable there."

"Damn, man! Why can't we just take the chick on a plane? We'll be in the car for almost a week."

"We can't risk anyone seeing her. What did you cats do with her wallet?"

Reggie handed it to him. Yohance looked through it. There was a little over $200, a black American Express card, a Visa US Bank card, and a Saks Fifth Avenue credit card in it.

"Maybe we should do a little shopping. She's caked up pretty good with plastic."

"No," Reggie told him. "Pastor Claude said if we use anything in the woman's wallet, her boyfriend will be able to track her whereabouts right away. The cards are off limits."

Bruce sat quietly looking at his poker hand, listening to the others' back and forth chatter. He had given his lady who lived in Phoenix, Arizona the numbers on that AMEX card right after they picked up the chick in the back last night. His lady had texted him and said she already ordered three pairs of red bottoms and a new Louis online, and the transactions went through like magic. Oh well, if the greedy skank got caught, it was on her. She shouldn't have bought so much damn merchandise. He spoke up.

"I'll go back and get the ho' out of the tub. I feel like getting my dick waxed. Yohance, take my hand in the game." Bruce reached into his pocket and pulled out a glassine baggie filled with pills, then went to the bar, poured a glass of Cognac, and mixed the pills in it. He opened the fridge and pulled out a pre-made sandwich. "I'll let her eat, then wash it down with this. These pills coupled with the heroin will send her to Mars. I want her to freak me real good. See you gentlemen in a bit."

Yohance's phone rang. It was Pastor Claude.

"Hello," Yohance answered.

"How are things going out there?" Pastor Claude asked.

"Pretty good. We've been keeping her so high that she's not fighting back."

"That's good, but be careful. I don't want her to overdose. That would defeat the whole purpose of this operation. Keep her naked until tomorrow. I have someone dropping off some cash to you in the morning. He will pay each of you and bring some clothes for her. I want you to be able to get on the road to New York as soon as he gets there. He's also going to trade trucks with you. The GPS will already be set with the road directions in it for your drive across country."

"How long do you think it will take us to get there?"

"Well, it is approximately 2,525 miles between Las Vegas and New York. I want you guys to stick to the sixty-five miles-per-hour speed limit, so you don't draw any attention to yourselves. You have a hostage that you are going to keep getting high while you're on the road. So, you cannot get stopped by the cops for any reason. The trip should take about forty hours. Since there will be three of you driving and you can sleep in shifts, you will only need to stop for gas, food, and to use the bathroom."

"Okay. Got it."

"If you stick to that plan, it should take you less than two days to get to the city. Then it will take you another two hours to get out to Sag Harbor where my church is."

"Okay. It sounds good. I've never been to New York, so I'm geeked up about seeing it. Are we driving the car back, or leaving it with you and coming home on a plane?" Yohance asked.

"We'll figure all that out when you get here. Call me as soon as you get the delivery tomorrow. I'll see you sometime on Friday evening or early on Saturday morning. Keep up the good work."

"Okay, Pastor Claude. I'll speak to you tomorrow." Yohance hung up the phone and looked at each man briefly but with intensity. "Y'all better not fuck this up. We could all go down for at least twenty-five years."

Twenty-five years settled in the air around the young men like a death threat.

Chapter Eighteen

Valerie

After some intense lovemaking, Val was listening to Victor quietly snore when her phone rang. It was the same source that texted her earlier. This source was so good that she called him Agent 88. In turn, like Rome, he referred to her as Agent 99. He must have finally gotten a lead on Turquoise.

"Hey, you got anything?"

"Yeah, two things. A source saw a woman that was a dead ringer for Turquoise Hobson, whose real estate business billboards are on all the benches at bus stops around town. She said the chick was at a trap house in South Central Los Angeles last night. The source says she was with two young guys who looked like gang bangers, and she seemed to be real high. The guys were copping heroin. They left in a burgundy Navigator. It happened too fast to get a license plate number."

"That's okay. Get me an address. There should be a surveillance camera somewhere on the block."

"I'm way ahead of you. The address is 2139 Florence Avenue. The guys were calling her Mahogany though, so I'm not sure if it was your girl, but my source says if it wasn't, she must have a twin sister."

"I don't think Turquoise uses drugs, but you never know. Rolondo was high on heroin the night they arrested him. Did your people tell you what the guys looked like?"

"Yes, they both seemed to be in their late teens or early twenties, tall, well built, and brown skinned. The guy that runs the trap house called one of them Yohance."

"That's good looking out. Let me see what I can dig up. Rome is on a flight that lands here in an hour. I will give him all of this information the minute I hear from him. I'll have Cantrese wire you $1,000 by Western Union right now. She'll call you with the transaction number in a little while. Call me if you hear anything else."

"Will do." Even though Cantrese was right in their makeshift office in their Ritz Carlton suite, Valerie called her on the cell phone. She picked up right away.

"Yes, Valerie?"

"Send '88' $1,000 by Western Union with the master card I gave you to use for expenses. Then hit him up with the MTCN number when you get it."

"I'm on it."

"Thanks."

Victor stretched, then sat up.

"I must be getting old. You knocked me out, baby."

"There is nothing old about you. Get up and get dressed. Rome will be here shortly, then we will head down to the Trump International to talk to Violet and her mother."

"This is one meeting that I am definitely dreading. The last time I saw that woman, she and my wife were tangled up naked in each other's arms in my bed. I vowed never to lay eyes on her again back then, and still don't want to see her."

"Victor, I'm afraid that this woman going to see Violet is a lot more serious than we originally thought it was. How did she even know that Violet was in Las Vegas? If Betty was Andrea's lover, then she had to, or maybe still has to, also be connected to your brother and Rolondo. Did Andrea ever mention who Violet's father was?"

"No she didn't. There is no name of a father on Violet's birth certificate. I made Andrea get it for me when we took her in."

"I think Betty's sudden appearance out of nowhere has something to do with Rolondo's escape. When we go down to their hotel, make sure all the security is heavily armed. I will be so glad when Rome gets here to the hotel."

"So will I, baby, so will I. Let's get ready. This is going to be another long night."

Chapter Nineteen

Columbus

Ariel looked around the living room of the bungalow at all of the shopping bags filled to the brim with all the new things Columbus had bought for the two of them. She was in awe. How much money was this Royale Jones really worth? He could probably afford to buy Crooked Island. It was unbelievable what a difference a day made. Twenty-four hours ago he was cleaning rooms and doing odd jobs for peanuts in the Bahamas, with absolutely no recollection that there was ten thousand dollars in cash hidden in his necklace. His one glance at the copy of *The New York Post* that she brought to show him had brought him back to life.

This morning, he had gone to the Sun Trust Bank where Columbus cashed in and transferred millions of dollars in certificates of deposit that were in his safe deposit box into new accounts. He explained to her the reason the box hadn't been confiscated in five years was because the monthly payment for it was automatically deducted from another one of his accounts.

Hitting almost every luxury store that the Bal Harbour Mall had to offer, including Balenciaga, Chanel, Giorgio Armani, Ermenegildo Zegna, Gucci, and Saks, where Columbus bought five pieces of Louis Vuitton luggage, including a suitcase, purse, wallet, and two pairs of shoes for her, Ariel had never seen such power shopping. Both of them now had new wardrobes. Ariel looked down at the Rolex watch that gleamed up at her from her wrist. Purchasing one for himself because he no longer had a watch, the man hadn't hesitated to also get one for her. The sound of Columbus' voice broke into her thoughts as he entered the bungalow accompanied by two maids from housekeeping.

"Ariel, why are you just standing there? We have to get this stuff packed into these suitcases. We have an eight o'clock flight to New York. These ladies are going to help. You can just slip into those jeans and one of the tops you got from Saks to travel in. I am anxious to get out of here."

"No problem. Ladies, why don't you start with his things? They need to go into those four suitcases."

Royale picked up the new briefcase and laptop, then headed upstairs. He had managed to catch up with one of his old connections who was able to get him a fake Michigan driver's license with the name Columbus Isley on it. His boy at the bank had also managed to open an account in that name and print out an instant debit card along with a Visa Gold card with no limit on it. He didn't want to tip off anyone that the real Royale Jones was back in a big way. By not touching any of his funds or CDs at Sun Trust for five years, his money had grown tremendously. There was now upwards of six million dollars at that bank. The real fortune, however, was in the safe buried beneath Claude's church.

Although not as bad, but similar to his three cousins, the love of the almighty dollar ran through Royale's veins. He was definitely going to get everything in it, and he was also going to take back the five years of his life that had been snatched away from him by Rolondo. Last, he was going for the real big gusto, Valerie Rollins. *Forbes* listed Victor Dumas' net worth at almost eight billion dollars. *Let the bastard buy himself another woman.* Royale had been deprived of real love for thirty-something years too long!

"Columbus, we've finished packing. We can leave," Ariel shouted.

"Okay, I'll be down in a minute, Ariel." He opened up his new laptop. He hadn't touched a computer in a long time, but everything came right back to him. He tried to google the name Ariel Pembrough once again. Nothing came up. He had figured out she definitely wasn't any supermodel now that his head was clear, and he saw that she had cheap clothes and shoes, wore no jewelry, and carried a cheap faux leather handbag. The bottom line, however, was that Ariel was beautiful, and her visits to Crooked Island, not to mention some real good sex, had been his only source of hope for the last couple of years. And in the end, it was the newspaper article that Ariel showed him that had brought him back to life. For now he would keep her as his woman. But if he could get his soul mate Valerie Rollins back, Ariel would be history.

He smiled, just thinking about the first time he laid eyes on Val. At his baseball game, she had been standing on the sidelines with her father. Columbus would never forget those jean shorts Val wore with a red sleeveless top. Although Val wasn't very tall, her legs were endless. He wanted to keep staring at them, but it was his turn at bat. It was the bottom of the ninth inning. The bases were loaded, and two men were out, and his team was losing to Michigan State, 2-1. Not knowing what possessed him to do so, he called out to Val, "This homerun is for you, beautiful." Columbus laughed as he remembered Val looking to the right and left of her, and then behind her as if he had addressed someone else. "Yes, I'm talking to you." He pointed his bat directly at her, before stepping up to home plate. Her father folded his arms, glaring at this showoff. Columbus then knocked the ball right out of the park, hitting a Grand Slam. His team won the Big Ten tournament, beating MSU, 5-2. When he ran over home base, Valerie was still standing on the sidelines cheering. He walked over to her and her father and introduced himself with a strong handshake. She smiled at him.

"Thank you for that. My name is Val." It was as if the heavens had opened up and sent him an angel.

"Can I call you Sweet Val?" he asked. She blushed and he had loved her ever since.

Royale closed the laptop, put it in the briefcase, then headed downstairs on his way to New York, with thoughts of finally claiming the contents of his buried safe, but more important, being reunited with Valerie.

Chapter Twenty

Rome

Rome and Amethyst, who did not get their secret hope to join the mile high club while jetting cross country, deplaned together at JFK Airport in Queens, New York. Val had emailed him the information about Betty Lum while he was on the flight, and he became so emerged in gathering all the goods on her via the internet that he didn't have any playtime. When Rome saw the Dumas security awaiting him as soon as he stepped into the terminal, he asked Amethyst, "Do you have a car or someone meeting you here?"

"No, I'll just take a cab. I don't have any checked luggage." Rome had to retrieve his gun from the airport security and his large suitcase. They would both be in baggage claim.

"If you don't mind waiting while I get my things, I can drop you off. We have to go right past Harlem to get to Midtown."

"Are you sure it's not a problem?"

"Not at all. In fact after I take you home, if you're free at seven-thirty tonight, my partner emailed me that we're having dinner at Ricardo's Steakhouse in East Harlem. Would you like to join us?"

"I love Ricardo's. Yes, I am free."

"Then it's a date," Rome said. "Fellows . . ." He handed his suit bag to one of Victor's guys, Stan. "This is an old friend of mine, Amethyst Printup. You don't mind dropping her off do you?"

"Of course not."

"Thanks, said Amethyst. "My house is on 127th Street and Madison Avenue."

As the group made their way down to baggage claim, a stunning looking woman who had been sitting in coach on the same flight stared at them intensely while chatting on her cell phone.

Claude

"Claude! You are not going to believe this. Rome Nyland was on my flight," Samantha said. "He's heading to baggage claim now with what looks like two security guys and a woman who looks familiar. Damn. I guess he wasn't as into his fiancée as she thought he was. He looks pretty cozy with what must be his side chick."

"Stay with them. I'm right downstairs. Most likely, he's headed to the Ritz Carlton where the rest of his crew is. Good looking out." Samantha headed downstairs and out of the terminal where she slipped into the front seat next to Claude as she watched Rome and his lady friend get into a black Escalade.

She looked at Claude and said, "I just overheard Rome invite the chick who's with him to dinner at Ricardo's Steak House tonight."

"I know the place. It's on Second Avenue in East Harlem. I guess that's where we will be breaking bread tonight too." Laughing, he drove off right behind Rome's car.

Chapter Twenty-one

Janvieve

Still keeping a low profile until she could exterminate Violet and Sincere, Janvieve retrieved her luggage over at Terminal B. She made her way outside the airport, then jumped into a cab. The Ritz Carlton had been sold-out, so she made a reservation around the corner from there.

"Please take me to the Trump International Hotel on Central Park West and Sixtieth Street in Manhattan." Janvieve had undergone even more transformations since escaping from the courthouse.

Once she got to the hotel, she called one of the Blades, who was a hairdresser. She came over to the hotel and gave her a full blonde weave that hung to her waist. Once she was finished, the hotel's concierge arranged for her to have a full body wax and tips put on her nails. Luckily some of the shops on Hollywood Boulevard stayed open 'round the clock, so she took a cab over there and picked up a few dresses, underwear, pairs of shoes, and a suitcase to put it all in. Janvieve Rochon was ready to get her revenge on. She needed to somehow shadow Claude and find out if the kidnapping of Turquoise had succeeded as planned and if Samantha, who also used the name Caressa, had gotten to New York. Sneaking up on them might also help her discover what Sincere was up to and where Violet was hiding out. It was time to let the games begin.

As Dumas II landed on the JFK runway for private planes, two black Cadillac Escalades pulled up not far from it. Three members of the Dumas security team got out and greeted Violet and Betty as they walked down the plane's steps. The first gentleman, Ben, stepped forward.

"Mrs. Dumas, Mrs. Lum, I am Ben. We all work for Dumas Electronics. We are here to escort the two of you ladies to the Trump International Hotel where you will be staying during your visit to New York."

"Trump International?" asked Violet. "Why are we staying there? My daughter and husband are staying at the Ritz Carlton. Take us there."

"I am sorry, Mrs. Dumas. My instructions are to take you to Trump International. Your luggage is in the car. Please get in. We can't hold up the runway."

Violet, followed by Betty, reluctantly got into the Cadillac Escalade. She punched up Vance on her cell phone, who picked up right away.

"I see your flight has landed safely."

"Cut the crap, Vance. My mother wants to see her granddaughter. Why are these stooges of your father's taking us to Trump International instead of the Ritz Carlton where Valencia is?"

"The Ritz Carlton is sold-out. I am going to meet you over at Trump."

"So what if it's sold-out? I'm sure you have a huge suite. Why can't I just stay with you?"

"That's not going to happen. You wanted your own suite. We're estranged. You left me, remember? I already have a roommate."

Violet did remember. Over the last few months, even a glance at Vance had turned her stomach. She cringed every time he wanted to make love to her. Soon she ran out of excuses to give him for not wanting to fuck. She couldn't be on her period or nauseous or have a migraine every day. So she just upped and left one night, joining her dad Sincere in Paris.

"I'll see you in a little while," Vance said.

"What do you mean you already have a roommate?" It was too late for him to answer her. Vance had already disconnected the call.

Betty sat there steaming and didn't want to ask her daughter anything about her conversation in front of the Dumas security men. She could offer her a little advice though, so she spoke just above a whisper.

"Look, I don't know what that conversation was all about, but you have become a little too spoiled and self-centered. It is almost as if you came out of Andrea's womb instead of mine. You're treating Vance the exact same way she treated Victor. I had some good times with her, but in the end, she was just another drug and sex-addicted whore. You need to straighten up."

"I couldn't care less about straightening up. Before yesterday, I didn't even know if you were alive or dead. I hate all of them and I hate you too!"

Chapter Twenty-two

Valerie

Valerie was on a conference call with two top publicists, Irene Gandy and Helen Shelton, tying up some loose ends for tomorrow's press conference. Her phone beeped. She looked at it.

"Okay ladies, that's Rome on my other line. Let me speak with him. He's probably going to need to speak with you all early in the morning about how he's going to need you to clear the press for security. I'll holler at you two later." She clicked on to the other line.

"Hey, kid. Are you here yet?"

"Yes, I am already in my suite with the maid you sent unpacking my clothes. This is some kind of swanky set-up, a maid and a butler. Thanks," Rome said.

"Great. I'm going to send Dwayne to your room to bring you here. I'm ready. Victor is on skype with his office in San Francisco, but they should be wrapping up soon. And Vance should be here any minute. I got the cash, and Victor wrote out the check that you wanted. We're good to go. Listen Rome, I got a call a little while ago from one of my more worldly sources. One of his connects saw a girl that looked just like Turquoise's photos on the billboards that are around town for her real estate agency. She was at a trap

140

house in South Central. I already texted the address to James Pace so that he can check it out. Have you ever known Turquoise to do drugs?"

"No, but at this point, there's nothing else you can tell me about her that would surprise me. I'm sure James will hit us up if he finds something there. I left a couple of messages for her sister. I'm waiting to hear back from her. I'll see you in a minute. Oh, and Val, I need to you to add one more person to your dinner reservation for tonight. Her name is Amethyst Printup."

"The figure skater?"

"Yeah. She and I sat together on the flight coming out here. She's a widow. I thought it would be nice to get to know her a little better. I used to see her around a lot when I was training for the Olympics."

"Oh you did, huh? I know that she's a widow. I did a story when her husband died from cancer. They hadn't been married very long. It was sad. No problem. Let me get Dwayne going. He has keys so that you can get up to this floor. There were no more rooms left up here."

"All right. Later."

"Later."

Val went into the suite's living room where Dwayne was deep in conversation with Cantrese. They got silent as soon as Val entered the room. She told Dwayne, "Rome is down in his room. You have his number."

Dwayne stood up.

"I'm on the way." With that, he was out of the door.

Val wondered what was up with Dwayne and Cantrese. Aloud she said, "Cantrese, you can start getting ready for dinner now. I'm going to run an errand with the guys. We'll be going straight to the restaurant from there, so you just grab a cab and go over on your own. It's Ricardo's Steakhouse on Second Avenue between 111th and 110th streets."

"All right. I'm going to head to my room. I'll see you in a couple of hours."

Just when Val thought she might possibly have two minutes of solitude, Vance came through the door.

"You look gorgeous, Val. I keep telling you that if you weren't with Dad, I would marry you myself."

Val smiled. The pink scoop neck Dolce & Gabbana dress flattered her body and matching Mary Jane shoes showed off her shapely legs.

"I keep telling you to leave my woman alone, son."

Both Vance and Valerie laughed as Victor entered the room at the same time that Rome and Dwayne walked through the door.

Valerie flew into Rome's arms.

"Thank God you are here and didn't get yourself killed in the process." The guys hugged Rome too.

"Hey, I'm glad to see all of you too." He patted his briefcase. "All of the ammunition we need is right here. Let's do this."

"I need to warn you all that Violet is not a happy camper about having to stay in a different hotel," Vance stated.

"Don't worry, Vance. When we finish with her mother, she probably won't want to stay anywhere near you. When we get there, just let Val and I do the talking and follow our lead. But there is one thing that I need to ask you before we go see Violet. My CI told me there is some buzz on the street that your ex-wife was involved with breaking Rolondo out of jail. You wouldn't happen to know where Roshonda is, would you?"

"Yes, Rome, I do. She's right down the hall in my room. We're sort of back together. Your CI is way off. Roshonda hasn't spoken to Rolondo since before he went to jail. And since we've hooked back up, she has been letting me look through her phone. I have the code for her voice mail and everything."

"This kid is usually pretty right on, but everyone has an off-day. All right, let's go get rid of Betty."

As Val listened to Rome and Vance, a light bulb went off in her head. She had a good inkling about which of Vance's wives Rome's informant was talking about. Andrea must have planted Violet on Vance and Victor for Valerian years ago. She prayed her hunch was wrong.

Accompanied by Dwayne and three other security guards, the four of them headed out to make their way up the street to the Trump International. Val didn't know if this Betty was dangerous or not, so just to be cautious, she had her gun tucked away in her purse.

Janvieve

After getting settled in her room at Trump Interntional, Janvieve decided to go down to the hotel's Jean Georges Restaurant to have a drink and chill for a minute while she plotted her next move. She had just read in the *New York Daily News' Confidential* column that the Dumas Diamonds Polo Club was having a press conference in the Central Park Boathouse tomorrow to announce its plans for the summer. She had already put a call in to a contact at the LAPD who would sell his own mother to get her a press credential so she could attend it.

Three brown Bentley SUVs suddenly pulled up in front of the hotel. Janvieve watched in astonishment as Rome Nyland, accompanied by two security guards got out of the first truck. Then, Valerie Rollins with Victor Dumas and one security guy embarked from the middle truck, with Vance Dumas and three more security guards exiting the last one. They all solemnly walked up the steps into the hotel as if they were headed to a funeral. Although she did not want any of them to see her, Janvieve had to find out what they were doing here. She practically ran through the revolving door to get close enough to hear whose room they asked for, but still managed to stay out of the group's eye sight.

Rome told the concierge, "The Dumas family is here to see Mrs. Violet Dumas."

Janvieve almost jumped for joy. *The conniving bitch is under the same roof as I am! Payback is such a sweet thing.* Janvieve grinned at the thought as she folded her arms. She would wait right here in the restaurant for Rome and his stooges to come back down, then slip the desk clerk a few hundred dollars to get Violet's room number. This would be the last five-star hotel that Violet would see alive.

Chapter Twenty-three

Violet

Why did he bring a miniature army with him, including Rome? Violet thought as she let everyone inside her suite. She assumed Vance was coming to talk to her alone.

"What's this about, Vance? What are they all doing with you?" she asked as she closed the door.

"Well hello to you, too, Violet," Vance responded.

Val stepped forward and hugged Violet.

"How are you, hon?"

"Not so damn good. What the fuck is going on, Val? Why couldn't I go straight to see my baby? I should call the cops and tell them that Victor's goons kidnapped me!"

"Hold on, Violet," Victor spoke up. "I practically raised you, and I taught you better manners than that. I won't have you speaking to Val like that. Apologize to her right now."

"My daughter will do nothing of the kind. Step away from her," a voice said.

They all looked up to see Betty Lum coming out of the suite's bedroom. Clad in a floral red and pink Gucci mini dress with pleated flowing sleeves and six-inch red Christian Louboutin stilettos, she looked like a print ad in a magazine.

"Victor, the years have certainly been good to you. The last time we met you looked like a skinny little nerd with huge glasses and buck teeth. Look at you now. You could pass for a model on the cover of *GQ Magazine*."

Victor glared at her.

"I didn't come here so that we could reminisce over the last time we met. Even though your daughter seems to have lost her mind, I have a little more respect for her than to describe the scenario you were involved in that particular day."

Val extended her hand to Betty.

"How are you? I'm Valerie Rollins, Victor's fiancée."

Betty ignored Val's hand.

"I know who you are."

"Why don't we all take a seat?" Rome said.

While Vance, Victor, Valerie and Rome sat on the couch and in a chair, Betty and Violet didn't move an inch.

"Betty, or shall I call you by your real name, Lisa Takeshita? I'm Rome Nyland. I head up the security for Dumas Electronics. Victor and Valerie were concerned that since you once had close ties to Andrea, your showing up at your daughter's hotel in Las Vegas, out of nowhere might mean that you had something to do with Rolondo Jemison shooting his way out of the courthouse in LA yesterday. I did some checking, and under your real name you were arrested along with Rolondo and Valerian Davidson many times back in the eighties and nineties. I'm sure you are aware that you still have warrants, most recently a desk ticket for prostitution in Chicago. So, are you going to tell us what's going on, or do I need to call the NYPD?"

"You think you are very clever, don't you, Mr. Nyland?" Betty walked over to the bar and poured herself a glass of champagne from an open bottle and took a long sip before continuing. "So what if I used to know Sincere and Rolondo. That was a long time ago. I'm not going to tell you a damn thing. Now, when can I see my granddaughter?"

"How did you know that Violet was in Las Vegas? Vance didn't even know where she was."

"That is none of your business," Betty replied.

Valerie was watching Violet throughout Rome and Betty's exchange. She didn't look the least bit surprised at the questions Rome was throwing out. Her hunch was correct. Violet was the ex-wife that Rome's informant was talking about. He must have known the two of them were separated. Everything was coming together now.

Valerie jumped into the conversation.

"Look, Betty, I know you don't know me from a can of paint."

"Oh, yes I do. I've seen your fat ass on television for years. I have to say, you are much prettier in person."

Val ignored the woman's diss and kept talking.

"I know that Rolondo and Valerian probably made you do a lot of things that you didn't want to do over the years. But for the sake of Valencia's mental and physical well-being, I have to ask you this question. Is one of those men Violet's father? They are both sociopaths, and if Valerian is her dad, that would make Violet and Vance first cousins. That also proposes physical and incestuous problems for Valencia. We would need to get a therapist and doctor to examine her right away. If she has inherited any of those men's traits, we have to begin working with her now. Please tell me the truth." She now realized that blatant incest was the true reason behind Violet being unable to barely even look at Valencia.

Betty remained silent. Violet looked as if she had seen a ghost. She didn't need to say a word. The look on her face told the whole story.

"Violet, you have known all along that Valerian is your father, haven't you?" Val spoke softly.

Instead of answering Val, Violet screamed, "I'm not telling you all anything! You're lucky that I don't have a gun on me, or I would kill you all right now. I'm out of here!" Before she could take one step toward the door, Betty grabbed Violet.

"Not so fast, daughter. Neither you nor I are walking away from these billion dollar clowns without getting paid. The only reason your father planted you down at Dumas Farms for all those years was to get what his brother owes him. Victor, I want $500 million dollars, or I will personally feed you and Vance to Sincere and Rolondo, wherever he is."

Valerie opened up her Birkin bag and pulled out a Louis Vuitton wallet that was filled with hundred dollar bills and a check. She extended it to Betty.

"Here is a certified check made out to Cash for $100,000. There is also $10,000 in cash inside the wallet. I advise you to take what Victor is offering you and slither back into whatever snake pit you crawled out of. One of those warrants you have under your real name is for manslaughter, so I know you don't want us to report your current whereabouts to the authorities." Val gave her a knowing look. "So, get your things and leave right now. You have twenty minutes. Security is waiting right outside of the door to escort you downstairs." Val was right. She did not want to go back to jail.

Betty snatched the wallet out of Val's hands and stormed into the bedroom. At least it matched her new luggage. Her exit from here would be faster than any twenty minutes. She had never even had time to unpack. She grabbed her new Gucci purse and Louis Vuitton suitcase and barreled out the door without even telling Violet good-bye.

"You low down dirty bitch!" Vance couldn't believe everything he had just heard. He didn't know what overcame him, but he jumped up, knocked Violet down on the floor, and started choking her as hard as he could. "How dare you do this to us? My dad took you in like you were a member of the family, put you through school, fed and clothed you. I made you my wife!"

Rome and Victor pulled Vance off Violet as Val helped her up.

"That's it!" Violet said between coughs. She picked up the phone on the table. "I'm calling the cops and telling them you tried to kill me. My father and cousin should have killed all of you long ago. But you just won't die!" Changing her mind, Violet hung up the phone, then reached into her bra and pulled a knife out on Vance. Rome, however, had the knife out of her hand before she had a chance to even try stabbing him.

"Rolondo is your cousin?" asked Rome. "You just acknowledged in front of all of us that he and your father have made numerous murderous attempts to take our lives in the past. Unless you want to go to jail for aiding and abetting your cousin yesterday and killing twelve people all together, you aren't calling anyone. Vance and Victor, it's up to you. What do you want to do with her?"

"Let Vance make that decision," said Victor.

"She's his wife and the mother of his child. If he wants to put her in jail, we can call the police," Rome said.

"I don't want to bring the family down. If you have her arrested, our new polo venture goes out the window. It could even have an effect on Dad's new video game deal. I want a divorce right away. And I don't want you anywhere near our daughter. I don't trust you, so until I finish my press conference tomorrow and get my guys out to the Hamptons, you are staying right here in this suite surrounded by security.

"After we leave the city safely on Friday, you're on your own. My lawyers will be in touch with you. Rome, let's roll. Good-bye, Violet."

Rolling her eyes at Vance, Violet got right up in his face.

"You had better watch your step, Vance, and keep a close eye on that little freak you call your daughter. When you least expect it, I'll be right there to stick a knife into each of your backs!"

"Nice. Very classy and loving for a mother, Violet," Vance said, turning away to keep from having to wrap his two hands around her neck and squeeze with all his might again.

They all turned and made their exit with Vance.

Violet kicked the door after she slammed it behind all of them. She looked at the security guard they had assigned to her standing righteously by the window. Right now, she was going to order some dinner, have a drink, and lay down.

Tomorrow she would figure out a way to get rid of him. She still planned to kidnap Valencia one way or the other!

Chapter Twenty-four

Janvieve

After rushing away from the unexpected disastrous scenario with the Dumas clan, Betty decided to regroup in the hotel bar and figure out her next move. She was so engrossed in her thoughts that she didn't notice a tall blonde woman sit on the vacant bar stool next to her.

"Hello, Betty. It's been a long time." Shocked that someone in New York knew her name, the first thing that came to mind was that Sincere had someone spying on her.

"Do I know you?" Betty asked.

Janvieve brushed the hair back from her face, put a napkin on her lap, and at the same time placed Betty's hand under it, right on his dick.

"Keep feeling and look closely."

A chill suddenly went swishing through Betty's body.

"Rolondo?"

"Shhh. My name is Janvieve."

"Can I get you two something to drink?" asked the bartender.

In a whispery voice that rang out like Marilyn Monroe singing "Happy Birthday" to President John F. Kennedy, Janvieve told the bartender, "We'll have a bottle of Cristal."

"What are you doing here, Betty?" She slowly caressed Betty's cheek with her hand.

Betty brushed Javieve's hand away.

"I should be asking you the same thing. Sincere is looking for you. He thinks that you and Violet pulled a con on him."

"No, Violet shot me. I thought Sincere was in on it. Luckily, I was wearing a bulletproof vest and was able to get out of Victor's house without being caught by the cops. If they catch me, I'm facing life with no parole or the death penalty. Where is your daughter now?"

Betty glared at Janvieve.

"You thought wrong. Sincere had nothing to do with Violet shooting you. That move was a one hundred percent decision made only by her. As I said, he thinks the two of you are in cahoots. That's why he sent me to Las Vegas to fetch her and bring her to New York. As for my daughter's whereabouts, a little while ago, as Victor and Vance Dumas, along with Rome Nyland and Valerie Rollins just tossed me out, she was still upstairs in a suite. But now that the cat is out of the bag I don't know what's going to happen to her. They're probably kicking her out now too."

"What do you mean, 'the cat is out of the bag?'"

"Meaning, they all know that Sincere is her father, making Vance her cousin. Hell, as much as Andrea was fucking Sincere, Vance could even be her brother."

Janvieve laughed.

"Shit, as much sex from men and women that Andrea used to run through, anybody could be Vance's father. Her mission on a daily basis was to get high and screw. If my memory serves me correctly, most of the time your ass was right with her. So let me ask you, Betty, are you going to tell Sincere that you saw me, or dime me out to Victor? I've always liked you. I would hate to kill you right here." This time Janvieve stroked Betty's hair, playfully pulling it hard.

Their conversation was interrupted as the waiter set a champagne bucket with the bottle of Cristal in front of them.

"You can go ahead and pour us two glasses," purred Janvieve. "So what's it going to be, Betty Lamb? Isn't that what Sincere used to call you?"

Draining the entire champagne flute in almost one gulp, Betty thought for a moment before answering Janvieve. Of the three cousins, Rolondo was the most vicious. Even masquerading as a woman, she had no doubt he had some way to exterminate her right here at this bar. She had to get away from him and fast. She set the empty champagne flute down and stood up.

"He actually still calls me Betty Lambie. I don't plan to be communicating with Sincere anytime soon. Coming to talk some sense into our daughter was a one-time favor. You have nothing to worry about. After all, I never saw Rolondo.

Thanks so much for the champagne. It was very nice meeting you, Ms. Janvieve." With those words, Betty picked up the handle to her new rolling Louis Vuitton suitcase and walked as fast as her legs could carry her onto Central Park West.

Satisfied with Betty's response, Janvieve downed the champagne and ordered another glass, smirking victoriously.

Ten minutes had passed, and Janvieve watched as Rome, Vance, Victor and Valerie left the hotel. Her first inclination was to follow them, but on second thought, Rome was too slick. Although he hadn't recognized her during their encounter the night before in Beverly Hills, she didn't want to push that he might figure out who she is now, despite the disguise. She would just hang here for a moment, and then try to get to Violet. She was going to have a good time killing that little traitor.

Chapter Twenty-five

Valerie

The scene in East Harlem, New York was lively as usual as the Dumas entourage walked into Ricardo's Steak House. The restaurant, named after the owners' dog Ricardo, was well known for its festive environment with live DJs spinning and an open kitchen where diners can see the eatery's grill masters cooking up delicious cuts of steak. Exposed brick walls highlighted the work of local urban artists, which only added to the fun, energetic atmosphere.

Val entered the restaurant as Michael Jackson's "Love Never Felt So Good" filled the air. The manager Jorge grabbed her and started dancing. It was Val's favorite song, so she started dancing with him. When the song ended, everyone clapped. She spotted her friend Marisa sitting at the bar and went over to give her a hug. Then her friend Damien grabbed her.

"It's so good to see you, Val."

"Oh! You too, Damien. I've missed you guys so much."

"Well, well, well . . . it's about time you surfaced," her favorite barmaid Darlene said as she came from behind the bar and hugged her.

More staff came to greet Val. She kissed the owner Eddie, and Regina, and her favorite waiter Marlon, then waved to the chefs. Val introduced Victor, Vance and Rome to her whole Ricardo's crew. It warmed her very soul to be home. Los Angeles was a beautiful city, but there was no place in the world like New York!

"Come on," Jorge told Val. "We have everything set up for you on the back porch. Your security and some of your guests are already back there."

As Val followed Jorge through the restaurant, a minister sitting at a table on the left-hand side of the bar caught her eye. A shiver ran through her. *Do I know him?* Although he was heavy-set with white hair, he bore an uncanny resemblance to Royale/Rolondo, or whatever his name really was. *Nah, couldn't be.* She needed to relax. All of this chaos was starting to get under her skin. As sinister as Rolondo was, there was no way he could have a minister in his family.

For the sake of their security in a public place, Val had reserved the entire back porch. Rome had guys at each of the side tables so that no one could approach Victor. She had sent Cantrese ahead with place cards, which turned out to be a smart move because she knew that Victor was tired of Vance and his revolving door of wives. She was glad she had told Cantrese to put Vance and Roshonda at the other end of the table.

"Victor and Val," said Rome. "This is Amethyst. We both trained at UCLA for the Olympics. We were on the same flight coming out here."

Victor stood up.

"It's a pleasure. I've always been a fan of yours."

Val couldn't believe that Rome seemed to be already on to the next girlfriend with Turquoise only missing for a day, but she stood up and smiled at the lovely woman.

"Welcome, Amethyst. I'm also a huge fan. I'm so happy that you could join us tonight. This is my Assistant, Cantrese, and Victor's son Vance and Roshonda. You and Rome are seated right next to me."

"Thank you. All Rome told me was that he was having dinner with friends. Never in my wildest dreams would I have thought he was talking about you or Victor and Vance Dumas. I hope I'm not underdressed."

"Of course you're not. Girl, I just love your blouse and matching walking shorts. White looks good on you. And those gold gladiator boots slay. Sit down and have a drink."

The servers started placing appetizers and salads on the tables. Vance grabbed the plate of fried calamari right away. Val laughed.

"Listen, if you are having lamb chops, the uptown rib eye or da chops, you have to give them the temperature that you want it cooked at. Otherwise, I took the liberty of ordering platters of salmon, chicken marsala, the Second Avenue special and pastas with either garlic and oil, carbonara, alfredo or spaghetti bolognese. They are bringing drinks around too. Bon appétit!"

Victor had been very quiet since they walked out of Violet's suite. He kissed Val on her cheek.

"Ordering the food ahead of time was good looking out, sweetheart. I want to go out to the Cedar Lane Stables in Queens to check on the horses and get back to the hotel and rest. Tomorrow is going to be a big day."

"I'm sorry for how bad things went back at the Trump Hotel. But like you told me, we are all here together, and it's going to be all right. Now enjoy your dinner. Do you want to split the rib eye steak?"

"Hell no. You get your own steak, woman."

Rome laughed at Victor as he helped himself to the Caesar salad and stuffed portobello mushrooms.

"Don't be shy, Amethyst. What can I get you?"

Looking at Rome as if he were a piece of meat she'd like to order from the menu, Amethyst answered, "I'll have some of that skirt steak salad. I've always heard that it was delicious. Victor, I have heard of the Cedar Lane Stables. Isn't it owned by the Federation of Black Cowboys?"

"Yes. It's actually on twenty-five acres of New York City owned land. Val suggested we use the location to board the horses as they arrived in the area until we move everything to Bridgehampton on Friday. Most of the guys who run it are from the Black Cowboy Association of Brooklyn. They have had a tough time maintaining the stables financially, so we want to help them out."

"I'm having a Christmas in July party the weekend of the fourth," Val told Amethyst. "Victor is going to make a donation to them there. It's a wonderful organization. The women in the federation are called the Cedar Lane Jewels."

Roshonda let out a loud yawn. She immediately excused herself.

"I am so sorry. The three-hour time difference between New York and LA must be catching up with me. Please forgive me for being so rude."

Val, along with the entire table, stared at Cantrese because her phone kept blowing up. Cantrese refused to look at it.

"Someone is calling you non-stop," exclaimed Roshonda, who was seated next to Cantrese. "Aren't you going to answer your phone?"

"No, we are in the middle of dinner," Cantrese replied.

"It's okay. Go ahead and answer your phone, Cantrese," Val advised. "It might be someone responding to some of the calls I had you make today."

Reluctantly, Cantrese hit the answer button.

"Hey, Elliott. How are you? I can't talk right now. I'm having dinner with my boss . . . Um that's not going to be possible right now. I'll speak to you tomorrow. Okay bye." Cantrese quickly ended the call.

Valerie had never seen the girl get that agitated over a phone call.

"Who is Elliott?" asked Val.

"That's just a guy I've been seeing out in LA. Nobody real important."

Val wasn't so sure Cantrese was telling the truth. The girl was almost shaking. Cantrese had been recommended to her by Violet. Now that she had turned out to be the enemy, Valerie would have to investigate Cantrese's past first thing in the morning. In the meantime, to ensure the baby's safety, she would take Cantrese's key to their suite and have the code on the lock changed as soon as they returned to the hotel.

"Yeah, Cantrese. Who is Elliott?" Vance asked, somewhat amused. "I see you're wearing a lovely new bracelet. Did Elliott give it to you? If he did, he must be a really cool cat who's definitely feeling you. You'll have to introduce him to all of us some time."

Cantrese answered, "We'll be here all summer, and he's in Los Angeles, so I doubt that it will be possible for you all to meet him anytime soon."

This was the first time Val had noticed the dazzling piece of jewelry. She observed Vance looking like the cat that swallowed the canary and a nervous Cantrese, then kicked Victor under the table. She couldn't believe Vance was screwing Cantrese right under Roshonda's nose. That boy was insatiable when it came to sex.

Having picked up on what was going on also, Victor didn't know whether to laugh at his son's brazen ways, or to shake his head in disgust. They were all saved by the waiter arriving with steaks and Rome's phone loudly ringing simultaneously. Rome listened intensely to whomever was on the other end, then told the table, "Excuse me. I need to take this call outside."

Val stood up.

"I'm going to follow Rome out to find out what's going on. Amethyst, why don't you tell these youngins' and my fiancé what you're doing these days? Rome and I will be right back." She strutted away in a hurry, following close on Rome's heels.

Val sat in the empty seat at the bar next to Rome, who stood talking on the phone.

"All right . . .. . . Thank you. No, I want you to leave the card on until I can pinpoint a location of the perp."

"What's up?" Val asked Rome.

"AMEX got a hit on my black card that has Turquoise's name on it. Someone charged $20,000 on it in Phoenix, Arizona. I'll eat the money. I just want to know where she is. They are going to email me the location that the packages were delivered to. I know a guy that does private work out there. I'll have him go check it out. Your people say they saw Turquoise last night. It only takes a few hours to drive to Phoenix. She could easily be there by now."

"I hate to say this, Rome, but I think whoever that client was who Turquoise had dinner with at Craig's was working for Rolondo. After all, they got into a Bugatti when they left there. Do you still have someone staking out the girl Samantha's apartment building? Those guys she was with the other night also sound like Blades."

"The kid told me this Samantha was headed to New York. I have his number. I'm going to have James send a sketch artist over to the kid tomorrow, so we can find out what she looks like. If we are going to find Turquoise and Rolondo, we need to find Samantha first."

"Val," said Cantrese as she approached them. "Vance just got a call from the Cedar Lane stables out in Queens. Dr. Henry says they are almost finished braiding all of the horses' tails for tomorrow, so if he wants to braid Wildin' Out's himself, he and Mr. Dumas need to head out to the stables now. He also wants to show Vance something on one of the horse's hoofs."

"Okay. Just have them wrap up my steak to take back to the hotel with me. Oh, I need your key to my suite. I'm going to have them changed due to the circumstances of the meeting we had with Violet earlier. And I have just one more thing to ask you."

"About what?" Cantrese said.

"So, Cantrese, how long have you been sleeping around with Vance?"

Still standing next to Val, Rome laughed. Leave it to Val to always discover what was going on in the dark.

"I-I-I'm sorry, Val. It just happened. He's so fine. Vance said you don't have any company rules against employees dating, and that if you did, it wouldn't matter because he owns the company along with his dad."

Rome stepped into the conversation.

"Come on, Cantrese. I think Vance being so rich is more of your attraction to him than 'so fine.'"

"No, it isn't. I really like him."

"Look," said Val. "As I told Vance and Roshonda. All of you are grown. Just take into consideration that he is just getting rid of one wife, whom I thought was a friend of yours, and has the first one sleeping in his bed every night. I like you. You have too much potential to be one of Vance's play things."

Rome couldn't resist making a wisecrack about the situation.

"I don't know, Val. If I had to bet on the weight of that bracelet she's sporting, I would say that your girl here is spending some quality time in my man's bed too."

Val elbowed Rome, who was cracking up at the entire scenario. After all he was going through between Turquoise missing, Rolondo being on the lam, and Violet turning out to be part of at least a fifteen year scheme to bring Victor down, it felt good to laugh.

Like a wind gust that was so hard it could shut a window, Talfor came breezing into the restaurant. Before she could catch herself, Val's eyes narrowed at the sight of her.

"Don't look so happy to see me, Valerie. I just came to pick up Roshonda. Since Nino has to rest to be ready for tomorrow, and Vance is headed out to the stables, I'm taking my girl to meet up with some of our old modeling crew at Ralph Lauren's Polo Lounge. Just because our men have to work doesn't mean we girls have to hold-up on our play time."

"That's nice," said Val. "Cantrese, tell everyone that I'm ready to leave also."

"Mr. Nyland, it's such a pleasure to make your acquaintance," Talfor told Rome, who was still standing next to Val. "Damn, you are finer now than you were back in your playing days." She extended her hand to him. "I'm Talfor Redd. Val, maybe I should start hanging around you with all these fine men you keep company with."

"Please, call me Rome. I always love getting compliments from a beautiful woman. I'm also a big fan of yours. Val, let's halt business for now and relax over some real drinks at the hotel. I didn't get to spend much time with Amethyst. Do you mind if I ask her to join us?" The way he was staring at Talfor, Valerie was surprised Rome even remembered Amethyst was on the restaurant's back porch.

"Of course not."

"Did I hear my name?" Amethyst asked as the entire group approached the bar. She told Rome, "I have to admit I'm a little disappointed we didn't get the chance for some one-on-one conversation, but it was a thrill to be in the midst of such esteemed company. I thoroughly enjoyed myself."

Rome bent down and kissed her on the cheek.

"I'm glad you did. I was wondering if you would care to join Val and me for a nightcap at the hotel?"

"I would love to."

"Great. Victor and Vance, I had the other drivers and one more security guy bring over the Escalades to take you cats over to Queens. After our meeting earlier, I wanted you to be riding in a little more armor than the Bentleys have to offer. Roshonda, you have the Town Car you rode over in to take you and your friend wherever you need to go. And Val and Cantrese can ride with me."

To Val's surprise, Vance took one disgusted look at Talfor, who just glared at him, kissed Roshonda, and the two ladies left. Val knew a rift was happening before her eyes.

"If you don't mind, Val, I need Cantrese to come with Dad and me. Doc Henry may need a secretary type out there to take notes on everything that's happening."

Victor, who now stood next to Val, couldn't believe what had just come out of his son's mouth.

"Who does this boy think he is fooling? What veterinarian needs a secretary at nine o'clock at night?" Victor whispered, before kissing Val on the lips. She grinned sheepishly. "Okay, sweetheart. We should be back about midnight. Don't wait up for me."

"You know I will. See you then. Cantrese, it's fine. Go with the guys. You need to learn the equestrian division of this operation anyway." Val hugged all of her friends in Ricardo's and followed the rest of her crew out of the restaurant's door.

Instantly Val turned, feeling eyes on her back. Cautious, she panned the entire restaurant. Her eyes met with the sharply slanted eyes of a beautiful female, who was summoning someone toward her. Val looked to her left to see a man wearing a wide smile and walking in the woman's direction. Even if the woman wasn't the culprit, someone was surely watching her every move. Val took a final glance, then turned and made her exit, grateful for Rome and the security team.

Chapter Twenty-six

Claude

W ell, Rolondo and Sincere are right about one thing. That damn Rome Nyland and Ms. Valerie Rollins do have smoother moves than Kobe Bryant." Claude stirred the cream and sugar around in his coffee. "They know Turquoise left the restaurant in a red Bugatti with a woman who was headed to New York City. Hell, they even know about the Blades' trap house. Let me text the guys and warn them so they can move the product out of there before the cops arrive. Otherwise, there goes a million dollars a week cash business straight down the drain." He sent the text immediately.

Caressa was in shock. She thought she had covered her tracks well.

"I can't believe they have all that information so fast. I thought you told Yohance and them not to touch her credit cards."

"I did. It doesn't matter. Do you know what kid they could be talking about sending a sketch artist to see? I have to send people to take care of him now. Rome cannot find out what you look like. He would probably piss on himself if he knew that he had been standing just a few feet away from you tonight."

There was no way that Caressa wanted to be responsible for the death of a child. But in this case, it was either his life or hers.

"His name is Antonio. He runs errands for people who live in my building after school. You don't have to have someone kill him though, Claude. The kid would never give me up."

"I'm sorry. I can't take that chance. Maybe the next time you'll keep your mouth shut. Come on. The check is paid. Let's blow this joint." He glanced around the restaurant. "Too many cell phones in here, and I can't be sure if people are taking pictures of their meals or us. We have a press conference to go to at noon tomorrow."

Chapter Twenty-seven

Columbus

After Ariel insisted upon taking a separate taxi to wherever the hell she lived from the airport, a weary Columbus was just finishing up checking into the Ritz Carlton as Rome, Valerie, and Amethyst walked into the hotel. He heard the one voice that had lingered in his ear for over thirty years say, "Rome, you and Amethyst get us a table in the lounge. I'm going to run downstairs to the ladies room." Columbus turned in the direction that the voice was coming from. He couldn't believe what his eyes definitely saw. Valerie was standing just a few feet away from him. He listened as the man she called Rome told her, "I'd better go downstairs with you."

"Don't be silly. Look at all of these people around. I'm just going to the bathroom. I'll be right back. You know what to order for me."

Rome followed her instructions, grabbed Amethyst's hand, and headed into the lounge.

"Where is the closest men's room?" Columbus asked the desk clerk.

"Just one floor down, Mr. Isley. You can take the elevators that are right over there. We'll get your bags right up to your room."

After he thrust a fifty dollar bill at the man, Columbus made a mad dash to the elevator. When he reached the floor, he headed straight into the ladies room. He didn't care how many women were in there. Luckily, it was empty. He locked the door behind him.

"Sweet Val, are you in here?"

Val was just coming out of a stall. She almost fainted when she heard the man standing in front of her call her by that name. Her 'oh so secret past' had come back to haunt her. The man whom she considered as the love of her life before she met Victor, the real Royale Jones, was alive and well. She could just barely get a whisper to emerge from her throat.

"Royale?"

He didn't want to waste time talking. He pulled Val into his arms and kissed her passionately. Caught up in a strange mixture of the past and the moment, Valerie didn't offer any resistance at first and returned his kisses. Reality sunk in when Royale tried to take it one step forward by squeezing her nipple. She pushed him off her. He let out a sinister laugh.

"Still the same Sweet Val, always playing hard to get."

"Where in God's name or in your case, the devil's name, did you come from?" She stepped back out of Royale's tight grasp.

"I've been on a deserted island in the Bahamas for the last five years suffering from clinical amnesia. A newspaper article that had a photo of my cousin Rolondo and a mention of you in it snapped me back to life. What I need to know is why you didn't tell anyone that Rolondo wasn't me? Baby, you know where every mole on my body is. Why didn't you tell anyone that he was masquerading as me? Did he threaten you?"

"First of all, Royale, we haven't seen each other in a long time. The first night that I saw *that* Royale I kept thinking he looked just like you but was thinner and a little lighter. But when he seemed to have no recollection of me, I just went along with it. I mentioned to Rome that I had met you years ago, and back then, you were darker and heavier. I thought since the man whom I presumed to be you was chasing Vance's wife Roshonda and Rome's girlfriend Turquoise so hard, maybe you had forgotten that old fat me—the one you deserted when I told you I was pregnant with your baby—ever existed."

"Baby, you know I could never forget you. I was young and dumb then. I have never stopped loving you. When I saw your name in the newspaper the other day, it was like time stood still. Look at me, Val. We are still the same two people. I know you still love me too." Royale pulled Valerie back into his arms and kissed her again.

Her mind told her to slap the shit out of him, and run out the door. However, his kisses felt so good that she allowed her body to take over.

Chapter Twenty-eight

Rome

R ome had become alarmed that Val was taking so long to join him and Amethyst. He grabbed one of the hotel security guards and flew down the stairs. He overheard a man's voice in the bathroom and tried to open the door, but it was locked. Rome pulled out his gun, then ordered the guard, "Open this door right now!" He stopped in his tracks as he saw Valerie in the arms of a man who was the spitting image of Rolondo. He, however, had just seen Rolondo the day before in court, and he had been clean shaven with a Caesar cut. This man's hair was long and curly. He was also darker. Keeping his gun on him, Rome snatched Val, put her behind him, then looked straight into the man's eyes.

"Royale?"

"They call me Columbus now. You can put away that gun. I would never hurt Valerie."

"Gentlemen," said the security guard. "There are no men allowed in here. You have to take this out in the hallway."

Royale grabbed Val's hand. She snatched it back. The security guard asked Rome, "Do I need to call the police?" Val shook her head no.

Still baffled, Rome looked at Val.

"Do you mind telling me what the fuck is going on? You better be glad I walked in on you and not your man. Have you gone crazy?"

"Now, I told you that I would never hurt Val. But that doesn't cover you, Rome Nyland. Keep talking to her like that, and I will beat the shit out of you." Columbus moved forward, now just inches away from Rome's face.

"Royale, hush. Rome, let's go back upstairs. I will tell you everything." She pulled Rome toward the door.

"I'm going with you, Val."

"No you are not, Royale. I can handle this by myself."

Rome told her, "No you can't. I want to talk to both of you. Let him come upstairs with us."

Just a few short minutes later, Rome approached the table with Val and Royale in tow. The three of them looked like someone had just died. Rome handed Amethyst his room key.

"Baby, I'm in suite 1018. Can you wait for me up there? Order whatever you want. I need to speak to Val and her friend alone for just a few minutes. I promise I'll be right up."

"Take your time. I'll be waiting. Good night, Valerie. Good night . . ."

"It's Columbus. Good night."

Val took a long sip of the chardonnay already waiting for her at the table.

"Rome, remember when we first met Royale who turned out to be Rolondo, and I told you I had met him, but back then he was darker and a little heavier?"

"Yes, keep talking."

"Well, Royale and I did more than just meet. We spent the summer after my junior year in college together. I thought we were both in love, but when I got pregnant, he kicked me to the curb. I lost the baby, and I never looked at men the same way again."

"So, you are telling me that you knew all of the time that, that imposter wasn't Royale, and you didn't tell any of us?"

"Are you listening to what I'm telling you? I told you the man looked slightly different. I let it go because when he walked into Mr. Chow that night and he looked at me as if he had never seen me before, all of the pain I endured all those years ago came flowing back. I was that same insecure college kid that lost the man I loved with all of my heart left." Val burst into tears.

Royale moved to put his arm around her, but Rome stopped him.

"Man, touch her again, and I will bust a cap in your ass."

"Listen, I don't know who you are to Sweet Val, but I am getting sick of your threats." Royale pointed at Rome but looked at Val. "This fool doesn't realize who he's fucking with."

"Obviously, you don't either. But the even bigger issue is where and why have you been hiding all these years?"

"I had an accident on my boat." Royale went on to explain the entire incident.

"So why are you calling yourself Columbus, and when are you going to tell the authorities that you're alive? That will give them an attempted murder charge against Rolondo."

"Columbus is the name the guys that pulled me out of the ocean gave me. I am still sort of using the name because I don't want any of my cousins to know that I'm alive until I find out what they are up to. I want to deal with Rolondo myself and Claude and Sincere owe me a whole lot of bread. I figure wherever Victor and his money are, those three greedy motherfuckers cannot be far behind. So for now, I am laying low, and Columbus is my name. Plus, I came to get my woman back." Both Valerie and Rome ignored Royale's last comment.

"Claude and Valerian are also your cousins?" Rome asked.

"Yes, we are all first cousins. Claude, Rolondo, and I are double cousins, and Sincere's mother is our moms' middle sister. Rolondo's and my mother are identical twins who married identical twins. That's why we look so much alike. Claude's mom married our dads' older brother, and I believe you all know who Sincere's father was."

"Royale, we are never going to be together again," Val spoke softly. "I am engaged to Victor Dumas. I love him. And I am begging you. Please don't make trouble for me after all of these years. For the first time in thirty years, I am happily in love."

"Sweet Val, you need to quit with this 'I left you' story. The way I remember it is that you stopped answering my calls after you suffered the miscarriage."

Rome didn't like what was transpiring here. When he ran up on Val and Royale in the bathroom, she was not resisting his kisses. Now she was sneaking strange looks at the cat. It was obvious she still had feelings for him.

"Look, Royale or Columbus, are you here to do any harm to Victor, Vance, or Valerie? If you are, I have to inform the authorities that you are no longer missing."

"Brother, I already told you that I would never hurt Val. I love her. And unlike my cousins, my mission in life is not to steal Victor Dumas' money or kill the geek. You don't have to worry about Vance. No one is ever going to bother Andrea's son. If that crazy trio planned to hurt Vance, they would have kidnapped him and held him for ransom when he was a baby. In fact, Andrea told Sincere that Vance is his son. She said Victor was so naive that he didn't even realize that they didn't have sex for months around the time that Vance was conceived."

Val and Rome looked at each other. When Valerian had been arrested for pointing a gun at Victor at the race track almost two years ago, his parting words to his brother had been, "Say hello to my son for me." But Victor insisted back then that he had Vance tested, and he was indeed, his son.

"How do you know so much about Victor and Andrea?" asked Val.

"Baby, I grew up with Andrea. All of us did. I was actually with her when she met Victor at the Kentucky Derby all those years ago."

There was so much tension at the table that Valerie jumped when her phone rang. It was Victor calling.

"Hi, darling. How did you guys make out with the horse? . . . No, I'm down in the lounge with Rome and an old friend that I just ran into . . . I'll wait for you here. I need to talk to you too . . . I love you too."

"Aww, isn't that sweet?" Royale teased.

Ignoring him once again, Val continued looking at her phone.

"I didn't hear all these texts going off. My friend Damien sent me this picture. Rome, he says the girl in it might be who we are looking for. He says he overheard them talking about us. She and the guy with her were in Ricardo's earlier tonight too."

Royale glanced at the picture.

"I don't know who the girl is, but that's my cousin Claude. Damn . . . that son of a bitch looks old. I guess his evil ways are finally showing up on his face."

Valerie took another look at the picture.

"Rome, look at that diamond heart ring that she has on. It looks just like the one Turquoise wears."

"You are so right. Forward me the picture so I can send it to Antonio and Cayenne and see if this chick is the infamous Bugatti driving Samantha."

Val was upset that she hadn't pointed this Claude out to Rome and Victor when they were at the restaurant.

"I saw him at Ricardo's earlier and noticed how much he looked like Rolondo. I thought I was simply imagining things."

"Naw, pretty lady, my cousin is not a figment of anyone's imagination. He is real. Why are you looking for that girl?"

Rome wasn't sure that they could trust Royale, so he answered, "She may know where a friend of mine is. Where can I find your cousin Claude?"

"He pastors a church out in Sag Harbor called the Holy Temple of Mary Magdalene. But I'm sure he's still lurking around here somewhere. They don't know you have that photo. My bet is they will show up at your press conference tomorrow."

Val suddenly had an idea.

"Royale, can you let us announce that we know you are alive and well tomorrow at the press conference? I know you don't want your cousins to know that you are alive, but this could bring them all out of hiding. Victor and I need to have this all end for the sake of Vance's daughter."

"Vance has a daughter? Who is his wife?" he asked.

"Violet McClean, the jockey. She and Vance are estranged though. He's actually back with his first wife and also seems to have something going on with my assistant. He gives being a player a whole new meaning. We just found out that Violet is Valerian's daughter today," Rome said.

"Discovering that Violet and Vance are cousins was ugly and incestuous enough. Now you are saying they could really be sister and brother. This is a horrible situation. I need to have tests run on the baby as soon as possible," Val added.

"I thought it was a bad idea when Andrea took that child to live with her and Victor years ago, but Sincere kept her so doped up that she was never in her right mind. I read online that Rolondo killed Andrea. I find that hard to believe. Sincere would have never allowed that to happen. None of them would have killed her. Somebody else would have had to."

"Somebody like Claude?" asked Rome.

"Not even Claude. Although the three of them pretty much all fucked the shit out of her throughout the years and used her up, they all still loved her in their own sordid way. The internet says she was killed at my bar in Las Vegas. I'm surprised that Rolondo kept it open. Who else was there when this happened?"

"Oh no," whispered Val, "Jermonna. She told me Sincere killed Andrea." Jermonna was an actress who was constantly in some sort of trouble, but was still Val's best friend. She somehow felt responsible for her.

"Either she lied to you as usual, or was so high she couldn't remember anything, which is exactly why the judge didn't allow her to testify. I keep telling you to drop that little wacko," said Rome.

"So if what I read is true," said Royale, "Sincere had a clear alibi, which means this Jermonna, whom I presume is the actress Jermonna Bradley, and her identification of him went out the window. He got off, so why did it get pinned on Rolondo?"

Val hated rehashing this terrible situation that happened almost two years ago all over once again. This was one story that just refused to go away.

"He kept bugging Roshonda for a necklace that Victor gave to her. It was actually stolen from Andrea the night of the murder. I saw it on a rap artist, Platinum Pizzazz. Her boyfriend, D.O.D., whose car Rome had seen the next day in Las Vegas, had all of the jewelry that Andrea was wearing that night on him when the police raided his house. He was killed on the way to the precinct. So with him dead, the police charged Rolondo."

"Sweet Lyrics' little nephew—D.O.D.? This is all too surreal. I leave for five years and all of these fools just went buck wild." Royale suddenly felt a sharp pain in his head and grimaced.

Val grabbed his hand.

"Royale, are you all right?"

He touched Val's cheek. "You know, they say you never forget your first. I knew you still cared about me."

"And just why would my fiancée still care about you? You are almost the spitting image of Rolondo Jemison, but I know you are not him. If you were, you wouldn't be sitting here with my fiancée and best friend. The police would already have you in custody."

The entire table looked up to see Victor standing in front of them flanked by four security guards.

Val quickly stood up and threw her arms around Victor.

"Baby, I am so glad to see you. This is the old friend I told you that Rome and I were talking to, the real Royale Jones. I kept telling you that I remembered him being darker. What I didn't tell you or Rome was that we dated in college, and I became pregnant, then suffered a miscarriage. Our relationship ended after that happened."

Royale stood up. He extended his hand to Victor, who didn't take it.

"Mr. Dumas. We met years ago at the Kentucky Derby. You are definitely one lucky man to be marrying this wonderful woman."

"Thank you, but I am fully aware of just how wonderful and kind she truly is," Victor replied.

Rome stood up too. "Well, I have a beautiful woman waiting for me upstairs. So I'll see you guys tomorrow."

Royale stared at Val in such an intense manner that Val had to turn away.

"I am going to say goodnight to you good people," Royale said, grinning slyly. "In answer to your earlier question, Val, yes, you can announce that I'm alive at your press conference. We'll see how those three rats react to that information. That ought to start sending them scurrying around their mazes."

Chapter Twenty-nine

Valerie

V
al, just what the hell is going on here?" Victor asked as he sat down with his arms folded.

"I'm sorry, sweetheart. As I explained to both Royale and Rome earlier, when Rolondo/Royale didn't seem to recognize me, I just didn't see any need to relive the pain that he caused me when I was a young girl. The real Royale appearing out of nowhere tonight was more than shocking, to say the least."

The waiter asked Victor, "Can I get you something to drink, Mr. Dumas?"

Although the doctor had told him to refrain from drinking alcohol, Victor told him, "A Long Island iced tea, and please bring my fiancée another glass of chardonnay." He took Val's hand into his. "Just where did Royale appear from?"

"He told Rome and I that he had amnesia for the past five years after having a fight on his boat with Rolondo, who is his cousin. He's been living on a deserted island in the Bahamas all of this time. He said he saw you and me on TV yesterday and came straight here." Val paused. "Victor . . . Valerian and some guy named Claude are also his cousins, which means he is related to you, Vance, and Valencia by blood."

"What does he want from us? There's no need for you to answer me. I saw the way the man looked at you. He wants you. I understand him. If you had been in my life thirty years ago, I would still want you too. So now my question is, do you still want him?"

"Of course not, darling. I hadn't even thought about Royale over the years until the man who I thought was him walked into Mr. Chow that evening. I love and want only you."

"Well, why don't you prove all of this undying love for me by marrying me on Friday?"

"This Friday, as in the day after tomorrow?" Val had to shake the shock and confusion from her head.

"Yes, this Friday. I haven't said anything to you or Vance, honey, because I didn't want to add more doom and gloom to all the madness that is already going on in our lives, but my health isn't good."

Hearing those words caused Val's heart to sink. Her countenance fell.

"I've always suffered with heart problems, which have worsened recently. On top of that, I never wanted either of you to know, but I have had colon cancer since before you and I met. I thought that I had beaten it, but a few months ago, I found out that cancer has now stricken other parts of my body."

"Victor, I can't believe that you withheld that kind of infor—"

"Life is too precious, sweetheart. I don't want to waste another moment of it without you as my wife. I went online earlier to see if we can just get married here with no fanfare or audience. We can go down to the Manhattan City Clerk's Office when they open at eight-thirty in the morning, then when everyone else heads to the Hamptons on Friday morning, we can go back down there at the same time and become husband and wife. We don't need a crowd. I just want this to be about us. What do you say?"

"Honey, why haven't you told me any of this?" Uncontrollable tears slid down Valerie's cheeks. She didn't care who was watching them. "I should have been with you every time you have had a doctor's appointment. I love you. I could have been helping you all of this time."

"I didn't want you or Vance to look at me as if I am a burden to either of you. It's hard enough on you that you have to take care of my grandchild, and the fact that everyday your life is in jeopardy because of my crazy brother."

"Victor, you changed my entire life when you came into it. You could never be a burden. I am a cancer survivor. You shouldn't have been handling this alone. From here on out we will fight this disease together."

"Does that mean you will marry me on Friday?"

"Yes . . . yes . . . yes!"

As the waiter brought back their drinks, Victor told him, "Bring us a bottle of Cristal, and also give a glass of Cristal to everyone here in the lounge. It's on me."

"You got it, Mr. Dumas."

Tears continued to stream down Val's face, but they were not only tears of sadness over Victor's illness. She was also happy tears. Whether it was a rogue brother, a love she had thought was long forgotten, cancer or heart trouble, she would never let anything come between her and Victor's happiness. Together, they could conquer any obstacle, big or small!

Early the following morning, Victor and Val walked out of the Ritz Carlton so they could arrive at the marriage license facility promptly at eight-thirty when it opened. They had to hurry back and get ready for the press conference once they obtained the license.

To both of their surprise, they ran smack dab into Royale accompanied by a stunning young blonde woman getting ready to head into the hotel. Royale looked at Valerie, who was dressed in a white silk maxi dress and matching high-heeled sandals, she looked closer to thirty than the fifty-six years old that he knew she was. Victor also wore white from head-to-toe.

"Good morning. Where are you two headed so early in the morning?"

As Victor frowned at the sight of Royale, Valerie answered, "Just running some quick errands to get ready for the press conference. I see you're up and out early too."

"Yes, my head was pounding last night, so I decided to go to the emergency room to get myself checked out. This is my friend Ariel, whom I told you and Rome about last night. She was kind enough to accompany me to the hospital."

Val smiled at the lovely young woman. She looked like a supermodel. There was something familiar about her.

"Aren't you Rebecca's daughter?"

"Yes, ma'am."

Before Val could ask how her old friend who used to run an escort service was, an Escalade pulled up and Vance and Cantrese, sans security jumped out. At the sight of Victor and Valerie, Cantrese froze right on the spot. Looking at Royale, Vance followed suit.

Seeing the look on both of their faces, Val said, "Relax, you two. First of all, Cantrese, have you lost your mind doing this walk of shame on such an important day? Give me your phone right now. I need to know if you are in contact with Violet and if this Elliot person exists."

"There is no Elliot. It was Violet. She's been paying me to spy on all of you. But I just can't do it anymore. I like you a lot, Val, and I'm in love with Vance. Please don't fire me, Val."

"No, we're not going to fire you," Vance intervened. "In fact, let Violet keep thinking that you're still her spy. I am going to turn the tables on that conniving skank. From now on, you are working for me. I want to know the bitch's every move. Do you understand me?"

"Yes." Cantrese nodded.

Val gave her a sympathetic sigh.

"I like you too much to fire you, but please be careful when you speak to Violet. And Vance, this is not Rolondo Jemison. This is the real Royale Jones. There is no need for you to be afraid."

"Good morning, Vance. I grew up with your mother, and although I hate to admit it, your Uncle Valerian, is my cousin. So I guess that makes the two of us cousins."

Suddenly Cantrese's phone, which Vance now had in his possession, rang loudly. He pulled it out of his pocket and saw the name that popped up on the screen.

"It's Violet."

Val reached for the phone.

"Let me talk to her."

Royale told her, "Put the phone on speaker. Let me handle this for you guys."

"Good morning, Violet," Royale said.

"Who the hell is this? Why are you answering Cantrese's phone?"

"This is your Uncle Royale."

For a moment, a huge silence lingered at the other end of the call.

"That's impossible. My uncle Royale is dead."

"Oh, so you think your uncle Rolondo killed me, do you? Well, as Mark Twain once said, my death has been grossly exaggerated! Now listen, you are going to straighten up and treat these nice people with respect. And you can tell your father and uncle that I am looking for them. We have unfinished business."

"I haven't heard from my father, and as I told my mother yesterday, I have no idea where Rolondo is. You can go straight to hell with the rest of them!"

"Violet . . . It looks like she disconnected the call. Was she talking about her real mother, Betty?" Royale asked.

"Yes," Val told him. "We met her yesterday. Victor paid her to get lost, but I doubt that she did. I'm sure she's still trolling around New York City somewhere."

"I would like to talk to her. I'm sure she knows where I can find Sincere."

"Call Rome in his room. He put a GPS tracking device in the wallet I gave her to keep tabs on her. He can find her for you," Val offered.

Victor remained silent throughout the entire conversation. However, listening to Royale's exchange with Violet had given him an idea.

"Listen, Royale, my fiancée and I have some place we really have to get to. But why don't you and your friend meet all of us for dinner at Jean George restaurant, shall I say at seven? It's right up the street from here in the Trump International Hotel. I have a proposition that I would like to run past you."

"That sounds good. I'll be there," Royale answered.

"Okay. Cantrese, make a reservation for eight people. For this one last time, call Violet and invite her. I want her to hear what I have to say also."

Looking at her fiancé as if he had lost his mind inviting Royale to dinner, Val told everyone, "Victor and I really have to leave. Cantrese, you have to be at The Boat House by ten. We'll discuss the rest of this after the press conference is over. Nice to see you again, Ariel. If you speak to your mom, give her my best. See you guys later." With those parting words, Valerie and Victor hopped into a waiting Rolls Royce.

Headed downtown to the City Clerk's office, Val looked at Victor with her face filled with worry.

"Sweetheart, what can you possibly want to discuss with Royale over dinner?"

"I watched him while he was talking to Violet. He seems to have a life-long relationship with all of these bad people. I can't take this anymore, Val. I am going to offer Valerian a billion dollars to go away and leave us alone. I am going to ask Royale to broker the deal for me. I'm not well, baby. I don't want all this constant madness to make my heart give out on me, or to exacerbate the cancer. This Valerian has been interfering with my life for almost twenty years, and I didn't have a clue that he even existed until you found that picture of him and Andrea in her dresser. If it wasn't for you and Rome, I'm positive he would have killed me by now. I am putting a stop to all of this sooner than later."

192

"All right, darling. We'll do what you think is best. Hey, we're here. Let's get us a marriage license." Val's phone buzzed. It was a text from Eighty-eight.

A woman who looked like Turquoise was seen being lifted into a black Escalade on the outskirts of Las Vegas. Unfortunately, my source thought the guys with her could make him and didn't get a license plate number. I'll keep you informed if I hear anything else.

Val didn't want Rome to ask her any questions about where she and Victor were headed so early in the morning, so she forwarded the text straight to James Pace. Victor was right. It was time for all this craziness to end.

Chapter Thirty

Rome

Rome opened the door of his suite to a candle-lit living room where two massage tables had been set up side-by-side with two men standing next to them. The sound of Luther Vandross played softly in the background. Swathed in a white terry cloth robe, Amethyst was lying seductively on the couch sipping a glass of champagne.

"You gave me permission to order up whatever I wanted. After flying across country and all the drama I witnessed you dealing with earlier tonight, I thought a massage would be just the thing you need to relax."

Rome walked over to her and for the first time, kissed her thoroughly. The tender mood was interrupted as his phone started beeping with text messages.

"I'll take this as I get out of these clothes. Baby, this is a wonderful idea. You start your massage now."

The texts were from Cayenne and Antonio. Both of them identified the woman in the photo as Samantha. It suddenly occurred to Rome that since she and Claude had overheard his and Val's conversation, Antonio could be in danger. He quickly dialed the kid.

"Hello, mister."

"Hey, Antonio. Listen, I don't think it's safe for you to watch Miss Samantha's car anymore. I don't want you to go back to her apartment under any circumstances. Do you hear me?"

"Yes."

"Does she know where you live?"

"No."

"Can I speak to your parents?"

"I don't have any parents. I lied to you about my mom. I stay on my own."

"Where?"

"Wherever I can that works for the time being. Right now I'm in the basement of my school."

"Where is the school?" Rome couldn't believe what he was hearing.

"It's John Burroughs High School on West Clark in Burbank."

"Okay, stay there. A lady named Davida is going to come and take you to her house. You'll be safe there. We'll talk in the morning."

"All right."

Rome quickly called his ex-girlfriend, who was now married to a doctor she had been two-timing him with for years.

Davida picked up on the first ring.

"It's about time you got in touch with someone. Romey called me, and he's worried to death about you."

Rome had meant to call his son the minute the flight landed in New York. So much had been going on that he never got a chance to.

"Let him know I'm fine. Listen, I need you to do me a favor. Go over to John Burroughs High School on West Clark in Burbank. I need you to pick up this kid Antonio and let him spend the night with you. I'll text him that you're on the way and to meet him out front."

"Who is he?"

"A kid who helped me last night that may have a hit out on him by now. Take your gun with you."

"Okay. I'm on the way."

"Thanks. Text me when he's safely in your car."

"I got you. Bye."

With Antonio's safety squared away, Rome stripped off his clothes and also put on a terry cloth robe that was hanging in the closet. For the first time he realized the bed had been turned down and was covered with red rose petals. Smiling, he went back into the living room and climbed on the massage table. This was the perfect ending to a harrowing day. He reached over to the next table and took the lovely lady's hand, then kissed it.

"Amethyst, you are truly a real jewel." Although he enjoyed the relaxation and lovemaking, he couldn't help but think of the innocent kid who had no clue his life was in danger.

The following morning, Rome started his day at five o'clock in the morning like always without needing an alarm clock. He got a nice long run in, followed by lifting weights and some fast cardio on his stationary bicycle. He reached over to touch Amethyst. Her side of the bed was empty. He then heard the shower running in the bathroom, so he bounced up and brushed his teeth in the powder room that was in the posh suite's hallway, then headed into the bathroom where Amethyst was. Pulling back the glass door of the shower, he asked her, "Want some company?"

Not saying a word, Amethyst reached for Rome's hand, pulling his body on top of hers, with one hand she poured the liquid soap onto his penis as she massaged it with her other hand. Growing hard instantly, Rome entered Amethyst, gently thrusting his throbbing manhood in and out until he exploded more than any powerful volcano would ever erupt! Something very special had happened between these two in a mere twenty-four hours.

As they toweled off and got out of the shower, Amethyst spoke softly, "Rome, you just made a fantasy that I have been carrying with me for thirty-five years come true. I fell in love with you the first time I saw you running around the track at UCLA. You always smiled at me and waved, but you only had eyes for your girlfriend Davida. And I thought that was so sad. You seemed like such a nice guy, and all she did back then was sleep around behind your back. I always thought you deserved so much more."

"Why didn't you say something to me?"

"What was I going to say? Davida had you under her spell. When I saw you on the flight yesterday, I thought it was some sort of kismet occurrence. Here you were all these years later sitting close enough for me to touch you. It's not every day a girl actually gets to meet her knight in shining armor."

"Baby, I have to be honest with you. I feel something different happening here too. But right now, I have a lot on my plate. My fiancée, or shall I say my ex-fiancée, is missing. Right now I don't know if she's dead or alive. Either way, that relationship is over. Even though I don't want to, I have to keep trying to find out what happened to her, and try to find Rolondo Jemison and put him back in jail. So all I can offer you until I get past all of that, is what's happening here and now. What is your schedule from today through Sunday?"

"I'm pretty free. I just got back in town, so I don't have any skating lessons scheduled or patients to take care of. Why?" Amethyst asked as Rome rubbed lotion on her back. She returned the favor.

"Well, why don't you come to the press conference this afternoon, have dinner with me tonight, then spend the weekend with me in the Hamptons? I have to make sure all the security is set up in the house that Victor bought for Val. I was going to stay with them all summer, but now I think I'll rent my own house. Do you feel like helping me look for something?" he asked as they both put on their clothes.

"I admit that I don't relish getting caught up with all the drama that seems to be surrounding you right now. But I used to dream about what it would be like to spend a weekend with you. It would be my pleasure."

"Okay. Let's order some breakfast and get this day going," Rome said, checking his phone for a message from Davida. There wasn't a single call or text. Davida should have reached out by now. Had she been able to find that kid?

Chapter Thirty-one

Royale

As Royale stood watching Val and Victor leave, Victor's statement about a proposition for Royale settled in his head, and he didn't like the idea of it. Somehow what he was thinking popped right out of Royale's mouth instead.

"The only thing you can propose to me, Mr. Dumas, is to give me my woman back."

Still trying to make sense of this new situation, his words startled Vance.

"Is that what you were going to say to my father?" he asked.

Royale smiled at Vance. This kid may have been raised by Victor, but he had ways just like Andrea.

"Look, baby cuz, I think you need to get your own house in order before you start concerning yourself with mine. Isn't that your extremely fine *first wife* pulling up in front in that town car? It looks like you need to get Rome to put a GPS tracking device in her wallet."

Almost losing her balance before breaking a fall, Cantrese looked like she was ready to faint at the sight of Roshonda. Royale quickly put his arm around her and pulled her next to him and Ariel.

"Don't worry. I got this."

With a staggering Talfor walking next to her, Roshonda approached Vance looking high and drunk at the same time. She grabbed on to Vance when she saw Royale standing there. At first she thought he was Rolondo, who had once been her pimp. But looking more intensely at him, she knew this had to be the actual Royale Jones.

"What are you doing out here, Vance? I thought you were spending the night with the horses," said Roshonda.

"I did. It's morning now. I thought you quit getting high and partying all night."

"Please, I just had a couple of drinks, right Talfor?"

Talfor looked at Royale as if she had seen a ghost.

"Royale Jones? I thought you were dead."

"So nice to see you too, Talfor. Good morning, Roshonda. As you can see, I am very much still among the living. Cantrese and my lady Ariel were kind enough to escort me to the hospital last night when I wasn't feeling well. I met Cantrese in the lobby bar."

Cantrese sighed with relief at his tall tale.

"I'm glad you're feeling better now. I'd better get to work. Vance, Roshonda, I'll see you at the press conference."

As she left, Vance looked at Roshonda in disgust.

"I need to start getting ready too. Let's go in. Nice meeting you, Royale. I'll see you at dinner."

"All right, baby boy." Royale's remark about Victor hadn't escaped Ariel.

"So, you are still in love with Valerie?"

"My feelings for Valerie are nothing for you to worry your pretty little head about. What you and I have together is our own special thing. Come on. The doctor said I need to rest and call the neurologist that he recommended at nine. Let's have some breakfast. I'm going to need some energy. I have a feeling a lot of shit is going to jump off today!"

Not knowing what to think about this Valerie situation, Ariel told him, "I don't understand what's going on, and this new you is so different, but I'm willing to follow your lead." With those words, Ariel begrudgingly followed Royale into the hotel.

Chapter Thirty-two

Sincere

Amere ten blocks south of the Ritz Carlton on Broadway and Forty-ninth Street, Sincere was looking out over the city from his room at the 'W' Hotel in Times Square. The slick New York hotel is a two-minute walk from the Forty-ninth Street subway, which is one of its features that Sincere loved most. It was always good to be able to make a quick exit into the subway when you had to. The iron horse, which was the MTA's nickname, was the easiest place to disappear in New York City. He also liked the stylish lobby bar. If he had some of his girls with him, the place would have made a great headquarters for his business.

So far this trip wasn't working out in his favor. Much to his dismay, both Betty and Violet's phone had been disconnected, which made the GPS tracking devices he had placed in both of them null and void. He also still didn't possess one single clue as to what had happened to Rolondo.

From watching the news, he did, however, know that Victor was having a huge press conference the next day, but he didn't think it was wise to make his presence known to his money bags half-brother yet. He was sure that Victor and that pain-in-the-ass Rome Nyland blamed Rolondo's courtroom escape on him, and he did not feel like being questioned by the police. His ringing phone broke into his thoughts. It was his cousin Claude.

"Hey man. What's up? Any word on Rolondo yet?"

"No, he still hasn't surfaced. I think your daughter killed him. Listen, we all need to lay low. We've had a couple of infiltrations out in LA. Rome was on the same flight to New York that Caressa was on last night. She overheard him telling this chick that he was having dinner at Ricardo's last night, so we showed up too. The whole crew was there, Victor, Vance, Valerie . . ."

"Okay. Go on."

"Caressa and I heard Rome tell Valerie that one of the Blades, a wannabe rapper named Cayenne, was selling information to him. He also told her about a kid that Caressa was paying to watch her car. He even knew that his woman left that restaurant Craig's in a red Bugatti. He sent the LAPD to try to get the kid to identify her."

"There's no way Violet would kill Rolondo if neither of us ordered the hit."

"I wouldn't be too sure about that. The word on the street is the Dumas' have her practically on house arrest at the Trump International Hotel. They suspect she had something to do with the home invasion in Bel Air where Victor's safe was cleaned out."

"That stupid little bitch! What are you going to do about Rome's stool pigeons?"

"Cayenne is already dead, but the kid Antonio has disappeared into thin air."

"Do you think Rome got to him first and has him hidden in a safe house?"

"There's no way. They never even noticed us at Ricardo's last night, and I was sitting close enough to where Valerie was standing to suck her big titties."

"Okay. I'm going to head over to the Trump International and see if I can talk to Violet. I also need to try to find Betty. She didn't follow my orders either. I would hate to have to kill my own daughter, but if she crossed me like this . . ." Sincere didn't finish his sentence because he had never trusted Claude. The last thing he wanted to do was let him know that Violet had to go. He also had people in place out in Sag Harbor to kill Claude in the next few days, so they could raid the church and try to dig up Royale's buried treasure.

"Sincere, are you still there?"

"Yeah, I'm still here. Where are you now?"

Claude didn't trust Sincere any more than his treacherous cousin trusted him. He wasn't about to give up his whereabouts.

"Just up in Harlem waiting to collect from some of my girls. I'll catch up with you later."

"All right. I'm out."

Sincere pulled a linen beige suit with a matching silk T-shirt out of the hotel's closet. It was time to get dressed and go handle his stupid daughter. He wouldn't feel bad about the untimely demise that she was about to meet. Hell, he never wanted a daughter anyway!

Chapter Thirty-three

Janvieve

After paying $500 to a clerk at the front desk to find out Violet's hotel room number, much to her dismay, Janvieve still hadn't been able to gain access to the girl's room. She had tried every trick in the book, from trying to convince several housekeepers to sell her their uniforms, to sneaking up the steps to Violet's floor. That plan was thwarted when she opened the door on the floor only to be met by a member of the Dumas security team. Before the man could ask to see her key, Janvieve sheepishly mumbled, "Wrong floor," then fled down the stairs to the lobby. The last thing she needed was for them to call the cops on her. Victor had put a five million dollar bounty on Rolondo's head, and after the multiple murders that he committed on Tuesday, if caught, a cocktail of life-ending drugs shot into his arm was the only future Rolondo faced. Because of that, Janvieve decided to move slowly, and devised a new plan to kill Violet.

She called four contacts here in the city and put out a $50,000 dollar hit on Violet. The plan was for them to pose as taxi drivers in front of the hotel and run down Violet the minute she hit the street. One of them had already picked up the down-payment. The Dumas' had to let the rat out of the cage at some point. As soon as they did, revenge would belong to Janvieve. It was early, so she decided to have breakfast. The contact had also dropped off some blow.

As Janvieve headed to the bathroom to take care of business, she saw Sincere walk into the hotel lobby. Darting behind a pillar, she watched as he approached the front desk and spoke to the clerk.

"Mrs. Vance Dumas, please. Tell her that John Allen Jackson is here to see her."

The clerk looked at his computer.

"I'm sorry, Mr. Jackson. We are only allowed to call up to Mrs. Dumas' suite for pre-approved visitors that are on a list that the security provided."

"Very well. Then I will leave a message for her."

"So sorry again, sir. We are not allowed to give her any messages that aren't from the pre-approved names on the list. In fact, I am going to have to ask you to step away from the desk, or I will have to call security."

Sincere quickly left without saying another word.

Putting on her sunglasses, Janvieve quickly followed Sincere out of the hotel. When she saw him get into a cab, she jumped in the one that was right behind it.

"I'm going to the same place that gentleman in the car in front of us is heading. Just stay with them." Both cars headed down Broadway until Sincere's cab stopped at Forty-ninth Street. Janvieve threw a twenty dollar bill at her driver, then hopped out, being very careful to stay out of Sincere's eye sight.

After waiting for ten minutes, she entered the 'W' Hotel. She didn't see her cousin anywhere in the lobby, so she figured it was safe to pick up a house phone. She gave the operator the name that she heard Sincere use back at Trump International when he asked for Violet's room.

"Mr. John Allen Jackson's room, please."

"One moment, ma'am. I will put you through."

Janvieve hung up before a connection could be made. Her day had just gotten so much better. Now that she knew where he was resting, the rat that just went upstairs was about to meet his exterminator real soon.

Chapter Thirty-four

Rome

R ome was in the middle of a final meeting with his guys about the security procedures for this afternoon's press conference when his phone rang. It was James Pace. He had to take the call.

"Gentlemen, excuse me for one minute." Rome stepped out into the hall. "Good morning, James. You got anything for me?"

"Hey, man. Yes, I have a lot. I got a hit on Samantha's picture. Her real name is Caressa Shabazz. She has a pretty extensive record for prostitution and one drug conviction. She got probation on that and never did any real time. The Bugatti was parked right where you said it would be, so I had it towed. We were able to lift her prints off of it as well as your girl Turquoise's fingerprints."

"Why did you have Turquoise's prints on file?"

"She has a record for two counts of fraud and passing bad checks."

"Are you serious?"

"I wish I wasn't. Anyway, that gave me enough to email the photo to the NYPD and have them pick Caressa up for us if they see her anywhere."

"Good going. The kid is with Davida. But she can't keep him there much longer. He's a runaway from foster care."

"Uh, Rome, I also have some bad news for you. The rapper Cayenne, whose real name was Carlton Jamal, is dead. It was ugly. His body was in a dumpster filled with rats. His tongue had been cut out. I don't know how the Blades knew about him."

"I do. Val's friend that took the photo of Caressa last night said she and who I now know is Rolondo and Royale's cousin, Claude, overheard Val's and my entire conversation. This is not good. Cayenne was a good kid. I tried over and over to get him to go legit. I did not mean for this to happen. He was not supposed to die like that."

"I know, man. But these gang bangers know they are living on borrowed time. Don't beat yourself up about it. What do you mean Rolondo and Royale's cousin?"

"Royale is alive, man! He's right here in New York. He says that he's had amnesia for the last five years after Rolondo thought he killed him. But here's the craziest part of the story. He and Val were college sweethearts. She says that in the back of her mind she knew that Rolondo wasn't Royale, but when he didn't act like he knew her, she was too hurt after all of those years to say anything. Val is going to announce that Royale is alive at the press conference we're having to announce the Dumas Diamonds Polo Team this afternoon."

"Damn! That's some drama right there."

"You don't know the half of it. James, I need a favor. I don't want anything to happen to this kid Antonio Wright. Can you call around and ask a few questions about him, see if I can become his foster parent? If we can make it work, I'll fly him out here, and he can spend the summer with me in the Hamptons. I can put him to work helping Vance with the horses. After what just happened to Cayenne, it is important to me to save this kid."

"No problem. I'm on it. Keep your eye out for Caressa. The sooner we have her in custody, the closer you'll be to finding Turquoise and possibly even Rolondo."

"Royale seems to think that Caressa and Claude will show up to this afternoon's press conference. It's at the Boathouse in Central Park. Will you alert the NYPD?"

"They will be my next phone call as soon as I hang up from you, and then I will phone Los Angeles County Department of Children and Family Services to find out what we need to do about Antonio."

"Thanks. I'll talk to you later."

With all the terrible information he kept discovering about Turquoise, Rome did not really want to find her that badly. But as usual, he would continue to do the right thing and keep looking for her. He looked at his watch. It was almost nine-thirty, which means it was time to get these guys in their positions in and around the Boat House in Central Park.

It was kind of strange that he hadn't heard from Val this morning. They normally spoke at seven a.m., but she hadn't answered her phone. Rome tried to call her again. It wasn't like her to be out of touch with him like this. He hadn't heard from Victor either. Val's phone went straight to voice mail again. Rome didn't like this one bit. He needed to find Val. He went back into the living room of the suite.

"Look, guys. I need to make a quick run to check on something. I'll be right back. He ran out the door hoping no evil had befallen his best friend.

Chapter Thirty-five

Valerie

It was a beautiful summer afternoon in Central Park, a perfect day for an indoor/outdoor press conference, and for a vengeful enemy to strike. Valerie had immediately agreed with Irene and Helen when they both suggested that the park would be the ideal spot to announce Vance's Polo Club. Since horseback riding was allowed there, they would be able to also showcase their gorgeous horses.

Boating on the lake in Central Park became popular in the 1860s, which naturally launched a need for a storage facility, or a boathouse. According to the history books and website, investment banker/philanthropist Carl M. Loeb and his wife generously donated $305,000 to help create The Loeb Boathouse that still stands today. Even though it has evolved into a landmark restaurant, it continues to provide boating enthusiasts with rowboats they can rent, so people can enjoy one of life's simple pleasures in the heart of the city.

It turned out to be a wise decision that Val and Victor had dressed in their white attire for the press conference this morning. Although they had filled out the application for their marriage license online last night to save time, still it had been a long process. They barely made it to Central Park ahead of the invited guests and media. As the almost married coosome-twosome approached the boathouse, waiters dressed as polo players wearing signature white Brooks Brothers polo shirts embroidered with Dumas Diamonds Polo Club, offered them mimosas, champagne, merlot, chardonnay, and water in glasses that bore the polo club's logo. Both of them declined. They were too anxious to make sure that everything was set up properly and in order for the festivities.

Cantrese, also clad in white, ushered them in and directed her bosses to the outside bar facing the lake. The scene they found awaiting them was spectacular. The boats that floated on the lake were filled with white and yellow roses, and lilacs. A gondola with a string quartet softly playing classical music floated in the midst of the boats. They were also clad in polo playing gear.

Once Victor and Valerie got inside, the décor only got better. The tables were covered in an ivory silk brocade with matching covered chairs. Just like the crystal for the drinks, Val had a china pattern created especially for today. The dishes were ivory with the polo club's logo engraved on them. To top everything off, each napkin on every table was held together with a broach that was also the logo. Designed by jeweler Lu Willard, each pin had a real two-point diamond in it.

Victor whispered in Val's ear, "You and your team have truly outdone yourselves, sweetheart. Everything looks so beautiful that we should probably be getting married here and now instead of at the courthouse tomorrow."

"Thank you, kind sir. We wanted to make today perfect for you and Vance. Tomorrow's going to be perfect. I can't believe we're going to finally be joined together for life in less than twenty-four hours."

"You have less than twenty-four hours until what?"

They had been gazing so intensely into each other's eyes that neither Victor nor Val had noticed Rome standing right behind them. He was also wearing white. In ten years, Val thought this had to be the first time she had ever seen him dressed in any color than black. She didn't even want Rome to know that she and Victor were getting married the next morning. Nothing was going to jinx this.

"Until we move out to the Hamptons. You're looking good. You should wear white more often. I see you have plenty of security guys in case Rolondo or Valerian show up. How many guys are with the baby and Esperanza?"

"Six. They should be arriving in about five minutes. I tried to reach you this morning. In fact, I've been looking for you. Why didn't you get back to me?" He waited for a response but didn't get one.

"Anyway, Royale called to tell me that he thinks Betty might know both Rolondo and Valerian's whereabouts. He told me that you said he should call me because of the GPS tracking device I have on her. Then he proceeded to say that you all had this conversation when he ran into you and Victor leaving the hotel around seven-thirty this morning. Where were you guys going so early?"

"We had to pick up a few things to take out to the Hamptons," Victor quickly told him. "Val thought it might get too hectic to get them later. If Royale thinks Betty might know where Rolondo is hiding, I'm going to up the reward money for information leading up to his capture to one hundred million dollars. That ought to loosen her tongue." Victor quickly nodded once. "Oh, Rome, I have scheduled a dinner meeting for all of us with Royale for tonight at seven at Jean George. I have something else to run by him that I think he can assist us in," he added.

A few more members of Victor's security team approached him, including Dwayne.

"Sir, the Black Cowboys are here. We just need you to watch as we pat them and their horses down," Dwayne informed him.

"No problem. Let's go."

As soon as Victor was out of ear shot, Rome leaned in close to Val so no one else could hear.

"We've been friends for over ten years, so you can avoid it as long as you want to, but you and I need to discuss what was happening when I broke into the bathroom on you and Royale last night. Today is the first time in a decade that I haven't spoken to you before the sun comes up. When we get to the Hamptons tomorrow, you and I are going to have lunch alone."

"Rome, there's really nothing to discuss. What you saw was just a reaction to long lost feelings. Please just forget that kiss ever happened."

"You know me too well to think I'm going to do that. But I will let it go for the time being. Oh, I think I want to rent my own house out in the Hamptons for the summer. I remember you telling me that your girl, Suzette, is a real estate agent these days. Can you give me her phone number?"

"Sure. Okay . . . I don't know why you want your own house. We have plenty of room, but I can do better than giving you Suzette's phone number. She just walked in. I'll introduce you to her as soon as we're finished with the program. Let's get this show on the road."

Rome grabbed Val's arm before she walked toward the podium, which was set up by the outside bar.

"For the record, baby girl, Royale seems like a pretty nice guy. I actually kind of like him. But what you have with Victor only comes around once in a lifetime. Make sure the past stays where it was."

"You don't have to worry about a thing." Val kissed Rome on the cheek.

As Val approached the podium to get the program started, it was old home week in New York. She waved to her friend, Jean, who was known as the 'Diva of Philanthropy,' then greeted all of her crew—Shelley and Joe, Karl, Lisa Arcella, Kenneth, Lu and Stan, Copper, Shannon, Dawne Marie, and Penny. The turn-out was amazing.

She smiled at Suzette and Jean. She would also be seeing the two of them at Saturday night's gala, a benefit for a breast cancer research foundation in Southampton. Like most summers, Jean was chairing the event, which raised much needed funds for cancer patients. An ovarian cancer survivor herself, Valerie felt blessed that for the first time she had been able to purchase tables to contribute to such an important cause. She and Victor had bought two tables, and Vance had also gotten one so that the members of his polo club could also attend the function.

Helen and Irene beckoned Valerie to the podium. Surrounded by more security than the president, Esperanza sat on the front row with Valencia on her lap. Val blew a kiss to the baby. Then she spied her colleagues from the media, Richard Johnson, Jawn Murray, Audrey Bernard, Don Thomas, Brian Niemietz, and her mentor Cindy Adams.

Oh my gosh! she thought, wanting to point in their direction, but knowing she shouldn't. *There's Norah Lawlor, Basha Riddick, and Soledad O'Brian.* Val kept gazing from one end of the audience to the other. Roshonda, resplendent in a tea-length white Balenciaga dress with black flowers on it, and matching black and white jeweled shoes, sat next to Esperanza and Valencia.

Val then addressed the crowd.

"Good afternoon, New York City. For those of you who don't know me. My name is Valerie Rollins. I am so happy to be back home for this monumental occasion in history as Vance and Victor Dumas introduce The Dumas Diamonds Polo Club, comprised of all black players, to the world."

She nearly gasped with glee when her eyes landed on even more of her media colleagues, Marcia Parris, Rita Cosby, Victoria Horsford, Geraldo Rivera, the gang from *Resident Magazine*, Gayle King, Elinor Tatum, James Edstrom, Christopher Pape from 25A, Keri D. Singleton, Tony Bowles, and so many more.

"Ladies and gentleman, let's also give a warm, Big Apple welcome to members of the Federation of Black Cowboys!"

The crowd cheered as a dozen black cowboys riding on their horses and waving banners galloped right past them doing a lap around the lake.

"And now I present to you the world-class athletes who make up The Dumas Diamonds Polo Club. Astride Florence, we have Nino Lopez! Riding the beautiful chestnut mare Pubica is Jamal Warren! On the magnificent Clavito is Lee Iger. And for this exciting moment in the world of polo, here is our fabulous and lovely female member of the team, all the way from Kenya, Falaki Obika, riding the gorgeous Palomino pony, Samadonna. Last but not least is my fiance's son, the legendary Vance Dumas on, in my opinion, the greatest horse to ever win the Kentucky Derby, Wildin' Out! Together, these wonderful equestrians and ponies are The Dumas Diamonds Polo Club!"

As the team and the horses rode back out of the park while the audience was busy giving them a standing ovation and cheering loudly, Caressa, who had no idea that Rome, Victor's security team, and members of the NYPD had been watching her closely, started edging toward the front row where Vance's baby was seated. Although neither she nor Claude had heard from Sincere or Rolondo since Tuesday, she knew both of their objectives still had to be to kidnap the kid and hold her for a ransom that would equal Victor Dumas' entire fortune. Caressa was determined to make a quick move while everyone was still on their feet, snatch the baby, and shoot anyone that got in her way. If Rolondo and Sincere never surfaced, Victor's billions would belong to her and Claude, who was waiting just outside the park with the car's engine still running. Keeping her eyes on the prize, she hustled forward just a little more. Out of nowhere, she felt a gun in her back and looked up at two uniformed cops in front of her.

A voice behind her whispered, "Don't even try to reach for that tiny gun you have stashed in your bra. I haven't been able to kill Rolondo as of yet, but since you are his associate, I will gladly blow you to smithereens. There is a silencer on my gun, and none of these nice people will know the difference."

The men in front of her moved so swiftly that the crowd never even noticed them taking her out of Central Park. As soon as the police officers got Caressa out of sight from the press conference, one of them read her the Miranda rights.

From the stage, Valerie had watched the entire scene. Acting on Royale's hunch that Caressa would show up today, Rome had purposely seated Esperanza and Valencia in the front row to lure her out front. Valerie thought, *One perpetrator down and two to go. They just need to find*

Rolondo and Valerian to end this madness. This Caressa girl let her hunger for money cloud her judgment by trying to kidnap the baby in front of hundreds of people. No matter what, greed always won over common sense.

Vance and Victor joined Valerie at the podium, where they were accompanied by the polo club players and members of the Black Cowboys, Nachos Figueras, and NBC Triple-Crown reporter, former female jockey, Donna Barton Brothers.

"I now turn this program over to Victor Dumas." Val handed the mic to Victor and took a few steps back.

It warmed her heart when she looked over the audience once more to see that her friends Ethel and Larry Stewart had driven in from Washington, DC, Renell Perry was here from Chicago, and her sister/friends Theresa Campbell, Jocelyn Allen, and Barbara Jean Patton had flown in from Detroit. Her dear friends Johnny Newman and Charles Oakley also happened to be in town for an NBA function, and it was a kind gesture that they attended the event to show their support.

Victor's voice grabbed Valerie's attention.

"Good afternoon. Thank you all so much for coming. I'm sure you are all ready to partake of the sumptuous lunch that the chefs here have prepared for you, so I will be brief. In the words of the legendary Argentinian Polo player Juan Carlos Harriott, 'It takes hot blood and a cool head to play polo.' So we have assembled some of the hottest and coolest young athletes in the sport to join us this summer in Bridgehampton.

"Today, on behalf of the Dumas Family Foundation, I would like to donate one million dollars to the Federation of Black Cowboys, so they can continue their work at Cedar Lane Stables." Victor paused, allowing the crowd's applause to die. Once he was satisfied he had the audience's full attention, he continued. "Then, as you know, gang and gun violence has been plaguing my family lately, and it is poisoning the minority youth all over America. To combat all of these deadly plays that kill innocent victims every day, we have purchased a housing complex here in New York City in the village of Harlem. This will be a $500 million project in which we intend to house, educate, as well as provide employment for these lost souls.

"Last, I'm sure that most of you sitting out there are also well aware of the home invasion that took place on my property in Los Angeles just the day before yesterday. A horrific tragedy, it took the lives of four innocent people.

"And I know this will come as a great shock to most of you, but I would like to announce that Royale Jones, whom career criminal Rolondo Jemison has been impersonating for five years, is alive and well. However, Jemison, who has been hunting down and torturing my loved ones for years, is still out there somewhere. I would like to increase the reward for any information that will lead to his capture to $100 million.

"Thank you, ladies and gentlemen. Please join us inside for lunch. See you out at polo in the Hamptons."

Val stepped down and picked up Valencia, holding her tightly as cameras flashed. She whispered to Victor, "Thank God no one in the crowd seemed to notice the cops hustle that girl out of here. Let's join everyone for lunch. I'm sure Rome will be back in soon to let us know what's happening. Hopefully her capture will be a big step in ending all this madness."

For once Val was wrong.

Chapter Thirty-six

Janvieve

A tall woman crouching down at the back of the Boathouse had also been watching Caressa closely from the moment she spotted her. Trying to make herself invisible, the woman was acutely aware of the extremely heavy presence of the NYPD. She had also heard every word of Victor's speech.

Moving swiftly away from the Boathouse, Janvieve knew she had to get her hands on Royale's buried fortune right away. She didn't know how he could still be alive, but if what Victor said was true, he could even be on his way to Sag Harbor right now to dig his safe up. Janvieve hoped that Victor was just bluffing. But if he wasn't, on top of all that, with Victor's offer of $100 million for Rolondo's head, she had to get out of the country fast. The five hundred grand was not enough money for her to live her life comfortably overseas forever. She needed her cousin's riches. But right now, she had to be about the business of killing Betty and Violet, the two people who could lead the police straight to Rolondo.

Chapter Thirty-seven

Rome

Outside on Fifth Avenue and Seventy-second Street, two detectives were putting Caressa into an unmarked black car. As they pushed her inside, Rome leaned down into the car.

"All right, Caressa. What did you do with Turquoise Hobson?"

Caressa was shocked that he knew her real name. In an attempt to keep her cool, he shot Rome a look that could kill.

"My name is Samantha. I don't know anyone by the name of Caressa or Turquoise."

"You can keep this Samantha masquerade going all that you want to. But the fact of the matter is the LAPD has already identified you as Caressa Shabazz, a member of the Bugatti Blades. You have a rap sheet dating back to when you were a juvenile. Now, you can play this game two ways: you can tell these nice detectives all you know about Rolondo Jemison and the kidnapping of Turquoise Hobson, who was last seen two nights ago in LA with you, and just maybe the LAPD will go easy on you and give you a deal.

"Or, you can keep acting like you have amnesia and be charged here in New York for the attempted kidnapping of

Valencia Dumas and in LA for the kidnapping of Turquoise Hobson and for the murder of Carlton 'Cayenne' Jamal. It's up to you, baby. I'm sure the girls out in San Quentin would just love to sample a sweet piece of meat like you." Rome handed each one of the detectives his business card, then showed them the photo of Caressa that Val's friend, Damien, had texted to her.

In a low voice so that Caressa couldn't hear him, he told them, "See this ring that she's wearing in the photo? My fiancée Turquoise wears one just like it. If you find it on your prisoner, call me ASAP."

They both nodded, shook Rome's hand, then got into the car and sped off down Fifth Avenue.

Back inside of the Boathouse, Rome pulled Valerie and Victor aside. Val still had Valencia in her arms, who had fallen asleep.

"That went pretty well. Caressa is still claiming that her name is Samantha, but as soon as they fingerprint her, she'll have to lay that act to rest. Hopefully, she'll fess up and tell the cops what happened to Turquoise and where Rolondo might be hiding."

"It sounds good to me," Val told him. "People are starting to leave. Let me say good-bye to a few of them, and then I will introduce you to Suzette. I sat Amethyst with her and Jean. I thought those three would get along well."

"All right. After this, maybe you and I can compare notes on all of this back at the hotel."

"I'm sorry, Rome, but I have more errands to run. I'm going up to East Harlem to the Sparkle Beauty Salon to get my hair done, and I've got some other stops to make."

"I can come with you."

"Sorry, no can do. This is girl stuff. You are not invited. I'll take two security guys along with Esperanza and the baby with me."

"What's with all of these errands? Aren't running errands what you two have Cantrese and Dwayne for?"

Victor laughed. He knew Val was trying to secretly get ready for their wedding ceremony tomorrow.

"Let her go, Rome. She'll be fine. I have a few things that I need to do myself, and then I'm going to rest until tonight's dinner with Royale. Come by the room and pick Val and me up around six thirty. Feel free to bring Amethyst with you. I want people around us looking on to think we're just out for a nice social evening."

"That's not a problem, Victor, but why are we really meeting with Royale?"

"I want to see if he can set up a meeting between my brother and me. Rome, I'm tired of all of us constantly looking over our shoulders for Valerian. I'm going to offer him a billion dollar settlement to leave us alone."

"Wow, Victor. I personally wouldn't give the creep a dime, but it's your money. Okay. As always, I got your back."

Esperanza wheeled Valencia's stroller over to where they were chatting. Val placed the sleeping toddler in it.

"Rome, let's get you introduced to Suzette so you can get your house on. And, instead of being all up in my business, why don't you take Amethyst shopping for a dress to wear to Jean's party on Saturday night? Make yourself useful that way. It will be Victor's and my treat. Brush the dust off that Dumas Electronics credit card that you have in your wallet." Pushing the baby's stroller, Val, along with Victor and Rome went to say their good-byes to people before heading out for the rest of the afternoon. Their mission here had been accomplished, on to the next thing.

They had never noticed the tall woman in the back of the crowd, nor knew that another enemy was waiting right outside of the park in his car. No matter what, the next thing was not going to be good.

Chapter Thirty-eight

Claude

Crouched down in his Jaguar that was parked two cars behind the unmarked car and three medallion police vehicles that accompanied it, Claude watched as Caressa was driven away, and Rome walked back into the park. He couldn't figure out how they had made her. His boys had gotten to Cayenne in time and put his lights out forever, or had they? It sure looked like Rome may have beaten them to the punch. The other kid was nowhere to be found. Perhaps Rome had him stashed someplace too. It was too late to worry about that now. Caressa was on her own. She had been too loose with her lips anyway. Let the skank rot in jail. He had to get back to Sag Harbor. His precious cargo from Las Vegas would be arriving late tonight/or early tomorrow morning. He had to put her to work and find someone who had a gold-finding device that would help him unearth Royale's safe.

Peeling out from his parking space, Claude noticed the tall, light-skinned woman with blonde hair walking out of the park. He raised his gun, but quickly put it away and drove off. Had her eyes been fixated on him, or was he being paranoid?

"Shit!" he cursed as he increased his speed, feeling as if he was a few miles closer to having Royale's fortune in his hands.

Chapter Thirty-nine

Violet

Although she rarely drank, Violet had almost consumed two entire bottles of Chivas Regal that were on the bar. After watching Vance and his silly polo club parade through Central Park on the news, she locked herself in the suite's bedroom away from the prying eyes of her father-in-law's goons and proceeded to get drunk out of her mind. Hell, there was nothing else to do. She had already tried to screw her way out of this prison by parading around naked in front of the guys. But Victor had them in deep check. They acted as if her perfectly shaped, petite body was invisible.

Violet was jarred out of her drunken stupor by the ringing house phone in the living room. Vance had the phone taken out of the bedroom so she couldn't make any calls. One of the goons answered it, then knocked on the bedroom door.

"Mrs. Dumas, the phone is for you."

It had to be Vance. They wouldn't put anyone else through. Maybe he had come to his senses and was letting her finally leave this God-forsaken hotel. She unlocked the door, then lay back on the bed spread eagle, masturbating and massaging her titty at the same time.

"Bring the phone in here," she shouted in a slurred manner.

The security guard wanted to laugh at her antics. This one refused to give in. She was fine as all get out. Any other time he would have been all up in her kitty cat, but he had a wife and three kids and needed this job. One piece of ass was not worth the security of his family. Since both of her hands were otherwise occupied, he set the cordless phone's receiver next to her on the nightstand and left the room, closing the door behind him.

Violet threw a glass at the door.

"You know you want this good stuff, ass hole!" She grabbed the phone.

"Hello, Vance. I know you want some of this good stuff between my legs too."

"This isn't Vance, Violet. It's Cantrese."

"Oh, Cantrese. Where is my husband? It ain't much, but I could use some of what he calls a dick right now."

"You are disgusting. Are you drunk?"

"What's it to you if I am? What do you want? And why did you guys think you could play a game with me this morning by having someone pretending to be Royale Jones answer your phone?"

"That wasn't anybody 'pretending' to be Royale Jones, Violet. That was the man in the flesh. He's alive, and it turns out that he knows Val. Anyway, the reason that he answered the phone is because he was standing there when you called and thought he could reason with you. Vance took my phone because I confessed to him that you had been paying me to spy on them. I can't do it anymore, Violet. I just can't."

"You ungrateful Judas bitch! I'm hanging up on you now."

"No wait! Victor asked me to call you and tell you to be ready to have dinner at Jean George Restaurant in your hotel at seven tonight. Your security detail will escort you downstairs."

"What does he want?"

"I have no idea. I'm just following orders."

Normally Violet would protest being told what to do, but she was going to lose her mind if she didn't get out of this room soon.

"No problem. Good-bye." She needed to sober up, so her high and mighty father-in-law wouldn't have one more thing to hold over her head. But first, she was determined to get her rocks off one way or the other.

Still butt naked, taking one last swig of scotch from the bottle that was next to the bed, Violet staggered into the living room. Falling into the other security guard's laps, letting out a wicked laugh, Violet stood up and started twerking in front of him and doing the Beyoncé bounce. Not as virtuous as his colleague was, this guard picked her up, hungrily sucking her bare breasts. He carried Violet into the bathroom where he locked the door. He wasn't one of

Victor's regular men, so he couldn't care less how long this job lasted.

"My man went to lunch. We have the place to ourselves. Let me show you what it feels like to have a real man in you, not some little jockey like that rich punk you're married to."

Violet was happy to oblige. At least she had a way to pass the time that would make her feel better than even two bottles of scotch had. Otherwise, she'd die of anxiety wondering if dinner would somehow turn out to be a trap worse than her current state.

Chapter Forty

Caressa

At the Twenty-second precinct house on Eighty-sixth Street and Traverse Road in Central Park, Caressa remained silent as the police officers, now joined by two detectives led her handcuffed into the station and up a flight of stairs. They kept walking until they reached an interview room. Caressa was directed to a chair, then proceeded to look through her Michael Kors purse. The first thing they pulled out was her wallet to look at her driver's license. Caressa knew this was going to be a problem. She hadn't had a clue or a warning that the NYPD could be looking for her. She had at least four different driver's licenses on her and Turquoise's two rings. She also hadn't been able to resist lifting Turquoise's Visa card right in front of Yohance and Shemar. She had been so quick that neither of those knuckleheads had noticed the sleight of hand trick she pulled.

"Well, looky here," said the black detective. "You must do quite a bit of driving to need all of these licenses . . . Samantha Stephenson, Caressa Shabazz, Stella Johnson, Soundra Usry. Oh, this one is the best out of them all . . . Jacqueline Bouvier Kennedy. I'll bet you are a First Lady . . . the First Lady of Rolondo Jemison or the Bugatti Blades.

I see that diamond Wildcat that's hanging around your neck."

Caressa remained quiet. She needed to think this one through thoroughly before making any move. Digging deeper, the detective pulled out a coin purse. He opened it and lo and behold, he pulled out the diamond heart ring that the guy Nyland showed him in the photo, along with one of the largest diamond engagement rings he had ever laid eyes on. He held both pieces of jewelry out to Caressa.

"Do you want to tell me where you got these two beautiful rings, because one of them looks exactly like a ring Mr. Nyland showed us that you were wearing in a picture. He told us that his fiancée, who just happens to be missing and was allegedly last seen in California with you, has a ring just like this."

Caressa couldn't believe what she was hearing. How could this Rome have a photo of her? Her only out here would be to blame all of this on Rolondo and try to make a deal with these cops. But there was one big problem. No one had heard from Rolondo in two days. She looked hard into the detective's eyes.

"I want a phone call and a lawyer."

Immediately after those words came out of Caressa's mouth, an Assistant District Attorney from Manhattan District Attorney Cyrus R. Vance, Jr.'s office entered the interrogation room. She was a stocky redhead wearing a red suit and sensible black heels. Caressa could tell this woman wasn't anyone to play with.

"My name is Patricia Ellison from the DA's office. We'll let you have your phone call and get your lawyer, but as for your gun, the fake IDs, and allegedly another woman's jewelry, things are not looking good for you, Ms. Shabazz. Guys, take her where she can make her calls, and then put her in a holding cell. The van should be here soon to take her downtown to central booking."

One detective followed Ms. Ellison's orders and removed Caressa from the room while the other one took her purse and jewelry with him to call Rome and file as evidence.

Rome

Not far from the Central Park Police precinct, thirty blocks down on Fifth Avenue, Rome was following Val's suggestion and was now in the middle of shopping at Saks Fifth Avenue with Amethyst, who kept insisting that she didn't need him to buy her anything.

"Rome, this really isn't my style. I'm a self-sufficient woman. I buy my own clothes."

"I love your self-sufficiency, but let Val and Victor treat you to something new to wear tomorrow night. She wants to do it. I rarely use their card, so it needs to get some air. In fact, let's not only get you an evening gown, bag, and a pair of shoes to wear tomorrow night, but something for dinner tonight too. I've had a rough couple of days. Cheer a brother up and indulge me. Here's the elevator. Let's look at the evening gowns first."

Amethyst decided to stop fighting him. The truth be told, she didn't even own an evening gown, because she rarely attended black-tie events. Once in a blue moon, when she did get invited to something that required formal attire, she simply threw on a black dress.

"Okay. I surrender. I would love two new beautiful outfits."

"That's what I'm talking about."

As they got ready to step on the elevator, Rome's cell phone went off.

"Rome Nyland."

"Hey, Mr. Nyland. This is officer Chet Ramsey. We found what looks like the ring you showed us earlier in the photograph in the suspect's purse, along with another ring. I think it may belong to your fiancée also. 'Love, Rome' is engraved on the band. The suspect has asked for an attorney, so we won't be able to interview her anymore until one gets here."

"I'm in the middle of something right now. Text me a picture of the rings and the name and number of her attorney when she gets one. Thanks so much."

"No. Thank you. I'll inform LAPD of this new development as well. Good-bye."

"Good-bye."

This was all getting so heavy, but Rome had always been a man that kept moving no matter how tough a challenge was placed in front of him. He put his arm around Amethyst.

"Here's another elevator. We are getting on this one. Let's get you some new threads."

Rome didn't know what emotion to feel. Should he be happy that he definitely now knew who took Turquoise, or sad that she might be dead?

Chapter Forty-one

Valerie

After the ordeal at the press conference, Val felt the need to keep Valencia in her sight for the rest of the afternoon. She had taken Esperanza and the baby on a whirlwind afternoon combined with beauty treatments and power shopping. Helping her get out of the Bentley SUV, Val's security guards had to get a bellman and a cart to take all of her purchases up to the suite. It was five-thirty. There was no way she was even secretly getting married the next day without having her hair done and getting a manicure/pedicure.

Their first stop had been her New York hairdresser Elsie's salon in East Harlem on 101st Street and Lexington Avenue, where she also treated Esperanza to a new hairstyle. After that, they headed further up Lexington Avenue to First Nails at 116th Street, where she had the ladies even paint Valencia's nails.

Leaving the nail salon, they drove straight downtown to Lord & Taylor on Fifth Avenue and Thirty-eighth Street. Val had seen a red lace dress by Adrianna Papell on the elegant department store's website. Back in the eighties, *Dynasty* had been one of her favorite television shows. On one particular episode, Joan Collins' devious character, Alexis Carrington Colby, had married Dex Dexter wearing a red lace dress. Val had never forgotten that scene and always wanted to emulate Alexis by getting married in red lace. Tomorrow, she would be doing exactly that.

While in the store, she picked up an evening gown and a few other dresses for herself and clothes for Esperanza and Valencia. They then headed to Van Cleef and Arpels, where she purchased a wedding band to give Victor. Their final stop was Christian Louboutin on Madison Avenue where she picked up red bottom shoes to match all of her outfits. She was going to have to hustle to be ready to leave the hotel at six-thirty for dinner. The thought of having to sit at a table with Royale did not appeal to her, but Victor must have had something extremely important to say to the man.

As they walked into the suite, Valerie instructed Esperanza to get the baby fed and bathed, then pack their clothes to be ready to leave for the Hamptons in the morning.

"Victor, we're back!"

"Your hair looks lovely." Victor was getting out of the shower. He kissed Val. "I was beginning to worry about you."

"I texted you several times. The girls and I covered a lot of ground. I am now more than ready to become Mrs. Dumas in the morning."

"I have an idea. Why don't we stay in the city tomorrow and have a sort of honeymoon, just you and me?"

"What about the baby?"

"For just one night my son can take care of his own daughter. He has a nanny, your assistant, who seems to also be his latest girlfriend, maybe Roshonda, and ten security guards to help him. When we leave here in the morning for the courthouse, we'll just send all of them text messages that we will be out to the Hamptons the next day. I have a lot of surprises planned for you. What do you say?"

Val was not so sure that she wanted to be separated from Valencia for a night, especially with the kidnapping attempt that had happened just a few hours ago. Plus, the dastardly trio were all still lurking out there somewhere to wreak havoc on their lives at any given moment. Maybe this wasn't the right time for a secret wedding. However, they had gone this far. Despite the nagging feeling she had that they should call tomorrow off and get married later, she told Victor, "I say I love surprises. Let's do it. Let me jump in the tub so we can get out of here on time."

In the meantime, she was going to ask Rome to send a local Private Investigator out to Claude's church in Sag Harbor. They needed to start keeping tabs on this man's every move.

PART 3

Chapter Forty-two

Claude

Instead of driving out to Sag Harbor right away, Claude decided to make a stop up in the Bronx to see his old friend Corey Jones, one of the last real hit men that really knew how to get a job done. He was sick of dealing with these young boys who were left over from the heydays when he and his cousins founded the Bugatti Blades. He was now in his mid-fifties. It was time to move away from all of those kids and move on to something else.

Corey's "office" was in the back room of a pool hall on East 141st Street in the Bronx's Mott Haven section. The crime rate in Bronx, New York, was considered the most violent in the nation, including rape, murder, non-negligent manslaughter, armed robbery and aggravated assault, as well as assault with a deadly weapon. Most of these crimes took place on the streets of Mott Haven.

Claude planned to take care of business, then get in and out of this joint faster than a heartbeat, or in this case, a gunshot. When Claude pulled his car up, Corey, a man of medium height, light-skinned, and who wore his jet-black hair pulled back in a ponytail was standing out in front of the pool house having a heated discussion with a stacked to the max brown–skinned chick with an afro.

"Look, I'm telling you, get that fool out of my house, or I am going to burn it down."

"You are no longer my man. You cannot tell me who can and cannot live with me and my kids!"

"Those are my kids too, and as long as I am paying the rent, I do not want the negro in my house!" He stopped yelling at the woman when he saw Claude. "I need to speak to my associate here. We'll talk about this later."

Mumbling "I got your later," the woman got into a silver BMW truck parked in front of Claude's car and drove off.

Corey embraced Claude.

"What can I do for you, man?"

"An associate of mine by the name of Caressa Shabazz got arrested in Central Park this afternoon. I need to make sure she doesn't make it down to central booking."

"You don't say? That precinct in Central Park is surrounded by trees and greenery. That will be an easy job. You got a picture of her?"

Claude looked through the photo album in his phone. Luckily, he had a picture of Caressa and Sincere that he had taken awhile back. He showed it to Corey.

"My cell is the same as it's always been. Text me that picture. For you, $3,000."

Claude pulled up his pants leg, reached into his sock, and pulled out his stash. He counted out twenty $100 bills.

"Here's two-grand. I'll give you the other thousand when the gig is completed. They popped her a couple hours ago, so you better get going. They should be ready to transfer her soon. She knows far too much about my business."

"I'm already packing and ready to jump in my car now. I got this. Don't worry about a thing. I'll be in touch with you soon."

"Thanks, man. Always nice doing business with you." Claude got back in his truck and continued his drive out to the Hamptons, certain Caressa's end would be quick.

Chapter Forty-three

Victor

After meeting in the lobby of the Ritz Carlton, although with some of the caravan riding in separate vehicles, Victor, Valerie, Rome, Amethyst, Vance, Royale, and Ariel, all arrived at the Trump International Hotel at one time and headed straight to the Jean George Restaurant.

Clad in a Saint Laurent red mini-dress with black polka dots on it, Violet was already seated at the table drinking a cucumber martini. While she had sobered up from her earlier alcohol escapade, she had decided that in order to deal with this group, she needed to get drunk again.

As the hostess led them to the table, Violet gave everyone an evil glare until she laid eyes upon Royale, leaving her mouth slightly open.

"Cantrese was telling the truth. You are alive. Where the hell did you come from after all of these years, and why are you hanging with the enemy?"

Val interceded. "Let's get everyone seated. Violet, you need to get up. You sit on the end with your Uncle Royale on one side of you and his friend on the other side. Victor, sweetheart, you are across from Royale. Rome, you are next to Victor. Amethyst is next to you. Vance, you are on the other side of Amethyst, and I am on the end, next to you."

As Violet stood up to move to the seat Val gave her, Royale grabbed her hand.

"I have been out of the country for the last five years suffering from amnesia. I haven't seen you since you were a little girl. Can I at least get a hug?"

Violet snatched her hand away from her uncle, rolled her eyes, then sat down.

"What are we all doing here anyway, Victor? When are you going to take me off this Dumas house arrest?" she asked.

"We are all here because I have some things that I want to tell all of you and a very important proposition to make to Royale. As for what you are calling house arrest, you are free to leave here with no security following you tomorrow morning. Now, I don't know where you intend to go, but I have paid for the hotel suite here for you until the end of July, so you are welcome to stay. However, you are no longer welcome in the house in Bel Air, which I have decided to put on the market, the farm in Kentucky, or the suite at Caesars Palace in Las Vegas. Now, before we get down to business, let's order dinner." A beat passed. "Cantrese told Valerie that Jean George has a pre-fixed menu, but feel free to order whatever you like," Victor said.

"Why? Is this the Last Supper?" Violet sneered.

They all chose to ignore her sarcastic question. As everyone looked over their menus, the waiter brought bottles of Billecart-Salmon Brut, chardonnay, merlot, sparkling and flat water to the table and opened each of them. Then they proceeded to offer them around.

"Would any of you care for any other drinks?"

Dressed in a brand new embroidered dress by Lanvin, Amethyst told him, "I'll have a raspberry-lychee bellini."

"That sounds delicious," Ariel piped in. "I'll have the same thing." Royale gazed at her briefly.

"Ariel, how is your mom? I haven't seen her since I ran into her in Las Vegas almost two years ago."

"I don't talk to her much, but I'm sure she's fine."

Royale snuck a look at Val. He thought she looked beautiful in the pink floral maxi dress she was wearing, but he didn't dare compliment her or ask how she and Ariel's mother knew each other. Instead he poured a glass of water for himself, then told the waiter he would have the baked Chatham oysters, grilled foie gras dumplings, and fragrant spiced lamb chops for dinner. He was anxious to see what Victor wanted, and then he was going get the hell out of here. Being close enough to Val to even smell her fragrance was driving him crazy. Everyone at the table must have felt the same way because they put in their orders fast.

"Do you want to tell us why we are all here, Dad?" Vance finally spoke up.

"All right. I'll just lay all of my cards on the table. I'm not feeling that well and haven't been for some time. I am tired of all the murders, kidnapping threats, and robbing going on. For the sake of my health and the safety of my family, I need to put an end to it all. I have decided to give my brother, Valerian, wherever he is, one billion dollars to make all of this mayhem go away. That's why I wanted to talk to you, Royale. I will pay you to find him and negotiate this deal. Will you help me?"

Insulted that Victor looked at him as some broke down hired help, Royale frowned before speaking.

"First of all, Victor. I don't need your money. I may not have billions like you, but I have quite enough millions to last me a lifetime, and I am still very capable of earning a lot more money. If I help you out with this, I will be doing it for Valerie. I don't want my cousins to hurt her or Vance and Valencia, who are my blood. I don't know where to find Sincere, but Claude may. I also think you all need to keep looking for Rolondo."

Remembering that remark Royale had made that morning about his father, Vance asked him, "What is it with you and Valerie?"

Royale looked Vance straight in his eyes.

"I have been in love with her for over thirty years."

Before anyone at the table could react to his statement, Royale fixated his attention on a man he saw head to the bar.

"Son of a bitch! Victor, you may get your bargaining session right now!" Royale jumped up from the table and ran to the bar. Rome quickly followed him.

"Sincere!" Royale shouted.

The man turned and looked as if a ghost was standing in front of him.

"Royale?" he whispered.

"Yes, cousin. It's me."

Sincere looked Royale up and down before noticing Rome standing behind him.

"Where did you come from, and why are you with this Shaft wannabe?"

"Rolondo tried to kill me, but I was rescued from the water. I had amnesia and have been in the Bahamas all of this time. I'm with Rome because your brother wanted me to try to find you. He wants to offer you a pretty sweet deal. What are you doing here?"

"A source told me that I could locate my daughter at this hotel. I've been trying to reach her by phone for a couple of days to no avail, so I decided to come in person to check things out. Where is Victor?"

"He's right inside of the restaurant."

Valerian didn't say another word to Royale. He walked right past him and headed into the direction that he pointed to. The security guards who were seated at two tables that flanked Victor's table stood up when they saw Valerian. Rome was right behind him with his hand on his gun.

Displaying no fear of his brother, Victor stood up.

"Valerian. This is a surprise. You're the last person that I expected to run into at this hotel. Would you care to join us?"

Ignoring Victor, Valerian focused on Violet, who was seated directly in front of him. He put his hands on her shoulders.

"Hello, daughter. My, you have been a naughty girl, disconnecting your phone, running away, then hiding from your father."

Not answering him, Violet reached for the bottle of merlot and poured it into a glass.

"I guess all those guilty feelings must have frozen your tongue so you can't speak. You need to be grateful that it hasn't been cut out of your mouth yet. All right, Victor. What is this all about? My cousin here, who I am so grateful has returned from the dead, just told me that you have a deal for me. What is it?"

"Don't you want to sit down first and have dinner or a drink with us? We all are your family."

"I normally don't eat or drink with my enemies, but I will have a glass of champagne to toast my cousin's resurrection from the grave."

Valerie poured Valerian a glass of the Billecart. He took a sip of it, pulled an empty chair from a nearby table up, then sat down.

"What kind of proposition do you have for me, big brother?"

"I am willing to pay you one billion dollars today to stop this madness and leave us all alone once and for all."

"You must be crazy! Our father's drugstores started your little empire, so I deserve at least half of what you have. Up the ante to four billion, and I will possibly consider staying off your ass."

"Valerian, those drug stores only sold for two hundred million dollars. I built the rest of this business on my own. When we found out that Violet is your daughter yesterday, my people pulled all of your financial records. I have your social security number. You have never made an honest dollar in your miserable life. You lived off of my wife until I cut her off, and then you or one of your henchmen killed her. Now you're living off Violet. We also went through her financial statements yesterday. She has, little by little, transferred the entire ten million dollars I personally gave her when she and Vance got married into an account in Switzerland that is linked to you. But she and Vance are getting divorced. She signed a prenuptial agreement. She isn't getting much more money. That gravy train is about to end. Take my offer."

Royale looked at Valerian.

"Sincere, you can't honestly be serious about rejecting an offer of one billion dollars. You are not even that pompous."

"Shut up! You are supposed to be dead! Rolondo can't do anything right. You are only trying to be so self-righteous in front of Valerie. That bump on your head must have affected your brain permanently. Do you think she still

254

wants you after all of these years when she's sleeping next to billions every night?"

Valerie stood up and faced Valerian.

"How dare you talk about me like that! You have no right to speak about who I'm sleeping next to. You don't know anything about me."

"Oh, but I do. You didn't just accidentally tumble down those stairs at your dormitory at Howard University all those years ago. I asked Dedra to push you. This fool actually drove to Washington, DC all the way from Ann Arbor to ask you to marry him. My future depended on all those millions he was about to sign for when he turned pro. The announcement was going to be made the next week. I wasn't about to let him share that money with you and some blood clot in your womb. She was supposed to kill you. Dedra was another worthless fool. She was also ordered to kill you the other year too, but couldn't get it right then either. Instead she offed herself."

"You've known Dee Dee all of this time. How?"

"I'm sorry, Val," Royale said. "She always claimed to be from Arizona, but Dee Dee also grew up with us in Illinois. My cousin here always had some kind of super power over her."

"It's okay, Royale. I let you and our baby go years ago. But Valerian, you have to let all of this pent up bitterness that's inside of you go too. Your brother is very generously offering you a new life. Please take it."

"No, it's half or nothing. If you all will excuse me, I have to head out to Sag Harbor. Fortunately, Victor, your offer isn't the only one I have on the table, or Royale, shall I say, hidden beneath the ground? Violet has my number. When your offer turns to *billions*, feel free to call me. In the meantime, you had better keep a close watch on our granddaughter. It was nice seeing you, Vance, or shall I call you son?"

"What's that supposed to mean?" Vance asked.

"Let's just say your mother and I knew each other in the biblical sense from around the age of twelve. You can take that for whatever you feel it's worth."

As her father left, Violet began to cry uncontrollably. She knew he was going to kill her. She just didn't know where or how.

"If you don't mind, can security take me back up to my room? Victor, I'll text you Dad's number right now. For what it's worth, I am sorry for the role I played in all of this. I confess that I helped break Rolondo out of jail. I also killed Amerani, and I stole everything in the safe, then my mother stole the money and jewelry from me," Violet confessed.

Vance couldn't believe what he was hearing.

"I gave you everything. Why would you need to steal from us?"

"My father raised me to. Now I see how wrong I was."

"Amerani isn't dead Violet," Val said. "In fact, she opened her eyes earlier today. She should be able to give the police her version of what happened at the house soon."

"Where is your Uncle Rolondo now, Violet?" asked Royale.

"I don't know. I thought I shot him, but obviously he got away. He's disguised as a woman by the name of Janvieve Rochon. He has a driver's license and a passport in her name. He could be anywhere."

"I'll notify the authorities in New York and LA of that right away," said Rome. "Violet, I'm going to have to take you down to a precinct here in New York tomorrow and have you arrested for committing these crimes you just confessed to. I'll be here to pick you up at nine. Vance, can you get her a lawyer?"

"No, Rome, I can't. I'm done with her. Violet, you will be hearing from my attorneys. "Fellows, take her upstairs."

Surrounded by security, Violet started walking out of the restaurant, then turned back.

"Vance, did you bring Tres Jolie to New York with you? If you did, I would like to see her one last time."

Vexed by Violet's request, he grimaced.

"You are some kind of piece of work. I can't believe you just asked to see your horse, and this is the second time I have seen you since you got to New York, and you haven't asked about your daughter.

"No, Tres Jolie is not in New York, and if she was, I wouldn't let you contaminate her any longer either. Get out of my face!"

One of the guys grabbed Violet's elbow and led her out.

"Whew!" sighed Val. "That Valerian is Satan in the form of a human being. I felt like I needed to wave a crucifix with every word that came out of his mouth. Sweetheart, it's hard to believe that you two have the same blood running through your veins. You think we need to try to get a DNA sample on him?" Val reached for the bottle of chardonnay and poured herself a glass. That had been one hell of an encounter. She was shaking. "I'm serious. He's worse than a snake. I need to use the ladies room."

Amethyst, who had been quiet through all of this, said, "So do I. I'll come with you, Val. Come on, Ariel. We might as well make it a girl thing."

Rome stood up. "I'll walk out with them and make sure they're all right."

In one of her swift moves that she was known so well for, Val put the champagne flute that Victor drank from in her Birkin bag without anyone else at the table noticing.

As soon as they left the table, Vance looked at Royale.

"How could you disrespect my father like that? Talking about how much you love his fiancée? And I was beginning to like the idea of having a real cousin."

Royale shook his head.

"Vance, I did not speak the truth to be disrespectful. I love her with all my might. I had no idea that Sincere and Dee Dee cooked up that plot to break Val and me up back then. But all of that stuff happened over three decades ago. I can't get the past back," Royale said. "Victor, I see how much you and Valerie mean to each other. I'm not going to do anything to mess up Valerie's happiness. In my opinion, you need to pay closer attention at how your best friend Rome looks at your woman. If he could have her for himself, all that inseparable friends thing he has going on with Val would fly right out of the window. And baby cuz, like I told you this morning, you need to put your own house in order and stop worrying about how I'm living. That young lady Cantrese seems to be too nice to just be somebody's side chick, even to a rich young studling like yourself. And I have known a lot about Roshonda for a long time. You cannot make a housewife out of a professional slut, no matter how fine she is. Your father tried to do the same thing with your mother, and we all know how well that worked out for him."

Victor laughed.

"I can't believe I'm saying this, but I like you, Royale. I tried to reason with my brother and failed. If he doesn't want my money, I'm not going to cry about it. I'll have to figure out another way to put a halt to his evil actions."

"He'll come around," said Royale. "I have known him all of my life. I could tell that he's bluffing. There is no way he is going to take a pass on caking up his bank account with one billion dollars."

Rome and the ladies arrived back at the table.

"That tip that Val's friend gave us last night was valid. A detective at the twenty-second precinct called me earlier. Caressa had Turquoise's diamond heart ring and engagement ring in her purse. She asked for a lawyer, so as soon as she gets one, they are going to text me so that I can show up at the arraignment."

"My gut tells me that Turquoise is still alive," Val told him.

"I agree. You have any idea what Caressa may have been doing with your cousin Claude, Royale?"

"Man, I have been living a vagrant's life on a deserted island for five years. These clowns have all seemed to have lost their minds. I can't believe they are still playing these New Jack City games, and all of them are over fifty years old. I would bet it's all connected with Rolondo breaking out of jail though."

"I'm still stuck on Sincere standing right in front of us and admitting to trying to kill me and Val. He takes being certifiably crazy to a whole new level, but I guess he always did. I'm going out to Sag Harbor to pay Claude a little visit tomorrow. You're free to join me."

"We're all headed to the Hamptons tomorrow, so I'll do that. I'll call you in the morning." Victor placed his right hand on his chest and grimaced.

Vance reached across the table and touched his father.

"Are you all right, Dad?"

"Just a little tired. Thank God I didn't grow up with my brother. Just spending a few minutes with him sucks the life out of you. Hanging around him, I would have been dead before I reached puberty." He helped Val up. "Come on sweetheart, let's go. The rest of you feel free to stay and enjoy dessert and some more drinks. The check has been put on the suite that Violet is staying in, so have a nice time."

As he and Val walked out of the restaurant, another sharp pain tore through Victor's chest. He knew his time on this earth was running out.

Chapter Forty-four

Valerie

Not needing an alarm clock that Friday morning on her wedding day, Valerie was wide awake and had already bathed and was getting dressed at six-thirty a.m. She wanted to take her time and make sure she looked her best. There was a knock on the door.

"Room service."

She was too excited to really eat, but she had ordered almost everything on the menu for Victor, including scrambled eggs, pancakes, and traditional eggs benedict. He loved them all. Awake also, he actually got to the door before she could and let the waiter in.

"Good morning, sir. Would you like me to set this up on the dining room table?"

"Yes please. Val, what is all of this? We're supposed to have a reception after the wedding, not before. This is enough food for an army." Victor signed the check as the waiter left.

"You fell asleep last night the minute your head hit the pillow, and with all of that drama with Valerian last night, you barely touched your dinner. I thought you might want to get your strength back up with a hearty breakfast. Eat before it gets cold."

"Your wish is my command. Then I will jump into the shower. We are leaving here at seven-thirty on the nose. You never know who may be lurking downstairs. I don't want to encounter all of those inquiring minds we ran into yesterday morning. It was like a convention out there."

"I know. Okay, I'll be in my office getting dressed. Let me know when you're ready to leave."

"Why are you dressing in your office?"

"So you won't see me until we're ready to go. It's bad luck for the groom to see the bride before she's ready to walk down the aisle."

Victor scoffed a pancake down with some juice and hurried into the bathroom. He was also anxious to get to the courthouse. Although he had wanted to keep this wedding a secret, he decided he had better let his assistant know what was happening. He dialed her quickly while Val was in her office.

"Charmion, listen carefully, but I want you to keep everything that I am telling you under wraps. Val and I are getting married today. There is just too much bedlam surrounding us. The only way I can protect Val and make sure she will be in charge of my empire if something happens to me is to make her my wife. And no matter what Royale claimed yesterday about not wanting to come between the two of us, I also know if she stays single, it is only a matter of time before that Rip Van Winkle Pretty Boy makes a move on her. Okay? I just needed someone to know what's going on, and I know I can trust you. I'll text you later."

She had no idea who Victor was talking to, but Valerie heard his every word. Once again, she wondered if today was the right day to get married. It was too late for that. She called out to Victor, "Let's go, sweetheart."

A beaming bride in red lace and a grinning groom wearing a black suit by Armani, white shirt and a red tie, Victor and Valerie walked happily into the city clerk's office as soon as it opened at eight-thirty. They were the third couple in line to get married. For their wedding day, Victor had hired a white limousine that Rome couldn't track, and had the driver pull over when they passed a flower stand at a deli and get Val a bouquet of red roses to match her dress. She took one of the flowers out of the bunch, broke the stem, then placed it on the lapel of his suit jacket.

"Victor Dumas and Valerie Rollins?"

After two years of being engaged, it was finally time to become Mr. and Mrs.

"Good morning, Your Honor," said Val. "If you don't mind, we have written our own vows. We actually wrote them awhile back. Luckily, I still had them in my email."

"That's fine. Are you ready to proceed?"

They both said, "Yes, your honor," at the same time.

"Dearly beloved, we are gathered here today to join Victor and Valerie in matrimony commended to be honorable among all; and therefore is not to be entered into lightly but reverently, passionately, lovingly and solemnly. Into this, these two persons present now come to be joined. Please read your vows now."

"I Valerie, take you Victor, to be my husband, my partner in life, and my one true love. I will cherish our union and love you more each day than I did the day before. I will trust you and respect you, laugh with you and cry with you, loving you faithfully through good times and bad, regardless of the obstacles we may face together. I give you my hand, my heart, and my love, from this day forward for as long as we both shall live."

"I, Victor, take you, Valerie, to be my partner, loving what I know of you, and trusting what I do not yet know. I eagerly anticipate the chance to continue to grow together, getting to know the even more wonderful of a woman you will become, and falling in love with you a little more every day."

"We will now have the exchange of rings," the judge said.

Tears began to stream down both Victor and Valerie's face. Val had already placed her engagement ring on her right hand, but she was not prepared for the huge piece of jewelry that Victor placed on the third finger of her left hand.

"I Victor, give you Valerie, this ring as an eternal symbol of my love and commitment to you."

Valerie then put the wedding band of diamonds on Victor's finger.

"I Valerie, give you, Victor, this ring as an eternal symbol of my love and commitment to you."

"By the power invested in me by the State of New York, I now pronounce you husband and wife. You may now kiss your bride." The judge smiled at the now newlyweds.

Unfortunately, as Val closed her eyes and lifted her lips to kiss Victor, all she could see was Royale smiling at her as he crossed home base after hitting a Grand Slam for her in Ann Arbor thirty years ago. What had she just done?

Chapter Forty-five

Violet

U nable to sleep the entire night, Violet saw that it was now six-thirty the next morning. Rome would be here in a little while to take her to the police precinct. She got out of bed, walked into the bathroom, and looked in the mirror. At twenty-eight years old her life was a terrible mess. All she had ever done was deceive people. She could blame it on her father making her secretly make the Dumas' lives a living hell. But the truth of the matter was, she did all those terrible things because she got a charge out of it. She hated those rich privileged idiots and that freak she and Vance conceived. The only being she ever truly loved was her horse, Tres Jolie. And she would never see or ride her again. She wasn't going to any police station with Rome to turn herself in. The way she saw things, from the moment she was born, life as she had experienced it, had never been worth living. It was time for her to take an endless nap.

Violet went into her cosmetic bag and pulled out the bottle of Vicodin the doctor had prescribed for her when she fell off Tres Jolie practicing a new jump, then emptied the entire contents of it into her hand. Next, she dumped an entire bottle of Aleve on top of those pills. Completing the pile of medicine in her hand with at least twenty Ambien capsules, she walked back into the bedroom and poured a glass of scotch, then slowly swallowed everything in her hand. When Violet finished drinking the one glass of liquor, she kept pouring additional shots until the bottle was empty, then lay back down. There was no need to leave a note for anyone. She had no regrets or wishes. It was going to feel so good to finally be able to fall asleep. She went on to dreamland riding Tres Jolie into a valley of blinding light. Her journey on this earth was complete.

Caressa

It was now nine-thirty on Friday morning and Caressa was still being held at the police precinct in Central Park. She had made countless calls to Claude and Sincere that had gone unanswered. The cell number she had for Rolondo had been disconnected since right after he shot up the courthouse on Tuesday. She hadn't even been able to report to him that some members of the Blades had that chick Turquoise. This was crazy.

A police officer unlocked her holding cell.

"Come on, Shabazz. Transportation is here to take you down to Central Booking. Since you have been unable to retain your own attorney, they will give you a court-appointed lawyer when you get downtown. Move it!" Officer Lomax led Caressa into the sunny park toward the van.

Two guys hid in the shrubbery waiting, their eyes clearly viewing their mark. Corey had called in reinforcements to help him stay focused and awake. He also had his girl call the station house this morning, claiming to be Caressa's cousin and inquiring about her well-being. The officer told her they would be taking Shabazz downtown within the next hour.

With their mark fixed perfectly within their killing view, the two men fired their glocks straight at her head.

"Pow! . . . Pow!"

This was easier than duck hunting. Caressa went down fast. They fired two more shots just to make sure she was dead.

"Pow! . . . Pow!"

To their horror, the cop went down too!

"Oh shit! Let's get out of here, fast!"

By the time the officers ran out of the station house to see what had happened to their prisoner and colleague, Corey and company were almost at Lexington Avenue, where they ran down into the Lexington Avenue subway heading back up to the Bronx on the number six train. They got off at 116th Street where Corey had parked his Mercedes the night before. They hopped in the car and drove down to East End Avenue and 83rd Street. After placing each gun into gift bags, Corey's assistant walked across the street to the park that ran along the East River. When he was sure that there was no one in sight, he threw both packages into the water and walked calmly back to the car.

Another morning. Another murder on the streets of New York City.

Chapter Forty-six

Rome

Val and Victor's phones went straight to voice mail several times. Rome decided then to stop by their suite before heading over to the Trump International Hotel to pick up Violet. He greeted the security guys he supervised once he got off the elevator at the hotel. When he got to the door of Victor and Valerie's suite, Esperanza wheeled Valencia out of the suite in her stroller followed by Vance, Cantrese, and two more security guards.

Rome kissed the baby, then asked the group, "Do you all know where Victor and Val are? I've been calling and texting them all morning, but both of their phones keep going straight to voicemail."

"They left here around seven-thirty this morning," Esperanza offered up, "but Miss Valerie didn't tell me where she was headed. She had on the beautiful red dress she bought yesterday."

Before Rome could ask the nanny another question, all of their phones beeped at once indicating they had text messages. Vance looked at his phone.

"It's from Dad. He says to take the baby and head out to Bridgehampton without him and Val. They'll join us tomorrow."

Cantrese also checked her phone. "I just got a message from Val. She says for me to go with Vance and Esperanza along with security and get the baby and Esperanza set up in the nursery. She also says she promised Sylvia in Turquoise's office that she would take care of paying her this week. She wants me to call her, and then wire her $1,000 by Western Union. Lastly, the staff from LA will meet us out in Bridgehampton, and Fresh Direct is delivering groceries, or we can feel free to eat out. She and Victor will meet us out there tomorrow."

Rome's phone had also beeped. His message from Val was similar. What was this all about? She had been avoiding him for the first time in ten years for two entire days.

"All right. You all go ahead. I have to deal with Violet, and I will meet you at the house in Bridgehampton this evening. Vance, have your guys already left?"

"Yes, with the exception of Nino and Falaki, who are riding out in a limo with Talfor and Roshonda, the van left with everyone around an hour ago. The staff Val hired for the farm are already there waiting, and the guys' rooms are in order. The horses are all being tended to also."

"Good going. Let's do this."

The group headed to the elevator, ready to hit the Hamptons for the summer and make history in the game of polo!

Outside the hotel, little Valencia grabbed Rome as Esperanza buckled her into a booster seat in the truck.

"Unc Rome . . . where GaGa?"

"GaGa had some things to do, sweetie. She'll see you later."

"I want GaGa." Valencia started to cry loudly.

Vance didn't know what to do.

"I've never seen her like this. She's usually so well behaved."

Esperanza handed the toddler a juice box and her talking Elmo, which quieted her down.

"She's not accustomed to not seeing Val when she wakes up in the morning."

Rome shook his head. None of this seemed like Val or Victor. Something was definitely happening that those two wanted kept a secret.

"I'll be glad when Val surfaces too. Okay, let me get Violet down to One Police Plaza. That's where Pace told me to take her, so that they can arrange for her to be extradited to Los Angeles."

As Vance got into the third seat of the car and sat next to his security guard, he told Rome, "As long as my daughter and I never have to set eyes on Violet again, you can take her to hell for all I care. I'll see you later."

Thinking about the way Turquoise had betrayed him, Rome understood just how Vance felt. He jumped into a waiting chauffeur-driven Escalade and headed up the street to pick up Violet. The guys Rome had guarding Violet looked a little worse for wear when they let him into the suite.

"Is everything okay here? You guys look like you've been to hell and back."

"That one in there is a piece of work. Her antics will wear anyone out." The one named Malik shook his head.

"Is she ready to leave?"

"She should be. I knocked on the door at seven-thirty and told her it was time to get up."

Rome knocked on the bedroom door.

"Violet, it's Rome. I'm here to take you downtown." There was no answer, so Rome knocked again. "Violet, it's Rome. Are you ready?" She still didn't answer. "Malik, when is the last time you saw her?"

"When we brought her back up from dinner last night."

Rome started banging hard on the door to no avail. He then turned the door knob only to find it locked. He picked up the telephone and dialed the operator.

"Hello. I'm in Suite 1128. Can you send security up here right away? I can't get the door to the bedroom open. I need to check on the woman inside. Thanks." Rome continued banging and yelling Violet's name with all of his might. He did not want to break the door down, so he hoped the hotel security hurried.

At that moment they knocked on the door. Malik let them in.

"Please open this door right now," Rome instructed.

The guy used a master key. Violet lay on the bed face down.

Rome saw the empty scotch and pill bottles on the nightstand next to her. As he picked her up, he yelled to Malik, "Call 911." Not taking the time to search for a pulse, Rome stepped into the shower with Violet and turned the cold water on full-blast.

"Come on. Stay with me, Violet."

She didn't respond. He took her out of the shower and laid her on the floor, then started to perform CPR on her. He stopped, then felt her neck. There was no pulse. Rome repeated the CPR. He felt her neck again. Still no pulse. There was a knock on the door. Malik let the paramedics in.

"They're in the bathroom."

"I think she took whatever was in those bottles on the nightstand. I can't get a pulse." The EMT workers lifted Violet's limp body onto a stretcher. Rome watched as they readied a defibrillator.

"Okay," said one of them, "stand clear!"

"Zap!" the defibrillator hit her chest.

Rome looked at the machine. There was nothing. The paramedics tried it again.

"Zap!"

"Okay, we have a faint heartbeat. Let's get her some oxygen and take her to the hospital."

"Can I ride with you?" Rome asked the paramedic.

"Are you a relative?" he responded.

"I might as well be. Her name is Violet Dumas. I work for her husband and father-in-law." Rome looked around the room until he saw Violet's purse. He picked it up. "Neither of you answered me. All of her information should be in here. Where are you taking her? Can I ride with you?"

"Yes, come on, sir. No problem. We're taking her to St. Luke's Roosevelt Hospital on Tenth Avenue and Fifty-eighth Street."

Forgetting that he was soaking wet and not even grabbing a towel, Rome rushed out the door behind them, onto the elevator, and through the lobby of curious onlookers, which included a tall, light-skinned woman that he didn't even notice staring him dead in the eyes.

As soon as they got Violet into the ambulance, her body went into a violent seizure, then suddenly went still. The paramedic checked her pulse, then her heart.

"I'm sorry, sir. She's gone."

It was only a two-block ride to the hospital that didn't even take five minutes, but to Rome it seemed like an eternity. Looking down at Violet's lifeless body, he remembered the beautiful young woman that had crossed the finish line first at the Kentucky Derby, year before last, standing proudly up on her horse, Tres Jolie, with her fist held high in victory. Now, she had taken her own life, leaving a helpless child with no mother. How in God's name had it come to this?

The sound of the paramedic's voice snapped Rome back to the present.

"Sir, we're going to have to take her to the ER so a doctor can officially pronounce her dead. What is your name?"

"Rome Nyland."

"Okay. Just have a seat and someone will call you."

Rome dialed Val as he walked to a seat. Since he was soaked from head-to-toe, people stared at him. He couldn't care less. He had played football many times in the pouring down rain, so he had been much wetter than this. Val's phone was still going straight to voice mail. He left her a message.

"I don't know what is going on with you, but there has been a tragic incident. Call me as soon as you get this message." Rome tried Victor's cell, which also went straight to voice mail. He left him an identical message. Then, dreading this next call, he dialed Vance, who picked up right away.

"What's up, Rome? Is my estranged wife locked up yet?"

"No Vance, she isn't. I'm at the hospital."

"What happened? Did she try to kill herself instead of going to jail?"

"I know you are just joking Vance, and I hate to be the one to tell you this, but yes, Violet did try to kill herself. I am so sorry, man. She's gone."

There was silence from the other end for just a moment, then Vance spoke.

"Rome, I wish I could be more Christian-like and be sad, but she has saved me from going to jail because I had illusions of killing her myself after all she did to my family. This may sound cold, but my daughter is much better off without her."

"Vance, you are still Violet's husband and the father of her child. You need to come to the hospital and identify her body."

"No, I am headed to my future. See if you can get Dad and Val to do it. Or better yet, call her loving parents. Offer them whatever's left in her bank account. I'm sure they'll come running to the hospital for that."

"Have you heard from your father and Valerie? I still can't reach them."

"Nope, Esperanza thinks they may be getting married."

"Married?"

"Yes. She said Val bought Dad a beautiful diamond ring yesterday. Cat got your tongue? Maybe Royale was right."

"What was Royale right about?"

"He thinks that you're in love with Val. Damn, it's too bad that she's my stepmother. The way she has the three of your noses wide open, even though I have never been into older women, I would love to try it just once to see what all the excitement is about. Her pussy must be platinum."

"Vance, this is no time for your sarcastic jokes. Your wife just died. If you hear from your father or Val, tell them that I'm at St. Luke's Roosevelt hospital on Tenth Avenue and Fifty-eighth Street. And no matter how cold and callous you are acting right now, you still have my condolences."

"All right, man. I'll let them know. Oh, and if Dad and Val did get married, you have my condolences too."

"Good-bye, Vance. I will see your wise-cracking ass tonight."

Maybe it wouldn't be a bad idea to try to reach Valerian or Betty and break the news to them about their daughter. Rome pulled Violet's phone out of her purse and scrolled through her most recent calls, seeing if he could locate numbers on them. The last time that he checked the GPS he had planted on Betty had been yesterday, and it showed her in motion up in Harlem. As he looked for their numbers, the phone rang.

"Hello?"

"Who is this and why are you answering my daughter's phone?"

Rome recognized the voice on the other end right away.

"Valerian, this is Rome."

"I would prefer if you call me Sincere. As I said, why do you have my daughter's phone?"

"I hate to be the one to tell you this, but Violet is dead. She committed suicide this morning. I'm at St. Luke's Roosevelt Hospital with her body. It's only around five minutes away from the hotel on Tenth Avenue and Fifty-eighth Street."

"I'm at the hotel. I'll be right there."

As Rome hit the disconnect button, he saw a "Breaking News" alert on the television that was on the wall in the waiting room. He started to ignore it and keep looking for numbers in Violet's phone, but the words, "Police Officer and Suspect Slain" along with a mugshot of Caressa flashed up on the screen.

"This is Sheldon Dutes reporting live from the twenty-second precinct in Central Park, the scene of a deadly shooting this morning where a police officer and attempted kidnapping suspect were shot by an unknown assailant. The shooter is still at large. I'll be back with more details after the break. This has been Sheldon Dutes with NBC News reporting live from the twenty-second precinct in Central Park."

Rome put his head in his hand.

"Tough day, huh?" a voice said.

"Royale. What are you doing here?"

"Vance called me and told me what happened to Violet and where you were. I thought that since I am related to her, you could use my help. Why are your clothes wet?"

Rome wanted to ask Royale how did he and Vance get so tight, but before he could get the words out of his mouth, or tell him why his clothes were soaked, Valerian came bursting into the emergency room like a bull in heat. He jerked Rome by the collar out of the chair.

"What did you do to my daughter, motherfucker?"

Rome twisted Valerian around and put him in a chokehold.

"Now, you know me and what I am capable of doing. I can break your neck right here. The only thing I did was try to save your daughter's life, which is more than I can say for you. If I let you go, are we going to talk about what happened to Violet man-to-man?"

Hospital security ran to them.

"Is everything all right here or do we need to call the police?"

Rome let Valerian loose. He turned to the officer.

"Everything is fine. We just lost a family member, so things are just a little tense right now."

Not convinced, the officer didn't budge.

Valerian noticed the Hermes Birkin bag on the chair where Rome had been sitting. He knew that it alone was worth thousands of dollars.

"Is that my daughter's purse?"

Rome told him, "Yes."

Valerian snatched the luxury bag out of the chair.

"I'll take care of it. Where are Vance and Victor? I'm surprised they're not here."

"Vance said he was leaving things up to me. He's on his way out to the Hamptons with the members of his polo club, and I can't locate Victor at the present time."

"Fine. I want you two to get the fuck away from me. Violet was my daughter. I will handle things from here."

Royale had been standing back observing things, but now felt the need to speak up.

"Are you sure, Sincere? All you've ever done was use that poor child to your own advantage. If we leave, are you really going to take care of business?"

"I am going to start pretending like you are still dead, cousin. Yes, I am sure. I want you two sorry ass motherfuckers to leave. Victor will surface soon. I'm sure she had an insurance policy worth millions that will take care of all of this. Tell my brother to get in touch with me as soon as you hear from him. Now get out of this hospital!"

"Cool. Royale, let's go. But before I leave, Sincere, a young lady by the name of Caressa Shabazz was shot and killed here this morning while in police custody. I had a CI in LA, who also conveniently was killed yesterday, that told me she was one of your women. Since you just happen to be here in New York showing concern for your daughter, you just didn't happen to murk that girl, did you?"

"Rome, just like you, your CI was stupid. Maybe that's why he's dead. I didn't know Caressa, but she used to sell a whole lot of pussy and move bricks for my cousins, including your new best friend, the Jesus-looking one standing right here. Now, for the last time, leave me alone to mourn my daughter's death!"

Rome and Royale left the hospital together where Rome's driver, along with a security guard, were waiting in the truck outside. Rome opened the truck's door and motioned Royale to get in too.

"I'll give you a ride back to the hotel. I need to shower and get out of these wet clothes. I put Violet under the shower trying to revive her when I found her unresponsive in her bed. Royale, the other night you told Val and me that you didn't know who Caressa was. Why did Valerian say that she worked for you?"

"I don't know her. I will admit that after I retired from playing baseball, I financed all of my cousins' illegal operations to keep long dollars flowing in. I rarely saw the people who worked for them. I've been gone for five years. You need to question Claude and look for Rolondo in his disguise as a woman."

"I'm already on that. But before we get back to the hotel, let me ask you one thing. Why did you tell Vance that I'm in love with Val?"

"Oh come on, man! I see the way that you look at her. I saw all of the pictures of you two that are on the internet that show you all palling around the country these past ten years. You all are too close for comfort. And from what I can surmise, with the stories out there, she really wasn't with anyone special for years until she hooked up with Victor. I know you had to hit that a few times."

"Since you are so perceptive, I'm not going to lie and say that I don't feel a certain way about her, but I never acted on those feelings and tried to get intimate with the woman."

"Brother, you are a damn fool. She gave me her virginity, and that was some powerful stuff she was putting down. Combined with her kind and generous spirit, I guess that's why I never stopped loving her."

"Well, it looks like we are both shit out of luck. Vance thinks the reason that Val and Victor have gone ghost is because they are somewhere getting married."

Royale let out a raucous laugh.

"Having a bank account stacked with almost eight billion dollars sure didn't give Victor the confidence that he could keep his woman away from me. I just reappeared in her life two days ago after not seeing her for more than thirty years, and he snatched her off and wifed her up. Wow!"

"Perhaps Victor checked out the way she looks at you. I also saw those intense kisses she was returning when you had your tongue down her throat in the bathroom the other night. I'm not saying that Val doesn't love Victor, but I do think she could still be in love with you. There is a big difference."

The truck pulled in front of the hotel.

"Let me get into some dry clothes and deal with all this stuff that's going on. It's noon now. I plan to head out to the Hamptons around four, after I talk to the police here and in LA. Once I find Val, I doubt that she's going to want to just leave Violet's remains with Valerian. This is all so sad. What time are you going to try to go see your cousin Claude?"

"I've got a limo coming to pick Ariel and me up around the same time. Are you familiar with Sag Harbor? I spent all of my summers out there as a kid."

"No, I'm not familiar with the town at all. This will be my first trip to the Hamptons."

"I got a room at the American Hotel on Main Street. We can hook up there. Call me when you get out there, and we'll set the time. Where are you staying?"

"For now, in Val and Victor's guest house in Bridgehampton, but I need a little more privacy. I am going to look into renting my own house for the summer."

"Yeah, you and the former ice skater look pretty chummy. She's still fine. I would want some privacy too."

"She and I were on the same Olympic team back in 1980. I just hooked back up with her the other day on the plane coming in. My fiancée did some pretty bad things behind my back, which makes Amethyst a welcome distraction."

"Vance told me your fiancée is the woman that you and Val are looking for. Maybe you should let her stay lost."

"No, if she's alive and in trouble, it wouldn't be right for me not to help her. Finding her could also lead to Rolondo. He's one of the bad things that she was doing behind my back. I'm going to head up to my room and take care of this business. I'll check you out tonight, Royale."

Chapter Forty-seven

Janvieve

On the Hampton jitney headed out to Sag Harbor, Janvieve pulled out a traveling water bottle filled with Jack Daniels and took a long swig. With Victor placing a $100 million bounty on Rolondo's head, coupled with watching Caressa get arrested, and Claude driving away from the park, then her coming face-to-face with Rome earlier in the lobby of the Trump International Hotel, she had made a hasty decision to hightail it out of New York City.

Not knowing whose idea it was for Violet to shoot Rolondo, she hadn't tried to reach Caressa or Claude to see where their hostage was located. Without sticking around to see whether Violet was dead or alive on that stretcher they carried her out of there on, Janvieve had packed her things, grabbed her duffle bag filled with money, and checked out of the hotel.

As she left, she did overhear one of the desk clerks say that the woman that was wheeled out had tried to commit suicide. She had never pegged Violet for someone who was weak enough to take her own life, but the stupid cunt had actually done her a favor. Now, she wouldn't have to kill her and have one more body on Rolondo's already too long list of casualties. The time had come to move on to bigger and more expensive things.

Janvieve planned to get in and out of Sag Harbor as fast as possible. Her plan was to rent a car, head straight to Claude's church, and then kill him. She had purchased a metal detector eXp 5000 over the internet that had been delivered to the hotel yesterday. The little gem had the reputation of being able to detect buried gold and silver right away. An Earth Imager, it was the star of "FS-Future Series." The only drawback to her plan was that Royale was the only person who knew the combination to the safe, and she had hoped that he was still dead. Now that she knew otherwise, she intended to buy a hatchet and somehow break the lock once she located it. Then she would dump Claude's body in the same hole and bury him, fill the trunk of the car with the silver and gold bars, and drive to Canada. Once she got there, she would sell everything, put the cash in a bank account and catch a flight to France. When she landed in Paris, she planned to catch a train to Switzerland, open an account at a bank, transfer the money, and let Rolondo live a glorious life snorting as much blow and fucking as many women as life threw at him. It was a thoroughbred blueprint.

The jitney stopped on Lexington Avenue right in front of Bloomingdale's to pick up more passengers. Taking another swig of bourbon, to her surprise, Janvieve watched Betty Lum get on the bus. There was only one reason that woman could also be heading out to Sag Harbor. She also had to see Claude and try to hone in on the contents in the buried safe.

Janvieve wondered if Betty had heard what had happened to Violet, or knew about Victor's huge reward offer for information about Rolondo. This Asian bitch was the only living person other than Sincere who could identify her as Rolondo. Possessing that knowledge meant she had to die. Janvieve's gun had a silencer on it. She would shoot her the moment they got off of this jitney. This day just kept getting better, so much so that she took one last swig of bourbon before falling into a deep nap.

Betty

Finding a seat at the front of the jitney, Betty had decided to head out to Sag Harbor without calling Claude first, just in case he spoke to Sincere. She had been to Sag Harbor plenty of times with Andrea and Sincere over the years, so she made a reservation at the Cove Inn and planned to relax this evening, maybe have dinner at the American Hotel, before seeking out Claude tomorrow. But right now, she needed to use the bathroom.

As she made her way to the back of the bus, she saw Rolondo in his Janvieve disguise sound asleep in a seat near the bathroom. Using the facilities would have to wait for now. She had seen Victor on television the previous day with his reward offer. This was her chance to hit the lottery. She sat back down and reached for her phone.

While Violet had been sleeping the other night in Las Vegas, she had gone through all of her things and written down Vance, Victor, Rome and Valerie's numbers. She even had her granddaughter's nanny's number. She quickly called Victor, but his phone went straight to voice mail. She tried calling Rome next.

"Hello?"

"Hi, Rome. This is Betty Lum."

"Hi, Betty. I guess you're calling about Violet. I am so sorry that she's dead."

"What did you say?" she whispered.

"That I'm sorry Violet killed herself. What can I do for you?"

"My daughter is dead?"

"Yes. Isn't that why you're calling me?"

"No. I am calling you because I can't reach Victor. I wanted to let him know that I am on the same Hampton jitney heading to Sag Harbor that Rolondo Jemison is on. He's disguised as a woman, but now I have to get off this bus and find out what happened to Violet. I need to collect the reward money that Victor offered as soon as possible. Where is my daughter?"

"Earlier today her body was at St. Luke's Roosevelt Hospital. Betty, what is the number of the bus that you're on, and what time did it leave New York?"

Betty looked at the number on the front dashboard.

"It's 9563. It left the city at two-thirty. I have to hang up now. I'll be in touch with Victor about the reward money."

"I'll let him know. And Betty, you should know that I left Valerian at the hospital with Violet's body. He says he wants to take care of the arrangements."

"Good-bye, Rome. Please tell Vance to take better care of his daughter than I did of mine." Betty asked the bus driver, "Do you stop anywhere that I can call a cab? I have an emergency and need to get back to New York."

"We're about to stop here in Queens to drop passengers off right now, ma'am. The stop is by a small strip mall. You can call a taxi to pick you up here. I'm pulling in now."

Betty practically jumped off the bus before the driver could open the door. She didn't want Rolondo to discover that she was on the same bus headed to Sag Harbor. It was obvious she was headed out there to see Claude.

Slowly she walked into a McDonald's and sat down. Tears began to flow down her face. She wished she hadn't been such a horrible person most of her life. There were people who didn't go through life, murdering, stealing, dealing and using drugs and hurting anyone who got in their way. She should have taught her daughter to live a straight way of life instead of just pawning her off on Sincere so she would have no responsibilities. Glancing out the window, she saw a taxi stand just a little ways away. She got up and walked toward it.

Also, she didn't know if she believed Rome's story about Violet committing suicide. Most likely, Sincere or Rolondo probably killed her.

Rome

After Valerie's phone still went straight to voice mail, Rome punched in Vance's number. He now realized that he should have called him first because no matter what, Violet was his wife. "How can I help you, Rome?"

"Violet's mom just called me. She said she's on the Hampton jitney headed toward Sag Harbor, and Rolondo is also on it disguised as a woman. The number of the bus is 9563." He paused briefly. "I am going to call the twenty-second precinct and tell the officers there that Rolondo may have something to do with this morning's double homicide. That should get them moving faster. Where are you now? It's not good that he is also headed to the Hamptons."

"I'm in the barn at the horse farm giving Wildin' Out a bath. Roshonda went shopping at the Tanger Outlets with Talfor, and Cantrese and Esperanza are at the house with Valencia. Christine and the staff from the California house just arrived. They brought Val's cat Lucky with them, so the baby has been playing with her all afternoon. We're all fine. Just go find that clown and put him back behind bars where he belongs."

"All right, but be careful. Have you heard from your father and Val yet?"

"No, I tried to call him a little while ago. There's still no answer. Maybe they flew to Las Vegas if they really are getting married."

"Naw, they're not in Las Vegas. I get text alerts as soon as any of your family's planes leave a hangar. All four of them are still over at Teterboro Airport in New Jersey. Let me get on this Rolondo info before he gets way. I'll see you in a few hours."

Hanging up from Vance, Rome called the precinct right away. The number was still in his phone after speaking with the officers there earlier. He would just give dispatch this information.

"Twenty-second Precinct."

"Hello. This is Rome Nyland, Head of Security for Dumas Electronics. I just received a tip that Rolondo Jemison, a fugitive from Los Angeles, that could be a suspect in the double homicide that occurred at your station house this morning, is on a Hampton jitney headed East with the number 9563 on it. Jemison is a tall, light-skinned African American man who is disguised as a woman. He is armed and extremely dangerous. Can you dispatch cars right away as well as alert the Hampton jitney that he is on one of their buses?"

"Yes, Mr. Nyland. I am also going to alert the State Police."

"Great. He is also wanted in Los Angeles, where he escaped from a courthouse the other morning after killing several people. I'll alert them also."

"Thank you, Mr. Nyland."

After sending Amethyst a text to tell her he had an emergency and would have someone drive her out to the Hamptons later, Rome's next call was to James Pace.

"What's up, Rome?"

"We may have Rolondo. He's been spotted disguised as a woman on a Hampton jitney. I just alerted the NYPD."

"All right. I'll follow that up with a call to them and the District Attorney's office here and there right now as well, and email them his wanted poster. Good going, Rome. Nice work."

"We have Violet's mother to thank for this information. She spotted him on the bus. Violet committed suicide this morning. I found her and tried to save her, but she was too far gone."

"I'm sorry, Rome."

"Thanks, man. We'll talk later."

Rome looked at his watch. It was now almost four. Where the hell were Valerie and Victor? He picked up the house phone.

"May I help you?"

"Yes. Can you connect me to Royale Jones' room?"

"I'm sorry, sir. We don't have a guest registered by that name."

"Try Columbus Isley."

"Thank you. I'll connect you now. Have a good day."

"Hello."

"Hey, man, it's Rome. I just got a tip that Rolondo is on a Hampton jitney headed to Sag Harbor. I called the cops and notified them, but I want to check things out too. You said you know the area. Do you want to roll with me?"

"Hell yeah. I'll meet you downstairs in twenty minutes."

Chapter Forty-eight

Valerie

As soon as she and her now husband got back into the white limousine following the ceremony, Valerie regretted going through with this quickie marriage without any of her friends, or Vance and Rome joining them at the County Clerk's office to witness her and Victor exchange vows. Her friend Copper was an ordained minister. Why hadn't she thought to ask her to perform the ceremony? Also, she could have asked Reverend Al Sharpton to marry them. She should have at least asked Shelley or Jean to come with her, or called LaToya out in LA to see what her schedule was like. If she had been free, Val could have sent a plane for her to come to New York for the wedding. Who was she trying to fool? She had agreed to marry Victor today without any of the people close to her because of Royale suddenly appearing back in her life. She could still feel his mouth bearing down on hers the other night and getting wet between her legs. She hadn't laid eyes on that man in over thirty something years, and the moment he touched her, she had been ready to tear her panties right off in that bathroom. If Rome hadn't come charging through that door when he did, she knew that would have happened. She couldn't betray Victor like that. So here she was, the wife of Victor Dumas. They didn't even have plans for a wedding lunch to celebrate. She was the queen of parties, with no soiree to go to on her own wedding day.

Val pulled her phone out of her purse to turn it back on. Victor snatched the phone right out of her hand.

"No cell phones until at least tomorrow, Mrs. Dumas. I told you I have a lot of surprises in store for you. Driver, we are going to 157 West 57th Street."

"Sweetheart, you have to at least let me check my messages. We are in the middle of a crisis. Rome is probably going out of his mind that he hasn't spoken to me since yesterday, and I need to see how the baby is."

"I told you that my son needs to start taking care of his own daughter, and you need to let Rome concentrate on his own woman."

"I need to let Rome do what? Where is this coming from?"

"Royale thinks that Rome is in love with you."

"Royale? When did you two get tight enough to start chatting about my best friend/partner and me behind our backs? You may have talked me into taking a hiatus from work this summer, but the last time I checked, I was the number one gossip columnist in America, not you or Royale! Honey, you have got to be joking."

"No, I'm not joking. But for now, can we just enjoy our first day as husband and wife alone? I promise to give you back to the rest of the world in the morning." Victor leaned over and kissed Val deeply as the car pulled in front of the address that he had given the driver.

Val held out the palm of her hand to Victor.

"I promise not to turn it on, but may I please have my phone back?"

Rolling his eyes, he handed it to her. Getting out of the limo, Val saw that they were in front of the flagship Park Hyatt Hotel. She assumed that in keeping up his need for their newlywed privacy, that Victor had booked a room here for them for their honeymoon night. But instead of going to the hotel's entrance, he steered her through the door of the adjoining building, where they were greeted by a uniformed concierge. She had been here several months ago when she was visiting New York for a magazine party and had raved to Victor about the apartment that it was held in. It had been unbelievable with five bedrooms and five-and-a-half bathrooms. The huge living room/dining room had floor-to-ceiling windows with views of Central Park to the north, midtown to the east, and south views over the Chrysler and Empire State buildings.

"Welcome home, Mr. and Mrs. Dumas."

"Thank you," said Victor. "Come on, darling. Let me show you wedding gift number one."

The elevator stopped on the 54th floor. Victor took Val's hand. He opened the door of the apartment that she had been in, 54B. With her mouth wide open, but speechless, Val walked through the front door. Victor poured them two glasses of champagne from a bottle of Cristal that was chilling in a bucket on the mantle. As they clinked glasses and took a sip, he picked up an envelope next to the champagne and handed it to her.

"The deed to this apartment is in your name. In the two years that we have been together, I have never seen you as happy as you were dancing with your friends at Ricardo's the other night, or laughing with all your girls at the press conference. So, I thought it was time for you to move back home to New York where you belong. Welcome to our new home, Mrs. Dumas. Since this apartment is the building's model, I took the liberty of buying it with all of the furniture. You can buy new things as we get settled."

Although she was thrilled, Valerie was slightly overwhelmed. She loved the idea of moving back to New York, but it would have been nice to have been in on the decision. The apartment was breathtaking, but Fifty-seventh Street was too busy for her. She would have preferred to live further east, where it was quiet.

Valerie took the bottle of champagne out of the bucket and followed Victor into the living room where he sat down at the table that had a checkbook and a Hermes wallet on it. He handed her the checkbook.

"Here are checks as well as a wallet filled with credit cards with your new name, Valerie Dumas on them."

"Victor, we never discussed me changing my name to Dumas. I have been Valerie Rollins all of my life. That is how people know me professionally."

"You don't need anyone to know you professionally anymore. You're my wife now. Your working days are behind you."

Val didn't want to upset Victor. They could talk about this later. She put the wallet and checkbook in her purse, then poured herself another glass of champagne, downed it in one gulp, kicked off her heels, and took off her dress, followed by the matching red lace panties and bra she wore under it.

"I need you to do me a favor, husband."

"And what favor might that be?"

"I want you to make love to me right here, right now."

As Victor took off his shoes, Val jerked off Victor's suit jacket, unbuttoned his shirt, and almost tore it off. Then she undid his pants and ripped his boxers off. She took the bottle of champagne off the table and emptied the bubbly left in it onto his dick, then proceeded to get down on her knees and engulf it entirely in her mouth. She sucked long and hard, thrusting in and out until his creamy milk poured down her throat. Wiping her mouth with a tissue, Val stood up and told Victor, "Let's see how good the mattress of one of these new beds is."

Practically running to the apartment's bedroom wing, they reached the master suite first. Whoever the decorator was had done a marvelous job. A globe-like chandelier hung over a king-size bed that was draped in a white comforter over white sheets. A white rug covered the room's floor. There were white nightstands with white lamps on both sides of the bed and a Lucite table set directly across from the bed with a white chair tucked neatly under it. The two of them fell on the bed, hungrily kissing each other. Victor moved down to the foot of the bed and softly kissed Val's vagina. He flicked his tongue between her meaty folds, then lovingly licked her clitoris as he slowly caressed her breasts. Val let out a throaty moan.

"Oh, baby. Baby, please make love to me now!"

He moved up and entered her. Their bodies moved in rhythm as if they were dancers on a private stage. The newlyweds couldn't hold it any longer. They came in unison like an exploding volcano. As he gently eased out of Val, Victor whispered, "I love you so much, Mrs. Dumas. I never knew that life could be filled with so much laughter and happiness until I met you."

"I love you too, sweetheart. I'm going to go take a shower. I hope we have towels here. I guess we can go pick up our clothes from the hotel in the morning."

"Yes, there are towels in all the bathrooms. The apartment comes with the hotel's amenities. We can even order room service. Our clothes should already be here. Check the closet."

Val opened the major walk-in closet door. Sure enough, all of her clothes were in it, including all of her and Victor's Louis Vuitton luggage that she had already started packing to move to the Hamptons.

"Thanks, darling."

She walked into the living room to get her purse. Valerie didn't care what Victor wanted her to do. She needed to check her phone. She hit the 'on' button. As soon as the phone came to life, it started beeping out of control. There were dozens of missed calls and text messages from Rome, Vance, Cantrese, Esperanza, and even some numbers that she didn't recognize. Before she could return anybody's call or text, the phone rang. It was Rome.

"Hey. I'm just looking at all these calls and messages. What's going on?"

"Don't even ask me that, Val. Where the hell have you been all day? Violet committed suicide this morning. The girl Caressa and a cop got killed on their way down to Central Booking, and we may have found Rolondo. Betty Lum called me and said that he's on a Hampton jitney headed to Sag Harbor disguised as a woman, just like Violet told us. I have the police on it, but Royale and I are getting ready to head out to the highway too. You didn't answer my question. Where the hell have you been all day?"

"Victor and I got married this morning. He made me keep my phone off. Poor Violet . . . I'm just a few blocks away from you. I'm coming with you. Give me a half hour. Pick me up at 157 West 57th Street. I'll be out in front."

"Okay. I'll be there. Since when did Victor start making you do anything?"

"Since this morning when I became his wife, but this is the first and last day I let that happen again. I'll be out in front of the building."

Ending the call, Val pulled out a velvet jewelry bag that she always carried. There was a special locket inside. She opened it and looked at a photo of her baby's sonogram on one side and her and Royale on the other. She closed the locket, then charged back into the bedroom. No longer in bed, Victor was in the shower. He smiled when she walked in.

"Care to join me?" Victor asked.

As she stepped in to the huge shower that was separate from the tub, Val told him, "Yes, but only because I'm in a hurry. All hell broke loose today. Violet committed suicide this morning. That girl Caressa was shot dead, and Rolondo is supposedly on a Hampton jitney headed to Sag Harbor."

"I'm so sorry, Val," Victor said. "Oh God! Violet is really dead . . ."

"Thank God I turned my phone on. I am getting dressed and going with Rome to see if the cops have apprehended Rolondo yet. You call the hotel's maids and have them pack up the rest of this stuff and bring it out to the Hamptons. Then call your security detail and get on the road too. I'll meet you at the house in Bridgehampton. I can't believe I let you talk me into keeping my phone off all day."

"I'm sorry, Val. Oh God! Did Rome tell you where Vance is?"

Valerie was already drying off and pulling underwear, a pair of white walking shorts and a matching top out of the closet, as well as toiletries out of her tote bag. She hurriedly got herself together, got dressed, and threw a white baseball hat with gold studs on her head. She completed the casual outfit with a pair of GG Bloom high-top sneakers.

"No. I suggest you turn on your phone and call your son as soon as you get out of that shower. I'm going downstairs to wait for Rome. I will call you as soon as I hear something. I'm out."

"Val, I love you."

"I know, Victor. I love you too." And with those parting words of endearment, their honeymoon was over.

Rome

Rome and Royale were already parked outside of the apartment building when Valerie walked out. Although Rome was furious at Val for leaving him out of her and Victor's plans, he started to laugh the moment that he saw her. Royale gave him a curious look.

"What's so funny?"

"The way you look at Val like she's a piece of meat on a plate. Put your tongue back in your mouth. She just married someone else."

Royale started to laugh too.

"I can't believe I'm so obvious."

Val climbed into the backseat of the truck.

"What are you two laughing about? I don't see anything funny happening around here today. Violet is dead. This is terrible. And how did Caressa get killed?"

Glancing at her in the rearview mirror as he pulled away from the curb, Rome told her, "Hello to you, too. I know you did not just get in this truck asking ninety-nine questions after the stunt you pulled today. What in God's name possessed you and Victor to get married this morning with all we have going on? And why were you so secretive about the whole thing? Hell, I'm offended that you didn't ask me to be your Best Man. I mean, Victor didn't even invite his own son to the wedding. Did you tell any of your girlfriends that you were getting married today? When did you all decide to do this anyway?"

Instead of answering all of Rome's questions, Valerie burst into tears.

Royale wanted to jump in the backseat and put his arms around her. Instead he told Rome, "Easy man. You don't need to be coming down so hard on her."

"I don't need you to speak up for me, Royale," Val said. "You should have done that when your cousin and my line sister were trying to kill me and our baby. Victor told me he wanted to get married today on Wednesday night after you two left the table. He has cancer and his heart is weak, so he said he didn't want to wait any longer. I was afraid to tell anyone what was going on because I didn't want to jinx it."

"I should have bet you some money, Rome. He saw me for five minutes, then raced her to the altar just like I told you. Valerie, you know I had no idea what Sincere and Dee Dee were up to."

Rome shook his head.

"I was wondering when Victor was going to tell you and Vance that he has cancer."

Val leaned into the front seat. "He told you? You knew and didn't tell me? How could you keep something like that from me, Rome?"

"The same way you kept Turquoise and Rolondo making a sex tape from me. I'm the Director of Security for Dumas Electronics. It's my job to know when any of you all sneeze. He didn't have to tell me. I know where all the cars are headed and where Victor is at all times. He was getting treatment over in Paris. The last time you two were there, every time he told you he had meetings, he was actually receiving an advanced form of chemotherapy that isn't available in the United States. Speaking of the infamous sex tape, who did you pay the million dollars to for it?"

Although she knew it was bound to come up sooner or later, Valerie had been dreading this question since Tuesday when she told Rome about the tape.

"Valerian."

"How did that happen?"

"He called me and told me he was in possession of it. The call was blocked, so I had no idea where he was calling from. After our initial conversation, I received instructions by text where to wire the money."

Royale was still stuck on the fact that Rome's fiancée and his twin cousin had been so deeply involved.

"If I'm correct, this Turquoise thought she was knocking boots with me at the same time that she was engaged to you, then Sincere beat you two out of a million dollars for a tape of the fake me and her boning?"

"Victor gave me the million dollars to buy the tape. I never told him that his brother was the seller because that would only have given him one more thing to worry about. Even though I didn't know he was as sick as he is, I've had a feeling for a long time that something wasn't quite right about his health.

"But forget this conversation for a minute. Royale, why would Rolondo and Betty both be on a bus headed to Sag Harbor, of all places?"

"I may as well tell you two this. When Rolondo thought he killed me, we were fighting over the contents of a safe that I had built beneath Claude's church. I presume that both of them are headed out there to try to find it and dig it up. I am the only one who has a map of the exact location, as well as the combination. I had both of those things hidden in my medallion all of these years, but because of the amnesia, I didn't remember."

The phone ringing on the dashboard interrupted them.

"Rome Nyland."

"It's Detective Mattioli. The jitney has been stopped on I-495 right by Jones Beach. Jemison is on the bus and he has taken a hostage."

Rome looked at his GPS, then also saw a sign for Jones Beach. As the flow of traffic almost came to a standstill, he could also see a roadblock up ahead.

"I'm just about there in a black Escalade. Can you get me through this roadblock? Jemison's cousin is with me, and I am very familiar with the perp. We can help with the hostage situation."

"Pull over to the side of the road and approach the roadblock driving up it. I'll see what I can do."

Rome followed his instructions. When he got up to the front of the stopped cars, the jitney was in full view. He looked at Royale.

"Are you up for this, man?"

"More than anything in this world. I am more than ready to help take this rat bastard down. You stay in the car, Val."

"Look, you are not my father or my husband, and after everything that happened today, he's never going to be able to tell me what to do again either. I'm coming with you guys."

Members of the NYPD highway patrol, SWAT cars and police vans and ambulances surrounded the jitney as they approached it. Rome spotted Detective Mattioli talking to a group of officers who had their guns drawn.

"What do we have going on here?" he asked.

"Jemison has a gun on him. He's right there at the front of the bus. He won't let any of the passengers get off."

"I'm Rolondo's cousin, Royale Jones. Let me try to talk to him."

The detective thought about it for a moment, then told him, "No. That's too dangerous. A negotiator is on the way to talk to Jemison."

From where they were standing, they could see a woman, who they presumed to be Rolondo standing almost in the doorway of the bus with a gun pointing at the bus driver.

"The hell with this. I'm not waiting for any negotiator. This bastard stole five years of my life from me!" Before anyone could stop him, Royale ran to the jitney and started banging on the door.

Startled, Rolondo turned around. When he saw Royale, he was so shocked that his hand holding the gun went to his side. In that split second, Detective Mattioli raised his gun, fired, and shot Rolondo in the middle of his head. Just to make sure his target was on point, he fired another shot right behind that one. Rolondo's body slammed hard against the door, causing it to open. He fell out, hitting the ground on the side of the highway.

What seemed like a small army of policemen, with their guns still drawn, surrounded him. One of them knelt down to feel his neck as two paramedics also knelt down next to him.

"There's no pulse. He's dead." The paramedics lifted Rolondo onto a stretcher, then rolled it to their ambulance.

All of her life Valerie believed that God always had a plan and purpose. Perhaps the purpose of Royale's coming back into her life out of nowhere was to end Victor being Rolondo's prey.

"Rome, it's over. Come on, guys, Let's go. The authorities can take it from here."

As the three of them walked back to the truck, the police took down the roadblock, and the traffic on the Long Island Expressway began to move slowly. An Escalade almost identical to the one they were riding in eased slowly up the road. There was a woman in the backseat. She looked directly into Val's eyes, then started banging on the window.

Val started to yell, then ran straight to the vehicle.

"Rome, that's Turquoise in that truck! It's Turquoise! Look!" Without thinking, Val reached into her purse, pulled out the tiniest gun imaginable, then shot at the truck's back tire that was closest to her. The SUV swerved. The police officer who was still parked not far in front of them ran back to Val, snatched the gun, and grabbed her. "Let me go! There is a kidnap victim in that SUV. Check my wallet. I have a license to carry this gun." She tried to break free of his grasp.

Rome had already reached the truck, which had come to a screeching halt as the car behind rear ended it. He pulled on the SUV's door handle, but it was locked.

Although she was in a drug-induced daze, Turquoise managed to open it, tumbling out of the truck and into Rome's arms. She looked up into Royale's face. Thinking he was Rolondo, she began to howl hysterically.

Yohance attempted to drive off, but there were cars in front and back prohibiting him from moving. Seeing how disheveled Turquoise looked, the police realized that Valerie was telling the truth about her being a kidnap victim, so they surrounded the truck with their guns drawn.

"Get out of the vehicle, all of you! Hands on your head!"

Instead of trying to fight back, Yohance and the guys followed the cops' orders. Sometimes even gangbangers like them knew when their time had run out. They all got out of the truck. The policemen grabbed each of them.

Turquoise collapsed onto the ground. Rome told one of the officers, "This is my fiancée, Turquoise Hobson. She has been missing since she was kidnapped in LA on Tuesday. Please call the EMT back here right away. Something's not right with her." Then he asked Turquoise, "Who did this to you, baby?"

"Boss, why are you just standing there? Get us out of here. Where are Pastor Claude and Sincere?" Yohance had not seen Rolondo the entire year that he had been in jail, so when he saw Royale standing there, he assumed he was the notorious leader of the Bugatti Blades.

"What! I'm not your boss. I'm the real Royale Jones. Rolondo can't help you. He was just killed. But your dumb ass, young blood, in front of all of these witnesses, has just incriminated my two cousins for this woman's kidnapping. Nobody, where you're headed, likes a snitch. Officers, this man just named Claude Hoskins and Valerian Davidson as two of the masterminds behind this woman's kidnapping. You will be able to find Hoskins and most likely Davidson at the Holy Temple of Mary Magdalene in Sag Harbor."

Several police vans along with another ambulance for Turquoise pulled along the side of the road. As each of the guys were read the Miranda warning, Rome helped a paramedic place Turquoise on a stretcher.

"She looks like she's on heroin," said Royale.

Starting an IV in her, the paramedic told Rome, "She's definitely under the influence of some narcotic. We'll find out what it is once we get her to the hospital."

Val took three $100 bills out of her purse and handed them to the paramedic.

"Can you take her to Southampton hospital? We'll pay whatever else it costs. We're headed out to Bridgehampton. My friend is on the board at the Southampton hospital and can make sure Miss Hobson gets top-notch care. Rome, do you want to ride with them so that Turquoise won't be alone?"

"No I don't. Guys, her name is Turquoise Hobson. She's forty-two years old. I am Rome Nyland. I am writing her sister's name and number and her assistant's name and number on the back of my card. Please give it to the desk clerks in the emergency room. They can get all of the information they need from the two of them. I'll call the hospital later to check on her. Val and Royale, let's go."

"Rome, are you sure that you want to leave her like this?"

"I've never been more sure of anything in my life. I now understand why Vance reacted the way he did this morning when I told him Violet was dead. Like he was finished with her, this chapter of my life is a wrap."

Chapter Forty-nine

Valerie

Due to the hostage situation and Rolondo being killed on the jitney, then the arrest of four members of the Bugatti Blades, and Turquoise being taken away in an ambulance, the traffic on the Long Island Expressway had been backed up for miles. It had taken Valerie, Rome, and Royale almost four hours to reach the Hamptons.

That Friday evening, Val was just finishing up a call with Victor, who was just now getting ready to leave Manhattan after forgetting he had an important meeting with the company that was buying his Urban War game and other digital Dumas Electronics content for almost seven billion dollars.

"Sweetie, I can't believe you almost let that meeting slip your mind. Why didn't Charmion remind you? She keeps your schedule."

"Getting married has been all I've been concentrating on for the last two days. But you were correct earlier today when you said we cannot turn off our phones. I will never try to keep you all to myself again. Dwayne had a van take the luggage slightly after you left, so it should be arriving in Bridgehampton soon. I'm very proud of you. As usual, you and Rome accomplished a lot. Rolondo is dead, and Turquoise has been found. I have to still figure out what we're going to do about arrangements for Violet. Vance has checked out of that situation."

"We'll worry about that tomorrow. It's not like she's going anywhere. We're pulling up in front of the American Hotel to drop Royale off. I'll see you later tonight."

"Bye, sweetheart."

Once Valerie ended the call with her husband, she turned to face Rome."

"Victor's just now heading out of the city. He just finished up a meeting that he had totally blown off with all of our wedding plans. I haven't had anything to eat all day. I'm starving. It may take us another hour to get to Bridgehampton. Let's eat here before we go to the house. I'll pick up something for Victor and call Cantrese to see if anybody out there wants us to bring them some food."

"It sounds good to me. I haven't eaten since this morning. Do you want to join us, Royale?"

"Yep. I can really use a good meal as well as some sleep right now. I'll give the cops a chance to get at Claude tonight before heading over to the church tomorrow."

When Val got out of the truck, she threw her arms around Royale's neck and hugged him tightly.

"Thank you for ridding our lives of Rolondo. I feel like a huge brick has been lifted off of my chest." Val's innocent gesture of gratitude didn't go unnoticed.

Talfor and Roshonda were sitting on the hotel's porch, when Talfor captured the two former lovers in each other's arms with her cell phone camera.

Royale broke out of Val's embrace as soon as possible. He could already feel the erection coming on with her pressed so closely against him, and that was something he didn't want her or Rome to observe.

"It's all good in the hood. My only regret is that I couldn't put a bullet through that bastard's skull myself."

Rome gave Royale a high-five.

"My sentiment exactly."

The three of them approached the porch where Talfor and Roshonda were seated.

Valerie loved the American Hotel's porch. When her friend Jocelyn had been an executive at an automobile company, they had stayed in Sag Harbor several times while attending Russell Simmons' Art for Life Gala. One of their favorite activities over the weekend had been sitting on this porch, where Valerie would regale everyone with some of her best stories about celebrities. It had been so much fun.

Val's new wedding and engagement ring caught Roshonda's eye.

"Dag, Val. When did Victor give you those new rings? You are blinding us out here. I don't think I've ever seen so many diamonds in one setting. Why are you also wearing that thick band of diamonds?"

So much had transpired since this morning that Valerie had forgotten about her new jewelry.

"Victor and I got married this morning. We wanted to surprise everyone."

"If you are a newlywed, then why are you with these two fine gentlemen? Where is your husband?" Talfor glared at her.

"There was an emergency, so I had to head out there with Rome. In case you haven't heard, Violet died this morning, Rolondo just got killed, and we found Rome's fiancée Turquoise on the Long Island Expressway. Victor had an important meeting in the city. He'll be out later tonight."

The host showed them to a table next to Talfor and Roshonda's, then handed them menus.

"The waiter will be right here to take your drink orders."

Rome took his phone out and started typing out a text message.

"I need to let Amethyst know that I'll have a driver pick her up around eight in the morning to bring her out here. It's too late for her to head out tonight. I am beat. I just want to see a bed. Do you want me to have the driver pick up Ariel for you too, Royale?"

"No. I've decided to take a break from her this weekend. I don't know how things are going to go with Claude tomorrow. I need to totally focus on getting into my safe. I don't need any distractions."

Val smirked.

"Isn't she a little young for you? At the most she just turned twenty-two, and you are fifty-six."

"I never asked her how old she is. On Crooked Island age did not matter. I had other things on my mind every time she came to visit."

"I bet you did. Her mom Rebecca told me that some man that her daughter Ariel was working for had gotten her hooked on heroin, and he was paying for the girl's rehab. She has been getting into trouble since she was around twelve."

"Is the man her agent or something?" Royale asked.

"Why would she need an agent? She never worked until she met this man. I believe he runs some sort of third-rate talent agency where he makes young people pay to go out on auditions. Rebecca told me that the man is real sleazy."

"Back on Crooked Island, Ariel told me she was a supermodel. However, the minute we got to Miami and set foot in the Delano Hotel, she looked like she was going to faint. I figured that she must be lying." Royale nodded slowly. "Hey, if she wouldn't have had that newspaper article with Rolondo's picture and your name in it, I would still be on Crooked Island. She got my life back for me," Royale added.

The waiter appeared at their table.

"Are you all ready to order?"

In unison, the three of them told him, "Yes!"

Valerie would be glad to leave Royale's presence for the evening. In spite of all that intense lovemaking she and Victor had earlier, her womanhood had started to tingle the moment she got in that truck and laid eyes on Royale. The sooner she got away from him, the better.

Chapter Fifty

Valerie

On Saturday morning, the sound of her phone ringing woke Valerie up from a sound sleep. She was in a bed in her new house in Bridgehampton, New York with Valencia curled up under her arm and her cat Lucky purring gently at the top of her head, but no Victor anywhere. She answered the phone.

"Good morning, Mrs. Dumas. I'm around thirty minutes away from there. How are you this morning?"

Val looked at the clock. It was almost ten a.m. For the second time this week, she had slept later than usual in years.

"I'm fine, but I will be much better when you get here. I can't believe we didn't spend our first night as husband and wife together. Victor, that is not a good thing. Don't do this to me again."

"Don't worry. We will never sleep apart again. What kind of plans do you have for today? Are you still planning to attend the gala tonight?"

"I don't know. I'm not really up to partying with all that happened yesterday. I'm going to go to the hospital and visit Turquoise. Rome doesn't want anything to do with her, but

I think we should check on her. And then I need to see what's happening with Violet's remains."

"You don't have to do that. Valerian called me demanding money to handle all of that. He already had her body taken to a crematory to be cremated today. He doesn't want us to go near her. I've already had cash delivered to him at the W Hotel. By the way, he still wants four billion dollars to leave us alone."

Valerie sighed and shook her head in frustrated pity.

"I'll talk to you more about it when I get there. I'm a little weary. I think I'll just rest today, if you don't mind."

"Of course I don't mind. I'll see you when you get here. We'll have brunch ready for you. I love you."

"I love you more."

Both Valencia and Lucky were now wide awake. They both jumped on top of Val. She laughed.

"Okay you two. Let's get this day going. I hope it will be easier than yesterday."

Royale

Sitting inside the house next to the Holy Temple of Mary Magdalene with Claude at the kitchen table, the two cousins were sharing a morning blunt in memory of Rolondo. Sincere was trying to figure out their next move to look for the safe now that Royale was alive.

Taking a long pull off the blunt, Sincere told Claude, "Royale must still have that map on him. Otherwise, he wouldn't be here in New York."

"How did he get hooked up with Victor and Rome? I still can't believe he survived that explosion and was on some island with amnesia all those years," Claude remarked.

"He didn't tell me. He always liked you more than Rolondo and me. Let's call that professional snitch, Valerie, and tell her you want to meet with Royale. Then tell him you just want a percentage of what's in the safe and see if he'll take you to it. Then I'll have some guys waiting, and this time we will kill him for real and make sure he stays dead. How does that sound to you?"

"Like a plan."

But before Sincere could call Val, Royale called him.

"Good morning, cousin. This is Royale."

"How did you get my number?"

"Rome gave it to me. Have you seen Claude? You know those kids you all had kidnap Rome's fiancée gave both of you up yesterday. The police should be over at the church sometime today. I'm coming with them."

"I don't know what kids you are referring to, or anything about your new best friend, Rome or his fiancée. I'm at the house next to the church with Claude. I'll let him talk to you." He put the phone on speaker, then handed it to Claude. "It's Royale," Sincere said.

"What's up, cousin? I'm glad to hear that after all of these years you are still among the living. What can I do for you?"

"You can cut the act, Claude. I already know that you and Sincere were in on Rolondo thinking that he killed me. I have decided I want to spend the summer out here in Sag Harbor, so I am taking my house back. You are getting arrested today for the kidnapping of Rome's fiancée and the murder of that kid Cayenne, so your address is about to change anyway."

Royale listened as Claude's kitchen was instantly filled with police, detectives, and dogs. Although he couldn't see what was going on with his cousins, he knew someone had snatched the phone out of Claude's hand, and he and Sincere were being handcuffed. An officer read them their Miranda warning, adding, "You both are being arrested for the kidnapping of Turquoise Hobson, the murders of NYPD Officer, Roger Lomax and Caressa Shabazz in New York and Carlton Jamal in Los Angeles."

Glad their arrest had occurred sooner rather than later, he knew most likely that he would have been their next target. That was one last deadly play these two would never get to orchestrate. With all those charges in two different cities, they would never be given bail, and once all of their evil crimes were shown to a jury, neither of them would ever see the light of day. There was now no hurry to get over to his house. Claude, Rolondo, and Sincere would never be able to get their hands on his life's earnings.

Chapter Fifty-one

Valerie

Two weeks later . . .

Valerie smiled as Victor and Vance held Valencia as
they walked her around the horse ring on a brand
new pony that Victor had just purchased for her.
They all looked so happy. Over the last two weeks since
they had gotten married, Val had watched Victor's health
take a sudden decline. Some days he didn't even have the
energy to get out of bed. Today was good though. He was
moving around the horse farm well. Victor admitted to her
and Vance that he didn't have much time to live. The night
they were married, instead of not remembering an important
meeting, Victor had actually been lying on a hospital bed at
the Ralph Lauren Cancer Center in Harlem, receiving a
radiation treatment that he had forgotten about. At least the
"forgetting something" part of his explanation to Val for
still being in the city was true. The doctor had told him to
quit lying to Valerie and Vance about his condition. So he
had been honest. He explained to her that the malignant
tumors had spread throughout his entire body. Val cried
rivers of tears, however, he told her to stop.

"Over the last two years you have shown me happiness that I never dreamed could exist," Victor had said.

"Sweetheart, it has been the same for me," Valerie replied as she held him in her arms.

Val thought about that conversation as Nino, Jamal, and Lee were all exercising their horses nearby. The first match was next Sunday. So far the team looked great and so did Victor and Valerie's new home.

Val also had turned their house into what resembled the North Pole. It wasn't so much about celebrating Christmas in July as it was about spending one more Christmas with her husband. She looked up in horror as Victor collapsed against the pony, causing both it and Valencia to fall. She ran to him as Vance picked up the baby who cried loudly. In a split second, Valerie knew that Victor was gone.

The following day, Valerie, Rome, and Vance all sat in Victor's office at the house in Bridgehampton as his attorney began to read his will. When Vance called him soon after they moved his father's body to Benta's Funeral Home in Harlem, Clifton Turner told him that Victor had wanted his will to be immediately executed, so Vance had sent a Dumas jet to fly him to New York last night.

"Good morning. I am so sorry about the loss you are suffering, Valerie and Vance. Victor's will is very simple. He never got the chance to put the house in Bel Air up for sale, so he left it along with the farm in Kentucky to his granddaughter Valencia. Vance, this horse farm, including separate properties in Kentucky, Paris, France and Ocho

Rios, Jamaica were left to you. Valerie, the deeds to the new apartment in New York and your Bridgehampton home are already in your name. Victor's holdings actually come to twenty-one billion dollars. With the exception of ten million dollars to you, Rome, and million dollar bequeaths to Dwayne, Christina, Esperanza and Cantrese, that twenty-one billion dollars is to be split equally between Valerie, Vance, and Valencia. The four planes are also to be divided between Vance and Valerie as well as the cars. Here are two letters that he left for Valerie and Vance. He also requested that he be cremated, that Valerie keep his ashes, and that in lieu of a service, that Val throw her Christmas in July party as a memorial to him. Lastly, Vance, he wants you to win the Bridgehampton Polo Championship this summer."

Vance started to cry. He had planned to abort the team and forget about polo, but he was happy to honor his father's wishes. Holding both Rome and Vance's hands as she sat between them, Val was stunned at how her life had turned out. Two years ago, she had been struggling to make ends meet. Now she was a widow worth billions of dollars. She didn't care about the money though. She would rather have Victor back. While Rome and Victor shook the attorney's hand, Val opened up Victor's letter.

My Dearest Valerie,

Don't mourn for me. Without your love, my life wouldn't have lasted as long as it did. I only have one request for you. Royale is a good man. Give love a second chance. I'll see you when we meet up in another lifetime. I love you with all of my heart.

Victor

One week later, Valerie clutched her wide-brimmed yellow straw hat as she sat next to Jean and Amethyst at a table in a tent on the polo grounds in Bridgehampton. They were taking a break from the hot sun until the Dumas Diamonds Polo Club was up. So far, Vance's team was ahead four to one for the day. She felt a large hand on top of hers and turned to see Royale sitting next to her.

"Vance told me where I could find you. Can I steal you away for a minute? I'm sure your friends won't mind."

Amethyst quickly said, "Go ahead, Val. We'll meet you back outside."

"All right," she replied, then allowed Royale to lead her out of the tent holding her hand. He walked over to a table and handed Val a glass of champagne.

"I'm starting a new minor league baseball team and need to fly to Miami in the morning to scout some prospects. Since I own the house Claude was living in, and don't really have any place else ready right now to live in, I've decided to spend the summer here. Rome and Vance told me about the letter Victor left for you that mentioned me. Maybe when I get back from Florida we can have dinner and talk."

He stopped and looked deep into her eyes. "As I told you that night at the Ritz Carlton, I've never stopped loving you."

Standing on her tiptoes, Val kissed him lightly on the lips. Victor was right. A second chance at true love shouldn't be passed up.

"It's too soon after losing Victor for us to get involved again, but I don't see any reason that we can't be friends who spend time together. I'll be here when you get back."

The two former college sweethearts smiled brightly at each other. Maybe it was time for both of them to create new memories.

* * * * * * * * * * * * * * *

About The Author

Flo Anthony

A multi-award winning journalist, Flo Anthony has hosts the daily nationally syndicated radio show "Gossip On The Go With Flo," heard in over 20 markets. Author of the Black Expressions Bestselling novel, "Deadly Stuff Players," Flo is also the Publisher/editor in chief of blacknoir.nyc and writes a weekly syndicated newspaper column "Go With The Flo," as well as a monthly column "Big Apple Buzz" in Resident Magazine.

A pioneer in the newspaper world, Flo is the first African American woman to work in the sports department of the New York Post, as well as the first African American to work in the New York Post's Entertainment Department and on the paper's world renowned Page Six. She worked at the New York Post for nearly a decade before leaving to helm her own column at Her New York for a six figure salary, which was groundbreaking for a woman of color in the newspaper industry prior to the millennium.

A familiar face on television, Flo can currently be seen on "Life After" on TV One and is a frequent contributor on "The Insider" and "Entertainment Tonight." She has appeared on over 25 television programs over the course of her career which began with a contract on the late Joan Rivers' Emmy award winning talk show.

A graduate of Howard University, with extended graduate studies at the University of Michigan, Flo resides in East Harlem.

Twitter @banananosekid

Facebook Florence Anthony